Burial deferred

Also by Johnathan Ross

Death's head
Dead eye
Dropped dead

Burial deferred

Jonathan Ross

St. Martin's Press
New York

Library of Congress Cataloging in Publication Data

Ross, Jonathan, 1916-
  Burial deferred.

  I. Title.
PR6068.0835B8   1986   823'.914   86-1822
ISBN 0-312-10879-6

First published in Great Britain by Constable & Company Ltd.

First U.S. Edition

10 9 8 7 6 5 4 3 2 1

Burial deferred

I

Even as a visitor, Detective Superintendent George Rogers had disliked hospitals, their smell and the painful things that the people in them did to those reluctantly in their care. He now realized that the desire of the imprisoned to be free went with it as well.

He was in his local hospital, for he could see through the window the squat towers of Abbotsburn Minster surrounded by the slate roofs and office blocks of the town. He had opened eyes that occasionally switched to seeing objects in duplicate to find himself pyjama'd in a strange bed, alone in a strange room and unable to remember what had happened to him or how he had got there. Although the pillow on which his head rested was reasonably soft, the back of his skull throbbed with a persistent ache that spread itself to whatever lay behind the sockets of his eyes. The top of his head wasn't anything to be happy about either and, touching it with his fingers, he could feel small ridges of pulled-together bristled flesh and the stiff projections of their suturing. If that wasn't enough, his breastbone was sore. Not too far away from vomiting and creaking with pain, he was in a mood to believe that somebody had opened up his damaged skull and packed it with layers of befogging cotton wool.

When he saw a bell-tit at the side of the bed, he pressed it. The nurse who came in briskly thrust a glass thermometer under his tongue, timed the pulse in his wrist against the fob watch pinned to her starched breasts and then told him that he had been involved in a road accident, that the ward doctor would be in to see him and would he please not try and sit up or ask so nonsensically for his clothes to go home. He accepted that she might otherwise be a pleasant enough woman, but her bossy schoolmistressy attitude irritated him.

He had decided to try and sleep again when the doctor arrived. He looked extremely youthful and a man, Rogers was certain, who must have been called in specially from the nearest postgraduate medical school to practise the recently-acquired mechanics of his profession on somebody they didn't mind losing. He confirmed the nurse's briefer information that Rogers had been involved in an accident in his car, having been brought into the Casualty Department during the dead hours of the morning – just over twelve hours previously, he explained on seeing Rogers's irritated incomprehension – suffering a cerebral concussion from one or both of the blows to the skull's parietal and occipital areas. Other than that he knew nothing of the circumstances or where it had happened. Then, after prodding at the injuries to the detective's head, he checked his blood pressure with the equipment he had brought in with him. Interrogating him about how he felt, he told Rogers that his inability to recall the accident was most probably the retrograde amnesia that often followed a concussion of the brain; that he might eventually remember in part, wholly, or not at all. 'It depends,' he added cautiously without explaining on what and seeming not to regard it as anything to worry about. The occasional double vision, also a result of the concussion, was nothing serious and he was cheerfully certain that it would correct itself in a matter of days. The soreness of Rogers's breastbone might, he suggested reprovingly, have been the result of driving without using the seat belt and banging into the steering wheel. Rogers should consider himself fortunate that he hadn't suffered broken ribs. His temperature, pulse rate and blood pressure were near enough normal, and his headache, obvious irritability and restlessness only symptomatic of what could happen to a brain that had been badly jolted.

Before he left, the doctor said that he had been asked to inform Detective Chief Inspector Lingard when his senior was well enough to be visited and talked to. Which, Rogers considered, couldn't be too soon, for the nearest thing to his coming-to in this bed he could remember was being in his car on the forecourt of the Headquarters building, not how he had got there or why, with a low reddening sun in his eyes and about to go somewhere. His loss of memory of what had happened in between, his physical feebleness, made him feel diminished and vulnerable to whatever might be going to happen to him.

'Dammit!' he growled at the ceiling, wondering whether he was going to be fed while inside, 'I've a bloody right to be irritable.'

2

Rogers was no man to accept being confined with patient fortitude while still possessing his legs and arms and the ability to move them. Lying on his back with all the held-back cantankerousness of somebody remanded in custody to police cells and waiting for people outside in God's free air to do things unlikely to contribute to his tranquillity of mind, he waited for Lingard's arrival.

He would probably be his only visitor, for Rogers's wife had left him more than five years earlier. Since one had discarded so completely six feet and more of reasonably muscular and flat-bellied constabulary bodywork fitted with black hair, dark brown eyes and its own teeth, a thin wedge of a nose fashioned by nature to be the instrument of a searching mind, the swarthy skin of a man who might have had a slight touch of Arab in his ancestry but hadn't, and what he considered defensively to be a well-bred and amiable approach in bed to sexual fastidious-nesses, he accepted that she had detected something unattract-ive in his inner persona. Not cursed with a permanent itch, it could, he believed, be that his hardly-held predisposition to asceticism, sometimes bordering on the priggish although be-leaguered often by his body's rebellion against it, was discern-ible to a woman's intuition and disliked. In his more brooding moments, he had thought himself to be similar to a library book, borrowed and never bought for long keeping or re-reading.

None of this worried Rogers so much as his present inability to recall some twenty hours of his recent activities; other than, perhaps, that he had been unconscious for more than half of them. Something like, he thought, having pages torn from the library book with which he had fancifully equated himself.

Other than that he accepted he had moral sanctions against doing it, he could have committed murder or rape or anything else pre-oblivion, and know nothing about it. This, as much as his physical feebleness – he was certain from the woolliness he felt in his head that they had been pumping drugs into his bloodstream – made him feel unarmoured and exposed.

Having thought out what the doctor had told him about the accident with his car, and having in his uniformed days dealt with enough of the deaths and mutilations caused by them, he couldn't understand how he had suffered the bang on the back of his head. How in the hell *could* it happen in the driver's seat? The cuts on the top of his head were explicable. He had no doubt that they were the result of the impact of his skull with the windscreen. It left him accepting the fact that he had been unbelted when it had happened; an unusual circumstance when, because of his experience of the gory consequences of road accidents, he had been always meticulous in using the seat belt, and even before it had been made obligatory it had already become an embedded habit for him to do so.

He was trying to convince himself that it couldn't happen to a do-it-by-the-book Rogers when the nurse opened the door, stared at him as if suspecting that she would find him doing something not allowed by hospital regulations, and let Lingard into the room.

Rogers's second-in-command, the man who took over his chair and assumed temporarily the county CID's overseeing when his senior was on leave or was, as in this instance, incapacitated, looked pleased with himself. He was a lean and elegant man of patrician appearance with blond hair, a high thin nose in narrow features and the intense blue eyes beloved by Chief Constables with lists of promotions on their desks. His dogtooth tweed suit was of comparable elegance, his handsewn shirt high in the collar and long in the cuffs, the olive-green waistcoat he wore elaborately embroidered with sprigs. His appearance was a paradox, for his eighteenth-century foppishness had often misled villains into using self-defeating violence against his unsuspected ability in unarmed combat.

'I'm told that you're back with us again, George,' he said smilingly. 'When I saw you this morning you were snorting like a baby pig and, I thought, breathing your last.' He took a tiny ivory box from his waistcoat pocket and pinched Attar of Roses snuff into his nostrils. 'How do you feel now?'

'Mad, bad and bloody-minded,' Rogers said heavily. 'How do you expect me to feel? I'm stuck here like a goddamned invalid. I don't know what happened and nobody can tell me anything other than that I was in some sort of an accident.'

'You don't know?' Lingard raised his eyebrows in surprise. 'You're not serious?'

'Of course I'm serious,' Rogers said testily. The throbbing in his head wasn't conducive to amiability, even with his colleague and friend, but he controlled much of his irritation at Lingard's understandable cavilling. 'I can't remember a damn' thing. All I've been told is that I was involved in a car accident, that I'm concussed and suffering from something called retrograde amnesia. I can remember *that*,' he added, a little defensively.

'You mean to say you don't know who did it?'

'For Christ's sake, David! Did what?'

'Walloped you on the head with a lump of wood, of course.' Lingard regarded Rogers with concern. 'Egad! You don't even remember that?'

'I don't remember it, David,' he said, spacing out his words for emphasis. 'I don't remember *anything* that happened after I left my office yesterday evening. If it was yesterday.'

'Yes, it was. I wasn't there, but you'd booked out to Thurnholme Bay at seven-thirty.'

Thurnholme Bay, once a fishing village but now a middle-sized resort of hotels, guesthouses and plastic pubs, was some sixteen miles from Police Headquarters and Rogers was necessarily familiar with it, although why he should have been visiting it on an evening baffled him.

'Right, we've got that settled,' he said. 'Suppose you now accept it and tell me what happened to get me into this place.'

Lingard sat himself on the foot of the bed, careful to avoid his irritable senior's feet, and refilled his sinuses with snuff. 'You were brought in here as a road accident case at three-thirty this morning. Thursday the 15th of August if you've forgotten that as well. Because it was you, I had the purple alert from HQ shortly afterwards and met up with Inspector Orris who was trying to sort it out in Casualty. You weren't the most beautiful sight in the world for a man got out of bed at four on a wet morning; blood all over, you'd thrown up on your trousers and weren't with us at all. It was as well I was there, too. Apart from the glass the vet was digging out of your scalp, he was hooking bits and pieces from the back of your head in cleaning it up and obviously wondering what the hell. Splinters of bark and fragments of lichen; not the sort of debris you can collect inside a car. You also had bits of dead leaves inside your jacket. So, for me, you stopped being an accident statistic as from then.' He cocked his head, looking quizzically at Rogers. 'Nothing coming back?'

'No, nothing other than it still hurts.' It did, too, and Lingard's voice, although not shouting out his information, resonated painfully in his brain. And, in his present trough of being, he wished Lingard would not be so flippant. 'You've done something about it?' he asked. He knew that he would have.

'Short of calling in MI5 and Scotland Yard's terrorist squad, I have,' Lingard assured him affably, 'and this is the picture so far as I can make it out. You left for Thurnholme Bay at seven-thirty, arriving at the sub-station at eight for an arranged interview with DPC Lewis about the spate of property thefts from hotels. You left him at eight-thirty with something of a flea in his ear for not doing much about them, saying that you had to be getting back to your office. Lewis saw you drive out of the yard – I imagine he was glad to see the back of you – turn in the right direction for home and that was the last seen of you until about three this morning.' Lingard searched his face for some recognition. 'Still nothing, George?'

Rogers shook his head, then grunted, wishing that he hadn't. 'Go on,' he said. 'I'll tell you when there is.'

'A lorry driver by the name of Frayling was hacking along the main road from Thurnholme, saw car lights – sidelights, not headlights – coming towards the road from a field in front of him and on his nearside. He thought it was odd that time of the morning, but odder still when the lights kept on coming through the boundary fence and over a ditch, the car finishing on its side in front of him. Luckily for you he had good brakes and a CB transmitter on board. He said that you had your head through the windscreen, were bleeding more than somewhat and unconscious. When an ambulance and a patrol car arrived and you were lifted out, it was seen that you hadn't been wearing your seat belt. That's significant now, don't you think?'

'I've already thought about it,' Rogers said, 'and it isn't me.' As he himself would put it, he was a long-time member of an Association of Pipe-smoking Bastards, and being concussed hadn't relieved him of his need for nicotine. And deprivation, he was sure, wasn't helping the recovery of his memory. 'When you've finished, will you smuggle me in my pipe and tobacco and something to light it with?' he asked.

'You haven't got it,' Lingard told him. 'At least, not your pipe you haven't. I've already checked your clothes and property. And it wasn't in the car either.'

'Find it, David, will you? It's my meerschaum and I love it more than my mother. Well, grandmother then,' he qualified. 'And I know this. If I didn't leave it in the car, it was either between my teeth or in my hand.'

'I'll look, but I don't know where,' Lingard promised him. 'They won't let you smoke it in here anyway, and you've interrupted my train of thought.' When Rogers merely grunted, he continued. 'Come daylight and with nothing useful I could do such as speaking to you, I drove out to the scene of your accident which, incidentally, was just past Cattes Cove. Following the wheeltracks you'd made, it seems you'd been up on the coast road, gone over the verge on the downhill bend and ploughed through a flock of bushes and a cow pasture to reach the main road.' He shook his head. 'It still baffles me why you hadn't rolled over on the way down and killed yourself.'

'My car's smashed, I suppose?' Rogers had had it only for a few months, the replacement for another that had died against a telephone pole, although through no carelessness on his part.

'A write-off, I'm afraid,' Lingard said. 'The side of the ditch that you hit with such a fair old whack was concrete. Still,' he added as if it would comfort Rogers, 'in view of the circumstances I've had it fingerprinted; results as yet unknown. It all seems to add up to this. After you left Lewis at Thurnholme you went to parts unknown, being at wherever it was for some six hours or so and finishing up three miles out of Thurnholme. You could have been poking your nose into some villainy or other, been banged on the head by somebody who didn't like what you were doing, dumped back in your car and sent careering down the slope where you finished up on the main road.'

Lingard paused. Rogers was manifestly searching among the blank spaces in his brain for some recollection of it and making no progress. From the expression on his face, Lingard knew it to be a time for treading softly. 'That's *my* version of what happened, George,' he said. 'The Traffic Department is playing around with a different one. And that's not going to please you. It's believed possible that being on the secondary road you'd been somewhere as a strictly private citizen and, returning home late after a few drinks, stopped somewhere along the road for a pee. In the dark you slipped, fell or otherwise accidentally banged your head against a tree and knocked yourself silly. You got back into your car in a daze, forgot to belt yourself in and drove off, losing control on the bend and diving over the top to run down to the lower road to your resulting concussion. I think they'd have liked to give you a breathalyser test to prove it.' He shook his head again. 'They don't seem to think it particularly significant that you were on sidelights, that the ignition key was in the off position and the gear lever in neutral. But they do think that all those things could have happened in the final bust-up. Does any of that help?'

'It helps, David,' Rogers said, surprisingly unruffled at what he could consider to be a disparagement of his driving. 'But only in my knowing in part what happened. So far as my remembering is concerned, you could be telling me about someone else having had it happen to him. I know this, though. I do take the coast road from Thurnholme, and only join the main road at Amford St Michael to get back here. I suppose I like a view of the sea with no commercial traffic to bother me. What I don't know is why in the hell I was there at that time.'

'Like I said, I think you ran into some late-night villainy and what you did about it got you clobbered.' Lingard knew that Rogers would never consider himself off duty if he stumbled against it, any more than he would.

'Assuming that I did, it must have been heavy stuff for someone to try to kill me. If you're right, that's how I read it. That's a bloody dangerous road to be let loose on in a runaway car.' Another's murderous malevolence, even hours old and its intent unsuccessful, could be unsettling and Rogers felt it. In bed, out of his professional milieu and sober grey suit, he was coffined helplessness, needing to be out and hunting his attacker, to exact a retribution that would satisfy his sense of injury. He was, beneath his constabulary skin, a normal vengeful member of the still partly primitive species *Homo* not-so-very-*sapiens*.

'It's a thought,' Lingard said. 'I wonder if he knew you were a police officer when he did it?'

'He needn't know now, need he? Not unless he had a look at my warrant card.'

'If he reads the *Post and Messenger* he'll know. At least, so far as your going over the slope is concerned. Whichever reporter wrote the snippet seemed to get a great deal of pleasure from your having the accident and from emphasizing that no other vehicle was involved.'

'That's the editor, David. He doesn't go for us much at any time and he's hanging it on me.'

'But nothing else. It's a certainty that nobody knows you've lost your memory of what happened.'

'That's true. You might make it more certain by persuading the doctor who's been practising on me not to write it up in *The Lancet*, or whatever they do. Or talking to the press, which he shouldn't do anyway.'

Lingard nodded his agreement. 'Something else, too,' he said lightly. 'When the chap – or it could be chaps, I suppose – who wanted you on the inactive list knows that you're still with us, he might make a more positive job of it. If, and when, he gets the opportunity, or comes looking for it. Particularly if he believes you know something not to his benefit.'

Rogers grimaced. 'You're a great comfort, David. He'll get his opportunity as soon as you bring in some clothes for me.

And do it today. I might just as well put up with my sore head doing something outside.'

'You're sure that's wise?' Lingard looked concerned. 'I doubt that they'll allow you to.'

'Allow me!' Rogers almost choked on his words. 'They don't have any bloody option. I'm not in jail, am I? There's only one way I shall get my memory back, and that's to go out looking for it; not by being stuck in here with people pushing needles into me.' That, so far as he knew, they had not done was beside the point.

Lingard stood from the bed, recognizing intractability when he saw it in the sudden lowering of black eyebrows. 'It's nice to have you back with us, George,' he murmured. 'It's been such a long time.'

3

It hadn't been easy to discharge himself from the hospital and, when he had, Rogers guessed that his name had been written up on the matron's black list as an obstinate ingrate not to be accommodated in the future other than as a terminal patient. The doctor, too, had been less than understanding, warning the detective of the consequences in exaggerated terms, suggesting (as Rogers had defined them) that he would undoubtedly drop dead on the steps as he passed out through the doors to an illusory well-being.

Hospitals, an otherwise healthy thirty-six-year-old Rogers had convinced himself, were for the helplessly ailing and the dying and not for a man who had only been banged on the head by some vicious bastard needing the remedial treatment of a prison cell. Too, in his view, only an amputation or clinical death could morally excuse a CID officer from working out his duties.

Wearing the fresh clothing delivered from his wardrobe, he was driven to his office in the dying daylight in Lingard's veteran Bentley. Getting his priorities right, he retrieved his spare pipe and staling tobacco – kept in a drawer of his desk against the unthinkable disaster of finding himself wholly bereft – and sat smoking while waiting for the thumping in his head to recede.

There were moments when he felt that the doctor had not exaggerated and he fought the nausea and pain by examining the clothes he had been wearing and the fragments of dried vegetation found in them, bagged in cellophane by Lingard as exhibits. Written on the labels was *Assault Occasioning Actual Bodily Harm: Det/Supt. G. Rogers. 15th Aug,* which, while confirming Lingard's faith in what had happened, didn't seem much of a charge for being knocked silly and toppled down the side of a hill. His examination of the clothing told him little other than that he wouldn't be wearing the stained trousers again and that it would be unlikely he would be compensated for their loss. That would prick his financial peace of mind as much as losing his car and his meerschaum. Not knowing one dead leaf fragment or growth of lichen from any other, they told him nothing other than that he had possibly been in or near a wood but, together with the possible finding of his meerschaum, would almost certainly indicate where he had been attacked. It was enough to justify his drafting instructions to Lingard for the following morning, squinting his troublesome eyes in the composing of them.

In a separate exhibit bag, he found what had been the contents of his pockets; his wallet, warrant card, cheque book, house keys, loose change and pens. There was nothing there that threw any light on where he had been or what he had done.

Before leaving in the patrol car waiting on his departure, he checked his booking-out duty board. It was there in his own writing that at 7.30 p.m. he was intending to visit Thurnholme Bay. Because he couldn't remember what preceded or followed it, he could have written it weeks ago. He was not far off staggering when he unlocked the door of his house, a house the Police Authority were pressing him to vacate in the continued absence of his wife and his known status as a single occupant. It had the unwelcoming emptiness of a womanless home for him, but he could think of no alternative that offered anything different.

Easing the swallowing of three paracetamol tablets with an extravagant dose of anaesthetizing whisky, he sat in an easy chair to stare at a wall until they took effect. When he thought he could move without falling over, he climbed the stairs and took a shower to wash the smell of hospital from his body. Looking at himself in the mirror, he thought that he had acquired overnight the gaunt face of an ascetic, even to the tonsure given him by the casualty doctor to allow the cleaning and stitching of his cuts, although this could be concealed by rearranging his hair. Using his shaving mirror, he could see a discoloured goose egg of a bruise in its nest of hair at the back of his head – two goose eggs, one overlapping the other, as he strained his eyes in looking. None of it concerned him so much as his emerging realization that he couldn't force his recollection to anything after he had visited the scene of the suicide of a dental mechanic in his greenhouse – he had stuffed a mass of hard-setting plaster of paris into his mouth while his wife was asleep in bed – which he felt had to be more than several days ago. Then the brief impression he had had in the middle of nothing of getting into his car against an evening's red sky – which might have been any evening – and the waking up in hospital. It was an unnerving condition in which to find himself. People had said words to him, had displayed attitudes: he had said words to them and, in turn, expressed his own attitudes. He could have done things, signed things – even cheques – for all of which he would be held accountable, and all of which had dropped into the brain's equivalent of a galactic Black Hole.

Deciding against a mowing of his whiskers, for with nobody in his bed to object it seemed pointless, he padded naked to it and slept dreamlessly.

4

When he woke at seven o'clock, surprised as always that the mosquito-buzzing of his wristwatch alarm could do it, he felt better. Apart from the soreness of his head – he knew that he would yell if anybody touched it – he felt fit enough to open moderately heavy doors without any assistance. Nothing of his memory had returned but he could, at least, remember how to get his own breakfast. Two cups of coffee, two pieces of toast – his customary culinary *chef d'ouevre* because cooking things baffled him – and a filling of his pipe were all that he could be bothered with.

It was a clear pale-blue of a morning with a sniff of approaching autumn in the air when Lingard braked his racing-green Bentley to a stop outside his house and sounded his klaxon above the heavy rumbling of the exhaust. When Rogers climbed into it, the canvas hood down as it was usually driven, he pushed himself into an excessive amiability towards Lingard to make amends for his short-fused irritability with him the previous evening. Too, he forbore knocking out the ash from his meerschaum on the door ledge, a habit in his own car. Although he had heard it described as the world's fastest lorry, the Bentley had been given feminine attributes by Lingard and he loved the monster immoderately. She was irreplaceable and, were it written in his destiny that he should break a man's arms in anger, he would certainly fulfil it on one who wilfully assaulted and damaged her.

There were eight men and two women, all detectives, waiting for him when he arrived at the summit of the road rising from Thurnholme. Having been briefed by Lingard, they knew well enough what had happened. Rogers told them that they were to search the verge of the road and the wood bordering it for a meerschaum pipe. Not, he was careful to say, because it was his and that he valued it – for in that case he could be accused of using them to his personal advantage – but because locating it would almost certainly indicate the spot where he had been attacked. And that was not to be the only object of the search. Anything, anything at all foreign to the natural environment, was to be marked and reported on. He was brief with his instructions because oddly, and he couldn't understand why, the reverberations of his own words touched against the aching on the inside of his head.

Cattes Cove was familiar to him only in knowing that it was there and in passing along the road above it to go somewhere else. The cove itself, and the sea, was screened from it by the long belt of wood; the inland side of the road, more open to a panoramic view of distant purple moors, being hedged with bushes, bracken and spaced-out silver birch trees. Walking with Lingard down the road to the bend, Rogers thought it an unlikely place to be the locus of dark villainy. There were no houses visible, no farming activities near enough for the smell of manure and silage to reach them, and traffic along the narrow road, because it passed through no villages, was minimal by day and almost non-existent by night. Other than, he qualified, for the occasional detective superintendent on his way home from places unknown. There were no signs on the road surface they had passed over to indicate that there had been an accident which he might have come across; nor, indeed, of anything else other than leaves fallen from the adjacent trees.

Standing with Lingard at his side, the scents of sun-warmed vegetation in his nostrils, he saw where his car's nearside wheels had hit the sloping bank before cannoning across to the offside of the bend and taking the verge in a tangle of smashed bushes not large enough to halt its progress. From there, the still-visible wheel tracks showed it to have ploughed into high bracken on the steep gradient, down across a narrow field of grass and finishing where it had burst through a four-strand wire fence on to the dual carriageway. Rogers could see the glinting of shattered glass and the discolouring patches of soil and dried liquid on the road surface where the car had come to rest. Sober and compos mentis, he wouldn't have chosen to go down there in daylight or in darkness in an armoured vehicle. He felt grateful for even the limited mercy of losing only some blood and his memory. And for not being conscious and subject to any uneasiness he might have felt in that plunge over the top. His guardian angel had certainly been on duty that night and doing what had obviously been her best. But that best wouldn't have kept her in his department as a policewoman.

'It's been photographed?' he asked Lingard.

'In definitive detail and colour,' Lingard assured him, wanting to add, 'Of course it has.'

'I can see how it'd support a fairish case of reckless driving against me,' he said thoughtfully, 'if the Traffic Department have their way. So far as the character who knocked me stupid is concerned, going over the top of this lot could be defended as adventitious rather than intended.' The thought that somebody had wanted him dead wasn't anything comfortable to live with, and his instinct was to reject it.

Lingard, to whom it hadn't happened, said, 'The lumps on your respected skull suggest there was plenty of malice in it to me.'

A car horn, sounded three times, reached them from where they had left the search party and they turned from the scene that hadn't told them any more than they already knew.

Detective Sergeant Millier, a blonde woman with such a smoothly soft and sensual mouth that Rogers considered her, however innocently, a disruptive influence in the department, was waiting near the utility van which had brought the party from Headquarters. 'I've found it, sir,' she said as Rogers approached. He didn't know, and would never be allowed to guess from her attitude, that she fantasized about him more than discipline regulations might approve. 'It was in among the trees.'

He smiled at her, something he found easy to do. Apart from the delectable mouth – she had dark-blue eyes as well – she was now his favourite sergeant. 'Good. You've left it where you found it?'

'I covered it with my handkerchief,' she said.

'Lead us to it, sergeant.' He thought that it might be his day after all.

Beneath the canopy of the trees it was shadowed a lucent green, bars of pale sunlight slanting in to the floor of dead leaves that crackled as Rogers and Lingard followed her. The sergeant's handkerchief lay in a hollow between the exposed roots of an oak and Rogers lifted it – it had an unconstabulary scent of jasmine in it – and returned it to her. His meerschaum, its golden-brown bowl not easy to identify on the dead leaves and lying apparently where he had dropped it, was unbroken. The bowl, half-full of tobacco ash, suggested that he had been smoking it when he entered the wood. Picking it up, looking at it with satisfaction and putting it in his pocket, he said, 'Thank you, sergeant, you can return to the wagon.' He had no wish to discuss his bodily functions in the presence of so attractive a woman.

When she was out of earshot, he spoke to Lingard. 'If I came in here for a pee, which I doubt, I don't think I'd come in this far. It's not too short of twenty-five yards and my objections to being seen peeing against a tree in the dark aren't all that dainty.'

'We could look for a stricken tree,' Lingard murmured, necessarily to himself. Aloud, he said, 'You could have been nearer the road, seen something moving and come in further to see what was what.'

'True,' Rogers agreed. 'Anything would sound possible to me at the moment. And if I did any bleeding here, it's not showing.' He was frowning his disappointment. 'Collect the party together and organize a search in this area. There must be something to be found other than leaves and rabbit manure.'

With Lingard gone, Rogers walked slowly towards where he could glimpse blue patches of sea – he could smell it, too – through the trunks and foliage of the trees, the ground sloping gently away from him. Apart from the distant sounds of the search party being rounded up by Lingard, there was a humming quietness in the wood with only the occasional thin piping of a bird and, away down below him, the subdued shirring of surf breaking on shingle.

He recognized the disturbance to the floor of leaves as soon as it came into his view. It had the appearance of having been scratched about by a large animal. Or, he thought, a hurried and careless concealment of something at night. And the night before last in particular. In an area of about the size of a single bed sheet, the dead leaves were jumbled together and not, as those around them, lying in flattened layers.

He crouched over it, ignoring the patches of shadow floating into his vision as he did so, reading things in what he saw, sniffing for the smell he anticipated. Crumbs of dried earth and brown leaf-mould were mixed in the leaves together with the wrinkled dead half of a blood-coloured worm. He brushed aside a patch of the leaves with his hands and scraped at the loose soil beneath it, not an activity about which he was happy, for he expected his fingers to touch decomposing flesh and his stomach to rebel against it.

He had burrowed to a depth of about eighteen inches and reached solid undisturbed soil when Lingard approached him. If he and the searchers trailing behind him were amused at the sight of a sober-suited detective superintendent on his knees and digging dirt with his hands, they took care not to show it. Rogers stood, his expectation of finding gruesome dead flesh vanished. 'You two clear the leaves from this patch,' he told the foremost two men. 'You others spread around and see what you can find.' He spoke to Lingard. 'If I had the sort of civilized mind that puts the nicest construction on things like this, I'd say that somebody was up here digging out leaf-mould for his chrysanthemums. As I haven't, I think this was intended for hiding a body. It's murder,' he said.

'And you disturbed him?' Lingard was nodding his agreement. 'Which was why he boffed you.'

Rogers was frowning as he watched the two DPCs clearing the leaves, but thinking things out. 'I suppose he was hard at it when he heard my car stop. Then the door being slammed when I got out. Perhaps I *was* stopping for a pee. He'd wait, probably sweating cold blood for me to finish and go. Perhaps he'd moved up towards where we found my pipe to see what was going on. Then, for some reason, I began to walk towards where he was. He'd hear me, of course. You can't tread on these leaves without making a noise, and at night they'd sound louder still. He wouldn't know who I was, naturally not. Just a passing car driver inadvertently poking his nose into where it wasn't wanted, but who could be a danger to him. People found digging in woods at night do tend to be suspected of doing something nasty or illegal.' That seemed to give him some relief, although it was all conjecture, for nothing of it brought any recall to his mind.

He was trying to remove leaf-mould from beneath his fingernails with his pocketknife, watching the uncovering of what he believed to be an intended grave at the same time. 'There are plenty of lumps of wood lying about which he could use,' he said, 'and presumably he did it from behind the tree. Or, perhaps not. Perhaps we came face to face and I said "What's going on here?" or something.' He shook his head in annoyance. 'No, of course we didn't. I wouldn't have a lump on the back of my skull if we had.'

The disturbed leaves, having been cleared, made it obvious that only part of the area had been dug. That part was no larger than would accommodate a child and, with a detective poking into it with a broken-off branch, had not been excavated any deeper than the hole made by Rogers.

Lingard said, 'Just knocking you unconscious wouldn't be the answer to his problem, would it? Not with you still breathing?'

'No, it wouldn't. But apart from killing me then and there – which'd pose the same problem he had already in getting rid of a body – he obviously wanted to get me well away from the scene. Which means he carried me to my car. He could have dragged me, I suppose, but there don't seem to be any marks of it. I'm a thirteen-stoner, David, which means that whatever else, he was no fairy; or that there were two of them.' That was a mollifying thought, if not a firm conclusion. Being felled by two men hadn't the indignity attached to its being only one. 'And then,' he said, 'I imagine that I was bundled into the driving seat, the handbrake released and sent off down the hill without even a God-go-with-you for company.' His mind produced a picture of his unconscious self in the car, gathering speed down the gradient in the darkness towards a chance collision with another car or to that steep fall into the road below. It was all forced imagery, and nothing of recall. 'I shouldn't be a policeman, David,' he added, shaking his head. 'I'd like to tear the bastard's liver out.'

'A good reason for you to leave it with me,' Lingard

suggested, 'although I know you won't.' When Rogers only grunted his disagreement of the possibility, he said, 'Are we agreed that when you'd been disposed of, chummy refilled the hole he'd dug? Then replaced the leaves and took the body away with him?'

'Yes. Panic stations intervening. He wouldn't dare go on with the burial.'

'Burying it somewhere else.' The two detectives, thinking alike, were pushing each other along with conjectures.

'He'd have to. Of course, it need never have been here in the wood in the first place. It's a bit hackneyed, but it could have been in the boot of his car tucked under the trees. Perhaps that's why I stopped. If I'd seen it parked there so late at night, I would've stopped to find out why.' He knew this with certainty. Any motivated detective would.

Lingard inhaled snuff, flapping away the grains his nose had missed with a crimson silk handkerchief. He moved always in an odour of Attar of Roses. 'You could,' he pointed out, 'have seen a light. It was dark that night; no moonlight because of an overcast, and it was raining. He had to be able to see what he was doing.'

Rogers shrugged. 'He'd be bloody daft if he used one,' he said drily. 'But anything to be rid of the idea that I'm the owner of an undisciplined bladder.' He had done as much as he could about his grubby hands and was preparing to leave. 'I think I've seen a house somewhere on the cliff top about here. If I have, whoever's living there might have heard or seen something. You carry on with the searching.' He smiled genially. 'You can't complain, David. At least I'm leaving all this to you.'

5

Rogers crouched, careful not to knock his head, to pass under the single bar fence – a reminder of privacy this, rather than able to prevent access – separating the wood from the greensward that sloped steeply to the house that stood a minute's fast walking distance below him. From the side it looked baroque Victorian; L-shaped in dark-red marlstone and big enough to be a hotel, the pitches of its grey slate roof broken by gabled dormers and squat chimney stacks, the tall windows in its two lower stories mullioned and topped with moulded architraves. At its rear was a paved yard enclosed by brick sheds and a walled kitchen garden, and a greenhouse with a few of its glass panes missing from one corner. Apart from a broad open space leading to the edge of the cliff and an unobstructed view of a glittering blue sea, there was a scattering of tall cypresses around the house – giving at first glance the impression of its being an Italian cemetery – with the further grounds thick with trees and shrubbery. A narrow greystone drive ran through them towards the road to Thurnholme Bay. A paved path in the turf leading to a natural cleft furnished with an iron handrail in the cliff's edge showed an access to the foreshore below. What appeared to be a structure of fence panelling stood near where the shrubbery began. The grass surrounding the house had the shagginess of a grazed paddock, the visible garden border filled with rose bushes. Three cars stood in the shade of a cedar of Lebanon near the forecourt of the house. The sun baked its midday heat on to what was, but for Rogers walking towards it, a scene devoid of human movement. Ignoring the cars, it looked very turn of the century; civilized and tranquil.

The double doors at the top of the steps, flanked by fluted pillars, were panelled and weathered to a neglected pale cinnamon. Rogers pulled at a brass knob set in the side stonework and waited. When his ringing went unanswered he left the door and looked at the house from the bottom of the steps. Three of the first-floor windows were shuttered and he could detect no movement through those on the ground floor. Moving to the seaward side of the building, he found another, smaller, door at the side of a lean-to conservatory which glassed in two house windows and almost obscured them with potted plants and flowers. With no bell-pull or knocker on the door, he rapped on its white paint with his knuckles.

The woman who answered his rapping was fragile-boned and slight, somewhere in her forties, and wore dark-tinted glasses. Her hair, a glossy bronze with lighter streaks in it, was worn long and tied in a ponytail behind her head, her skin milk coffee against her sleeveless white dress and the flimsy scarf held around her throat by a gold circlet. She wore no make-up on a thin face with high cheekbones, a narrow nose that gave her a well-bred attractiveness and a smiling mouth that showed beautifully white teeth.

Rogers smiled back at her. 'Good morning,' he said, producing his warrant card and displaying it to her. 'Detective Superintendent Rogers. I'm sorry to bother you but I've a small enquiry to make and I couldn't get a reply at the front.'

'The bell probably doesn't work,' she said. She hadn't looked at his warrant card. 'I believe they sometimes disconnect it so that they aren't woken up.' Her voice was cultured, and pleasurable to ears accustomed more often to the coarser accents of villainy. 'Won't you come in?'

He followed in the wake of her heady scent – strong, he considered, for the time of the day – into the cool twilight of a shaded room with its windows opened to the view of the sea. The furniture in it was reproduction Regency, the stuffed easy chairs chintz-covered. A black grand piano and a hi-fi music deck stacked with discs and tapes stood against one wall; a book case containing unfamiliar-looking books, the spines of which had lettering only at the base, against another. Vases and bowls of flowers rested in profusion on the window sills and on an otherwise unoccupied coffee table. There was conspicuously no television set. Nor were there any pictures hanging on the green-papered walls, but a solitary photograph in a silver frame of a bristle-moustached soldier with a brigadier's three pips and crown on his shoulders – he thought, possibly her father – stood between vases of flowers on the mantelshelf above the fire hearth. Two inner doors, both closed, he noted, and a small alcove occupied by a small dining table and two chairs. If there were anyone else at home, he or she was being remarkably quiet about it. A cream-coloured Labrador bitch with gentle dark eyes lay by one of the chairs, giving a couple of lazy flicks of her tail when she saw Rogers.

With the woman standing close to him, an amused smile on her mouth and her eyes still shielded from him by her impenetrable dark glasses, the room's contents and the dog made what he thought about her almost a certainty. He felt himself to be a stupid and undiscerning oaf, staring into her blank gaze with frowning uncertainty. 'I'm sorry . . . I didn't realize,' he said.

'That's always so much better, isn't it?' she told him calmly. 'Don't allow it to disturb you or I shall be offended.' She had removed her glasses as she spoke. Her eyes, a deep lustrous green and held in a stare as expressionless as the glasses she had discarded, made it difficult for him to believe that they were sightless. 'It's silly,' she said, 'but bright light can still hurt my eyes.'

'But otherwise completely?' He kept the pity he felt out of his voice.

'Completely.' She was as matter-of-fact as though she were talking about a minor cold. Then she said, 'You have a nice voice, Mr Rogers, and you are tall. That's all I know. Would you mind terribly if I see to whom I'm speaking?'

'Of course not.' Her use of the word 'see' provoked the thought that he was misunderstanding her, that he had been only partly right.

She moved closer, facing him, the scent on her skin strong in his nostrils. Her slightness so near made him feel ponderous and awkward. She reached up to him, her fingers brushing lightly over the contours of his features, touching gently along his mouth. 'You're smiling at me,' she said, and then moved her hands to his shoulders, pressing her fingers into his biceps and pinching together the fabric of his jacket before ceasing her tactile reading of what he looked like and what he was wearing.

It had been a sensually empathic experience for him. He thought it absurd, but whatever it was that homed distant male moths and panting dogs on to the females of their species, she had it in abundance for him. He hoped that the milk delivery man and the electricity meter reader were not similarly privileged.

'You've been in among the trees somewhere,' she said, 'and you smoke a pipe. I can smell the smoke in your clothing.' She was smiling at him, apparently deciding that he was a man with whom she could continue to be amiable.

'I was under the impression that I smelled of harebells and butterfly wings,' he answered her with a put-on ruefulness.

She returned his flippancy. 'I think you might if you didn't smoke. But do so if you wish. I don't dislike it. Now please sit down and ask me your questions.' She moved confidently to an easy chair facing one of the windows and sat, the dog padding over to her and lying near her feet.

Rogers took its twin to one side of her. From it he could see the sea which she could not, smell the perfume of the flowers drifting in on the warm air. He took out his notebook and pen. 'May I have your name, please?' he asked her.

'You may write down Phaedra Haggar; a widow of undisclosed age,' she said pleasantly. She had identified the meaning of his movements exactly.

Her hearing had been hypersensitive and Rogers knew that he would have to tread carefully in what he did. 'I'm investigating an incident which happened in the wood above here the night before last,' he said. 'Possibly about three in the morning. It could be that you heard something unusual enough to wake you.'

She thought about that, then shook her head. 'If you mean from Ridge Clump behind us, I'm afraid not.'

'But you could hear if you were awake and there were?' It was odd to have her turn her sightless eyes to him when she spoke, impossible to read anything in the expressionless green stare.

'I'm a light sleeper, Mr Rogers. Noises here can wake me. Sometimes traffic passing on the road does, although there isn't much of it.' She pushed her shoes off with her toes and curled her legs on to the seat of her chair as if settling in for a long and absorbing conversation. 'Was there a particular noise I should have heard?'

He thought, such as that coming from the digging of a grave? An unsuspecting skull being thumped with a log of wood? It was unlikely and nothing with which he could prompt her. 'Just noises,' he said smiling, then realizing that a facial communication could mean nothing to her.

'Like those I've been hearing this morning?' Her mouth curved her amusement. 'I heard men talking and, I'm sure, a woman too; a car with a loud exhaust that stopped up on the road and probably a van with sliding doors. Did somebody sound a horn from one of them?'

'You've remarkably good hearing, Mrs Haggar,' he said, ready to conceal his surprise should she also have smelled Lingard's snuff. 'Or we must have been making a devil of a row.'

'Not really. It's very quiet here and sounds carry. Are you going to tell me what's been going on? You're being terribly mysterious.' In repose, when she was neither speaking nor smiling, her mouth showed a gentle sadness.

'Nothing at the moment that's very important,' he said cautiously, 'and if I'm being mysterious it's because I don't yet know what happened. Does the wood belong to the house? I'm afraid I skulked under the fence to get here.' He and his sore head needed a smoke, but her remark about his smelling of tobacco decided him against it.

'No. It's council property. My ground runs from its boundary to the foreshore.'

'Are you alone here?' A silly question with three cars under the cedar of Lebanon. 'Or is there anybody else who might have heard or seen something unusual?' He didn't have too much justification for digging into the circumstances of her living, other than that he was attracted to her as a woman he could admire for the gallant way in which she carried the misfortune of her blindness.

She leaned forward, smoothing the nape of the dog's neck with the fingers that had done things to his breathing. 'Emily might have, but I'm afraid she hasn't learned to speak intelligibly yet.' She shook her head. 'Oh , dear, I mustn't make jokes about your investigations, must I? All the seven bedrooms in the house are occupied – eight guests in all. I can't speak for them, naturally.' He must have given out waves of non-understanding. 'When my husband died,' she explained, 'I was left with a house and land I couldn't afford to run, that I couldn't sell because it is entailed to his daughter and I wouldn't wish to lose it anyway. And so, I'm here in what you might call wrongly the dower annex; or rightly, the landlady's retreat.'

While she talked, he had watched her. For her age, she had an unusually youthful body; slender with a girl's small breasts, and the legs that she had tucked under her were long and slim. The lower reaches of his mind had been wondering whether it had retained the lusts of its earlier days, the fate of all but the most elderly of widows in becoming the subject of male speculations about their accessibility. At the same time he felt guilty, suffering some of the shame of the voyeur because she could not be aware of his interest.

'I may wish to speak to them later when I can find them,' he said. 'Will they be here for the rest of the week?'

'Apart from a married couple, they are all in the same party,' she replied, 'and they've ten days more.' Her mouth smiled again in his direction. 'Some of them are probably in now, but they expect the daily woman to answer the bell when it can ring. She won't because she insists it isn't part of her job to do it.'

'She probably belongs to a union.' He was reluctant to leave her, but could think of nothing further to ask her. She seemed not about to offer him coffee or something a little more exhilarating like whisky, so he stood. 'I'm grateful,' he said. 'Perhaps I could call on you again if I get any further information about what happened.'

She stood as well. There was none of the uncertainty he expected from a blind person in her smooth litheness. 'Please do,' she said. 'I really would like to know. I'm so incurably inquisitive about things that go bump in the night.' She held out her hand and he took it, feeling it warm and soft in his own big paw, and now determined that he would return with or without a reason for doing so.

Letting himself out into the sunshine – it seemed brighter and more friendly than it had been before he had seen her – he recalled the title of a book he had read; *In Praise of Older Women*, or something similar. He could now appreciate its appositeness, thinking that it had a lot going for its point of view, and that Phaedra Haggar, young-looking widow, might be the exemplar of why it had been written. Nothing of which, however, was forwarding the investigation on which he had set what was left of the professional part of his mind.

6

Having been driven to his office in a patrol car and now sitting at his desk wreathed in comforting smoke, Rogers worked out his frustrations in renewing his dislike of his surroundings.

Boxed in the grey stone, aluminium and glass of the new Headquarters structure foisted on the force by a with-it Chief Constable and an architecturally innovative Police Authority, his furniture of soulless plastic and metal, the computers and their datadisks and peripherals he was required to use to ask for any information he required, he suspected that the day would come when he would be identified by a sterile number and officially communicated with only by print-outs.

He missed his office in the old Headquarters with its scarred wooden and leather furniture, its ceiling marinaded a familiar saffron from years of rising tobacco smoke; the building itself comfortably ancient with the unseen shades of generations of forgotten policemen about its corridors, offices and parade room; even the whitewashed cells that emanated the despairing odours of imprisoned villainy. Although he would never admit it, he even missed the brainless mouse which was occasionally trapped in his waste paper basket, and which he released regularly to its home behind the wooden skirting after sharing with it any sandwiches he ate in the office.

In part, his frustration had arisen in Lingard's reporting to him that although the wood had been searched meticulously in its length and breadth, nothing more significant than a few empty beer cans, torn-open food packaging and a rusty cycle wheel had been found. Rogers was – his own phrase to Lingard – buggered without a body. He had to have one, or specific information about one, in order to trigger off the routine preliminaries of a murder investigation. Surmise and suspicions over a few spadefuls of disinterred leaf-mould were not enough, for it could be argued that other things than dead bodies could be buried at night in quiet woods; other things that could necessitate a banging on the head of a nosy intruder.

A murdered body, seemingly heavier than when alive and unco-operative in being moved, was an encumbrance; an unwieldy conglomeration of solid flesh, tissue, bone and blood to hide or otherwise dispose of; containing in its intractability not only the seeds of its own dissolution, but those of its murderer as well. In thinking around the problem, he could accept that the body intended to be buried need never have been taken into the wood. Were he himself anxious to dispose of one, he would certainly dig the grave first and bring the body to it afterwards. To be discovered digging a hole in the ground, however suspicious, would not have quite the same connotation of red-handed guilt as if there were a corpse present and patently waiting to go into it. Whichever way it had been, the body had been disposed of or buried somewhere else, and neither he nor Lingard had the most lightweight of ideas about where to have it searched for.

Although hunches were not anything he would lay claim to, Rogers did feel intuitively that he might find an answer connected with Phaedra Haggar's rather odd establishment that was neither a private house nor an hotel. Before leaving for his office he had sent for DPC Lewis who, with his ear not too close to the local ground, had known nothing of the police activity in Ridge Clump. In answer to Roger's questioning he said that he knew Mrs Haggar, had met her when she had reported the theft of a dinghy from her boathouse. In his extreme youth and seemingly unaware that he was courting his senior's extreme displeasure, he had spoken of her as if she were a withered old crone, confirming Rogers's earlier distrust of his judgement. Trimmed of Lewis's wordiness, it appeared that she was the widow of a retired brigadier who had died in his seventies some six years earlier. She had been much younger than him and was his second wife. They had arrived in the Thurnholme Bay area several years before that and had bought Catteshead House which hitherto had been unoccupied. Since the brigadier's death, she had been letting part of the house off and on to mainly professional people visiting the coast. So far as he knew, few of them came into Thurnholme and, when they did, it was to do their shopping or to eat, for, because of Mrs Haggar's blindness, they fed and looked after themselves. He had heard, he said in answer to Rogers's question, that she had gone progressively blind and had been totally so for years. It had been a little more than Rogers had expected from a man whose inefficiency he had apparently chewed at a couple of days earlier for his failure to detect a spate of thefts from hotels, but not a lot more than he already knew. Before he sent him back to Thurnholme, Rogers asked him if he had recovered the stolen boat, not being too surprised when Lewis said that he had not. Although he would have liked to, he didn't ask him whether or not Phaedra Haggar had 'seen' him by exploring his features intimately with her fingers.

On reaching his desk, Rogers had sent for the Missing Persons Register. This, now in the format of uneasily clipped-together print-outs instead of the more convenient filed forms, gave him no assistance. Nobody had been reported missing during the past ten days he was allowing as reasonable, and those who had been before then had vanished from districts other than that in which Thurnholme Bay lay.

It was while he was grunting dismissively through the flimsy paper sheets that he heard the words . . . *and I think you should go.* . . in a woman's voice; an echo in a dark cave and fugitive, gone as soon as he tried to hold them. Because there was no fitting them to the voice of any woman to whom he could remember having spoken, it worried him; even although they held the promise of a gradual return of his lost recall.

Putting it to one side for the more immediately important, he had filled in an accident notification form to his insurance company for his wrecked car – which he had seen in the Workshop's garage and sorrowed over – and had had a non-productive interview with the Chief Superintendent, Administration, about a replacement charcoal-grey suit. Ignoring the matter of a torn seam or two, making a penny-pinching sugges-tion about having the suit – which was now a crime exhibit – dry-cleaned, and manifestly considering that it had been spoiled by Rogers's carelessness in having the accident at all, the Chief Superintendent did nothing soothing for the growing malaise that the detective had been feeling.

32

With, he was certain, the stitches coming adrift on the top of his scalp, Rogers made the decision to retire temporarily from an investigation bogged down by the absence of its victim and go to bed, hoping to recover enough enthusiasm to visit Ridge Clump at three a.m. He couldn't imagine what it could tell him, probably nothing, but he wouldn't know even that unless he went there.

Driving himself home in the hotted-up yellow tradesman's van known ironically as the Banana Wagon and commandeered from the department, he set his wristwatch alarm and drank a generous medicinal dose of undiluted whisky which he hoped would stun him enough to sleep in daylight.

7

It was with a pin-point of soundless awareness that he felt hands pushing at his back, bending his legs into a sitting position; felt moist breath on the skin of his cheek and heard hard breathing close to his ears. Spongy softness beneath him, his shoulder against unyielding hardness, as he fought sluggishly against the paralysis that held him fearful and flaccid. Small green globules of light seen through half-closed eyelids floated like distant planets in infinite space, the floor under his feet vibrating, lifting sharply and settling with a jolt. Then the deep sonorous tolling of a bell, remote in the blackness and growing louder until he struggled from the dark pit of his sleep to an awareness of the telephone ringing at the side of his bed.

Daylight seeped through the drawn curtains and hurt his eyes that felt full of sand. His watch, read with difficulty, showed twenty past seven and he had overslept, his intended night visit to Ridge Clump aborted by it. 'Rogers here,' he croaked into the mouthpiece.

It was Lingard. 'You sound rough, George,' he said. 'Are you all right?'

'I was until you woke me up.' He was in a mood to be irritable. 'What's gone wrong?'

'Nothing that I can think of.' Lingard sounded light-hearted. 'It's all going right for you. We've got our body. I think,' he added as a personal insurance against his being wrong.

'Ah!' Rogers pulled his mind back on duty and swung his naked legs out of the bed. 'Stop thinking and tell me.'

'A woman. Shot in the face with a 12-bore or similar. Seen submerged against the breakwater at Thurnholme by a boatman at about six-thirty this evening. And God rot whoever did it, George, she's in a terrible mess.'

'You're there, David?' he asked.

'I have been. I'm now ringing from the quayside. She's been hooked out on to the breakwater and I'll wait for you there. The local inspector's calling out friend Twite and notifying the Chief Constable, the coroner and the rest of the needing-to-knows.'

Twite was the stand-in pathologist required, prior to his dissecting it in the mortuary, to examine any violently-dead body *in situ*, and Rogers needed to be there before him. 'Twenty minutes,' he said as alertly as he was able. 'I'm already on my way.'

Replacing the receiver, he tried to reorientate himself in time to Lingard's remark about the body being recovered that evening. Pulling the curtains open, he saw an orange sun low in the sky, long shadows and the feel of late day deadness in the warm air coming in through the window.

'You're a bloody fool, Rogers,' he muttered to himself. He had been in bed all of three hours and the only profit he could dredge from it was that he had no need to shave before doing his thing in an investigation that now promised him much into which he could sink his teeth.

8

Thurnholme Bay, no longer a village and not yet a town, was a place to be avoided by those – of whom Rogers was one – with a distaste for large flocks of garishly-dressed and sun-peeling holidaying humanity. Built in the half-bowl of a limestone fold,

34

and the distinction is ??
Even the Brits can't tell you.

its rows of houses mounted the sides in overlapping crescents of white, blue and brown plastered frontages and slate-grey roofs, most of which were guesthouses or bed-and-breakfast establishments. On the slopes of the rocky headlands, the two horns of a crescent, were inset large houses and hotels that had distanced themselves from what was a growing commercial disfigurement below them. Cafés, pubs, fried fish bars, souvenir shops and ice-cream parlours were separated from the harbour only by the nose-to-tail parked cars. In the harbour, created by the building of a breakwater, cabin cruisers, sailing dinghies and small yachts, tethered to orange mooring buoys, heaved gently on green water filmed by oil slick. Black-backed gulls, floating low in the air that smelled of seaweed and frying fish, screamed for food. Hanging over the hazy rim of the sea, the sun glinted light from the windows of the houses and daubed them with the pink tinge of a dying day.

Parking his van on the No Waiting yellow lines at the edge of the harbour in the absence of anywhere else, Rogers made his way to the breakwater. Built of huge stone blocks and green with seaweed at water-level, it curved across the opening to the sea like a crooked finger. A uniformed PC in shirtsleeve order, holding back the knots of curious spectators, saluted Rogers as he passed through. He could see Lingard and DPC Lewis standing at the far end with a body at their feet. It lay on its back as though waiting on a sacrificial ceremony to a sea god, shadowed against the reddening sky and containing in it the absolute inertness of death. A third man in a dirty blue shirt and trousers and wearing a peaked cap stood apart, leaning his back against a rusty iron rail that ran along the seaward side of the breakwater.

'Do we know who she is?' Rogers asked Lingard as he joined him, lighting his pipe and shielding the flame from the warm inshore breeze with a cupped hand.

Lingard shook his head. 'Not yet. Lewis thinks he might have seen her about the town, but he can't be sure.'

'That's the boatman over there?' The man in blue was out of earshot. 'He looks like a pirate.'

'He probably is in his spare time. I kept him here for you. His name's Scullian and you won't find him very talkative.'

Rogers stood over the body, a grimace twisting his mouth. Few men could be callous to what he saw. A loose dress of pale blue with shoulder straps, stained with blood that the sea hadn't washed out and clinging to the body, showed it to be naked but for a gold watch and loop chain bracelets on both wrists. Both arms and the sides of the thighs were striped with deep-pink horizontal abrasions. Her black hair, tangled in wet strands around the head, had been worn long and straight. The impact of shot to the face had pushed up into the skull the left side of the forehead, the whole of the orbital socket and eyeball, the base of the nose and the cheekbone, leaving a semi-circular crater that exposed shredded grey brain material pierced by flakes of bone. The ear and the parts of the hair that would cover it were missing. Sea water had soaked away the blood that must have flowed down the face and the pellet holes scattered around the torn flesh of the wound were pallid. The right eye, partly open, showed a dark-brown iris; the gaping mouth, the white even teeth of a young woman. Even as Rogers scrutinized the terrible lesion – a nightmarish sight even for a man accustomed to the torn flesh and disfigurement of violent death – a tiny olive crab appeared from beneath the broken bone and scuttled sideways to fall over the side of the breakwater into the sea below.

'The obvious,' Rogers said to Lingard. 'Shot from a few yards at most and not enough to allow the pellets to spread more than about seven inches. At a bit of an angle, too, which suggests that she was lying on her back. Probably in bed, don't you think?'

'Wearing a nightdress, I imagine she could have been,' Lingard agreed.

'But it doesn't explain the shape of the shot pattern, does it?' He was narrowing his eyes at the wound. 'It should be circular, and it isn't. There's a definite cut-off on the lower edge with no stray pellet holes.'

'Suggesting that something was in the way of part of the shot,' Lingard said. 'Like the end of the bed?'

'It could be, and the lower third of the spread I'd guess. Even then I wouldn't expect there to be such a clean edge to it.' This was a problem Rogers hoped he could leave to the pathologist.

The ache in his head was worsening, taking the sharpness from his thinking. 'I think that we'll have to assume she's the one who was to be buried in the wood, but more immediately important is to find out how she got here in the water.'

'And why,' Lingard said. 'Dumping her in the sea is about the most inept way of concealing a body I can imagine. And if she was tied to a lump of concrete it certainly doesn't show.'

'Whether or not, it's against the odds that she was put in just here. Cattes Cove is around the headland and she could drift. Have you asked the boatman about it?'

'Everything but that, what with one thing and another.' Lingard looked slightly chagrined. 'But he did say that she couldn't have been where he found her for long. His boat was here and he'd have seen her.'

'Leave him to me, David. You get on the telephone and chase up friend Twite. I don't want the body lying around here for much longer.'

Scullian was still leaning against the breakwater rail when Rogers approached him. The colour of a varnished door-post, his features where seamed and pitted, his chin and jowls thick with a white stubble. He looked hard and durable and cunning, his clothing at close quarters smelling rankly of dead fish and sea salt.

There was no need for Rogers to introduce himself, Scullian being the sort of man who would have the need to identify plain-clothes policemen on dark nights. 'You're the chap who found the body?' Rogers asked him.

'I've told the other'n.' His scowl seemed fixed in perpetuity and he was obviously inclined to taciturnity.

'So tell me as well,' Rogers said with amiability, although not feeling it.

'Her was in the water, midway under and hucked against the stones.'

'And you pulled her out?'

'Me and my mates. It takes more'n one.' He turned his head and spat into the water, watching the blob of sputum float away as though the detective were not there.

'She wouldn't have been dropped in where you found her?'

Rogers suspected that he had been classed among the untouch-
ables in the boatman's life.

'Her weren't there before.'

'When was before?'

'Six, near enough.' He spat again, wiping his mouth with the
back of his hand. 'Her came in with the tide. The current brings
'em in. Loosten lobster traps an' all.'

'And where does the current bring them from?'

'Along the coast.' He bobbed his head as though in recognition that the detective was asking the right question.

'From the direction of Cattes Cove?'

'Ar. An' further than that. Through Stutt Rocks.'

Rogers had never heard of Stutt Rocks, but wasn't about to
admit that to Scullian. 'As I thought,' he said. 'She was
floating?'

'Naw.' He showed his derision of Rogers's apparent
ignorance. 'Bumpin' and rollin' along the bottom more like.'

Rogers, seeing Twite's cream shark-nosed Citroën brake to
a halt on the harbour road, decided that he had obtained all that
he needed from Scullian to connect the body with his own
misfortune in meeting its murderer. 'Thank you,' he said. 'See
DPC Lewis before you leave. He'll want a statement in writing
from you for the coroner.'

Doctor Wilfred Twite, graduate in morbid pathology and
excessively bonhomous with it, was short and fat, had tightly-
waved black hair, an incongruous Mexican-style moustache
and sweated copiously. Wearing his summer uniform of a tan
safari suit with an open-neck shirt and a yellow cravat, he
matched in his own way the absent Lingard's dandyism. A
gourmand, he carried a briefcase that Rogers had never seen
opened and which he was cynical enough to believe contained a
Michelin food guide and smoked salmon sandwiches against the
catastrophe of his finding himself hungry and out of reach of a
recommended restaurant.

Meeting him, Rogers took the outstretched pudgy hand.
'Sorry to drag you out, Wilfred,' he said. 'There's nothing
much to do other than to confirm that she's dead and that her
death was caused by a gunshot wound. And when it happened,
of course, if that's possible now.' Even with a long-dead and

ripely decomposed corpse, it needed a medical man's say-so, and not a policeman's, to make it officially dead.

Twite beamed at him. 'Good. Ten minutes at the most, old George. I'm on my way to a conference.'

Which, Rogers guessed, was an equivocation for his eating somewhere. He filled him in with the brief details of the body's recovery and said, 'You can do the full examination tonight, I hope?'

'Not a chance.' Glancing only briefly at the body, he lit one of his cigarettes which smelled of smouldering incense. 'She certainly won't be going anywhere in the meantime.'

'No, but *I* want to. You could find something significant that I need for my investigation.' Rogers wasn't surprised at Twite's inclination for delay. He couldn't be expected to get hysterical about spending an evening cutting up a body to satisfy an impatient policeman as an alternative to a pleasurable meal and whatever was to follow it.

'So I could, so let me have a look at her,' he said cheerfully, not committing himself to anything.

Their shadows were now long in a sun that touched the horizon as they stood at the side of the body, and coolness was in the air. While Rogers watched in silence, Twite crouched, his buttocks straining dangerously tight the fabric of his trousers, and stared intently at the dead face, then put a forefinger in the wound and moved a piece of splintered bone back and forth. With the same finger he pushed up the lid of the uninjured eye, putting his face to within inches of it and peering at it. Turning one of the hands palm upwards, he rubbed his thumb over the pad of one of the fingers, moving to the feet and using his thumb similarly on the sole of one of them, making small sounds with his mouth as he did so. Turning the body on to its side, he examined the back, giving it a light smack of apparent satisfaction with the flat of his hand before letting it settle into its original position.

He stood, breathing a little harder, and said, 'For your report, old George, she's indubitably dead, and I'd swear to that on a stack of Glaister's Jurisprudences.' The cigarette between his lips wagged as he spoke, scattering ash on the lapels of his jacket. 'There're no external signs of putrefaction, but I'd guess

39

she's been dead for at least two days, possibly three. The skin corrugations on the plantar surfaces of the feet and fingers suggest that she's been in the water for at least twenty-four hours.'

'Just to avoid any future embarrassment, Wilfred,' Rogers said, 'I don't suppose that she was drowned first and shot afterwards?'

'Ah! The old hypercautious copper! That could happen, couldn't it?' He shook his head and more cigarette ash dropped. 'But not with this one. There's no signs of asphyxia that I can see.'

'But for certain when you do the examination tonight?' Rogers asked pointedly.

'Come off it, you pushful sod!' Twite was wiping his fingers with a handkerchief and smiling. 'You've had my preliminary opinion and I said that she'd keep for tomorrow. My conference and the lady I'm seeing afterwards won't.'

He was unexpectedly firm and Rogers accepted defeat. 'My apologies,' he said drily. 'I didn't realize that your sex life was involved. Do you have an opinion about the actual wound before you go? The direction of the shot, the shape of the shot pattern?'

Twite flipped away the cigarette stub and pursed his mouth. 'I'd be guessing again, but entry from a position a little below the horizontal, and the gun fired from a few feet away. Ballistics aren't my strong point so I wouldn't know about the patterning other than that I'd have expected it to be more circular.'

When the pathologist left him – moving with a fat man's briskness and waving a hand to Lingard who was on his way back – Rogers stared down at the pathetic body of the unknown woman, trying to read from it more than Twite had told him. Stronger than the prospect of a future legal justice, he fancied that a non-physical entity that had been her was at his side, a ghostly prompter that would never leave him until he had found her murderer. By the manner of her death she had, albeit unknowingly, burdened a man she had never known with that accountability, adding herself to the graveyard of similar corpses he carried in the back of his skull. Neat-breasted, flat-stomached and slim, she couldn't be more than twenty-five and was to be presumed unmarried if the absence of a finger ring meant anything. Her features, before the hideous ruin done to them, must have been decidedly attractive. And dammit, he said to himself, there had to be someone with nous enough to have noticed her absence from wherever she had lived.

He spoke to Lingard who had joined him. 'I'll leave you to get her to the mortuary, David. And I'll attend at the post-mortem examination when Twite decides that he'll do it. In the meantime, you find some brilliant bugger who knows everything about shotguns and have him brief us on the spread of shot, distances fired from and so forth. I think another talk with Mrs Haggar seems to be necessary before we do much else.' He would have preferred to return to his bed, but decided that he was a policeman first and a convalescent a poor second.

Preparing to leave, he saw an open-top red sports car stopping on the wrong side of the harbour road below him. With the engine still running, the woman in it was turning her head to stare at him. Although the light was fading, he could see her clearly enough and what he saw was vaguely familiar. Dressed in lemon-yellow with a head-scarf covering dark hair, she was sharp-featured, looked married and, in Rogers's reading of her, patently arrogant in her good looks. A woman, he judged, likely to treat a man with a greater contempt for his shortcomings than he need deserve, and the type of woman with whom he would always avoid entanglement.

As he stared blankly back at her obvious interest in him, searching his mind for recognition, she broke the brief contact between them and drove off. But she had stared at him as though she knew him, and not as a woman being curious about what was happening on the breakwater.

9

The gateless drive entrance into which Rogers turned his van was far enough away from Catteshead House not to be associated with it, but more easily with the small cottage set back in the trees and picked out in the beams of the headlights.

Travelling the short distance from Thurnholme Bay into descended night, he had fretted at his hasty decision not yet to have Lingard organize a Murder Investigation Room and staff, arguing with himself that with no real evidence that the unidentified woman's body had come from Cattes Cove, or even that its disposal into the sea was connected with the digging of a presumed grave in Ridge Clump, it seemed sufficient that he and Lingard could do what had to be done until the uncertainties were resolved. That an uncharacteristic irresolution was there at all might, he accepted, might be due to the soreness of his head, his unrecovered memory and the shadow of a Chief Constable, critical of failure, which too often rode with him.

When he drew up on the forecourt of the house, he saw that two cars, a blue Vauxhall Cavalier and a brown Mini, remained of the three he had seen parked there earlier. No lights were visible from the windows of the house, but an outside light, buffeted by moths, illuminated the front doors. Smoothing his hair disarranged by the wind of his driving and straightening his tie – and they were damned silly things to do for a blind woman, he told himself – he walked round the corner of the house and knocked on the white door.

He was about to knock again when a light above his head was switched on. 'Yes?' he heard her say from behind the door. 'Who is it, please?'

'Detective Superintendent Rogers,' he said to the wood panel in front of him. 'I'm sorry to disturb you, but could I speak to you?'

He heard a bolt being drawn, the rattle of a safety chain being unhooked, and the door opened. She was not wearing her dark glasses and he preferred her without them, her eyes being perfectly normal in appearance and a deep green. Still in her white dress but without the neck scarf, she smiled. Feeling grossly meaty and gauche against her slightness, he smiled a useless smile back at her. 'Please come in,' she said as if happy that he had called. 'You aren't disturbing me in the slightest.'

As she closed the door and rebolted it, her slim fingers moving with a deft sureness, he said reprovingly, 'You should be very careful about allowing strangers in, Mrs Haggar, merely on their giving a name. I could have been anybody.' He was conscious of her scent again, and the attraction of the fine-boned face and young-girl body. His memory of her hadn't exaggerated her niceness and the fascination she held for him.

'No, you could not, Mr Rogers. I can recognize voices once I've heard them. I need to, don't I?' She smiled teasingly at him. 'In any case, I could smell the harebells and butterfly wings on you.'

He followed her to the room into which she had taken him earlier. It was in darkness until she switched on a low-wattage wall light for which she would have no need on her own. Its weak illumination gave her an even more youthful appearance, and he wondered whether that was by a feminine intent. The dark-eyed Labrador dog, lying in one of the chairs, flicked her tail for him and he went across and stroked her ears. He liked her as much as he did her owner and he said, 'Hello, Emily. I'd love it if you'd choose to run away with me.'

Mrs Haggar smiled at his foolishness. 'Please sit down,' she said. 'May I get you a drink? I was about to have one myself.'

'Thank you.' He chose the chair near the window which he had used before. 'I don't normally touch the stuff,' he lied straight-faced, 'but I'd like a whisky, if I may. Undiluted, please.'

There were several bottles in the wall cabinet cupboard she opened and she chose the whisky as though she could see it, measuring it apparently by sound into two tumblers. Rogers knew that she would resent any offer to help and he chose not to do so. After she had handed him the tumbler with the most whisky in it and they had said 'Good health' to each other, she sat opposite to him. The Labrador, leaving her own chair, laid herself at her feet.

'Well?' she said, 'I'm sure you've come to tell me that something's happened.'

'I'm afraid I was less than forthcoming with you this morning,' he said, choosing his words carefully and with no wish to be overly forthcoming now. 'Necessarily so then; not, I feel, so necessary now. I mentioned that there'd been an incident on Wednesday night in the wood. That incident involved one of our officers being knocked unconscious by an unidentified man while investigating a matter he thought suspicious. By the time

43

he came round the man had gone and we didn't know exactly what he was up to. But we thought something rather serious. As you know, being so close to your house it was naturally assumed that somebody here could have heard the noise of its happening.'

Her expressionless stare was fixed on him and he could only read the concern in her voice. 'And is he all right? The poor officer, I mean.'

'I believe so. He thinks he'll live,' he said, smiling despite himself, then realizing how that must sound to her and adding, 'I'm sorry, I was joking. It wasn't much and he's back at work none the worse for it.'

'I heard you smile, so I guessed it wasn't terribly serious.' She had, as she had done before, pushed off her shoes and curled her legs beneath her.

'No, it wasn't. But what we found out later was. This afternoon the body of a young woman was taken from the sea at Thurnholme. She'd been killed with a shotgun, Mrs Haggar, and apparently put in the water along this stretch of the coast.'

That obviously meant nothing emotionally personal or disturbing to her and she said, 'Oh dear! That *is* nasty and terribly sad. Has it to do with your officer being injured?'

'The time of her death more or less coincides with it, and they could be connected,' he said noncommittally. 'Which, of course, is why I've come to see you again. We haven't so far identified the dead woman or, obviously, found out from where she came.'

'And you think that she might have come from here? Or from somewhere near here?' Her eyes were fixed on him and still he found it difficult to accept that she was not seeing him.

'In the absence of anything else, it's a likely supposition. But not necessarily so.' He drank some of the whisky he hadn't really wanted, but had taken as an acknowledgement of her hospitality. 'Possibly you might have known her, or heard of her? I'd say that she's twenty to twenty-five years old, slim build, long black hair, brown eyes, and wearing a blue . . .' Damn! He had allowed himself to forget again. 'I'm sorry,' he said. 'I'm being very stupid.'

She had smiled at him. 'I wouldn't know, would I? But don't

be sorry.' Her expression changed to one of concern. 'Are you thinking that she might be one of my guests?'

'Could she be?'

'Please God, I hope not.' She shook her head vigorously. 'No. I'd have been told if one had gone.'

'There is one, then? Or more?'

'Three,' she replied. 'And two of them are, I suppose, what you would call young. You have me worried, Mr Rogers.'

'I'm sorry.' He wanted very much not to have her consider him as doom and disaster, for few people developed an affection for the bearers of bad news. 'Don't think the worst. This is as much an elimination enquiry as anything else. They're out at the moment?'

'Yes, they are. They eat out in the evenings at Thurnholme.'

'You told me that there were eight, Mrs Haggar. Could I have their names, please? I shall need to speak to them.' Her scent had drifted to him and a separate part of his mind, difficult to control, had wondered how a man who wished to make unsolicited love to her could indicate it when she was unable to see the message written clear in his expression and eyes. If she could sense or smell the satyriasis in him she showed nothing.

'Of course you must.' Although she appeared composed, there was a tiny frown creasing her forehead. 'There are Mr and Mrs Tolliver, Mr Player, Mr Gough, Mr Quennell, Mr Whitaker, Mrs Horn and Miss Foxton.'

'Is Miss Foxton the younger?'

'I don't know. Mrs Horn and she are about the same age, but I believe Mrs Tolliver to be older.'

'Have you seen . . . well, had contact with the women during the past couple of days?'

She thought about that, pulling at the tail of her hair in concentration. 'That's difficult to say. I don't have all that much contact with them; other than, perhaps, when they arrive and when they leave. Mr Grice does whatever paperwork there is and organizes things.'

'Mr Grice?'

'Yes. He rents the cottage at the end of the drive.'

'I see. You were about to tell me whether you'd spoken to any of the women here.'

'Yes, of course. Mrs Tolliver this morning, certainly. I think Mrs Horn – I believe I heard her and Mr Player talking together earlier this evening. I'm not at all certain about Miss Foxton.' She grimaced. 'Oh, dear. I hope that doesn't mean anything.'

'It need not,' he assured her, believing that it possibly might.

It was a soft warm darkness outside now and the sea, seen through the shadowed fronds and giant leaves in the conservatory, gleamed a smooth inky-blue under a moon shining from behind the house. The air was heavy with the scent of her flowers. The unwanted whisky had apparently anaesthetized his sore head to an acceptable numbness, the chair he sat in was comfortable and, with this attractive woman to question, he felt that his investigation had something in it that could lift it above the squalid ordinary. But that, he thought, might soon be spoiled.

'Are you here every night?' he asked her.

'Yes.' She appeared surprised at the question. 'I go away very seldom.'

'Although you told me that you are a light sleeper, Mrs Haggar, would you necessarily have heard a shotgun fired in such a large house? Or in the vicinity?'

'I would in the house, obviously. I would hear it outside were it close enough, because I do.'

He raised his eyebrows. 'You do?'

'Yes. There are two of my husband's guns in the house. I've kept them because they were his and because they are an attraction for my guests.' She smiled briefly. 'And, of course, there's a sordid profit for myself in providing the cartridges and clay pigeons. They shoot at them over the sea, so there's no danger to anyone. And quite definitely the guns are not to be used for shooting at birds.'

'Have they been used at all during these past few days?' With the mention of guns he had become inquisitorial, although still amiable.

'Yes. I've heard them being used several times.'

'Would you know by whom?'

She shook her head. 'No, I wouldn't. Nor, of course, am I always here in the mornings. When I can get someone to take me, I do go out. I did on Wednesday morning when I visited my dentist.' She leaned forward, serious-faced. 'Mr Rogers, please tell me. You're beginning to believe it happened here, aren't you?'

'I'm beginning to believe that it's a strong possibility,' he conceded, 'and I'm asking you to co-operate in letting me see the bedrooms. I don't intend touching any personal belongings, and I'd like to do it before they return.'

'Could I ask what you would be looking for?'

'The woman was apparently shot in bed or, at least, in a bedroom. If she was, there would be signs of it, something that couldn't be hidden or cleaned up.' He had to be careful in what he said because he couldn't quite believe it himself. 'Despite what you've told me, there might be circumstances when you wouldn't or couldn't hear a shot from a different part of the building. Or, because I don't know when it happened, you could have been somewhere else.'

'Or that I wasn't being truthful?' She sounded more amused than offended.

'Cross my heart and hope to die, I'd never suggest it,' he said diplomatically. 'It really is a fact that we can't take things as read. If we aren't suspicious of most everything, we aren't doing our job properly.' Pontificating Rogers, he thought. He could be moving her to tears of boredom with his platitudes. 'May I see them?' he asked again.

'Yes, of course. Why not?' She uncurled herself from the chair and stood. 'No, Emily, not now,' she said when she heard the dog stirring, stooping and fondling the cream-coloured head with obvious affection.

Rogers had risen also and they stood facing each other. She said lightly, 'I do hope that I'm not embarrassing you, but do you mind terribly if I see you again? Knowing somebody by his voice and a recollection of the shape of his face isn't always enough.'

'Of course.' Although he wasn't going to be embarrassed, he would certainly be unsettled.

She moved close to him – too close, he thought, for his lower self's comfort – her scent heady in his nostrils and her mouth within a courageous man's kissing distance. She reached up, her eyelids closed, her fingers smoothing lightly over the

47

contours of his face. He felt again the sensuousness of her touch. It was hypereroticism for him and all the more so because it was one-sided. Under any other circumstances he thought that he would have groaned.

'Mud-brown eyes that are probably bloodshot,' he said exaggeratedly, for he did now feel some embarrassment, 'blackish hair and a nose that you can't possibly miss.' The fingers were brushing gently along his moving lips. 'All my own teeth and I'm close to being thirteen stone stark . . . well, you know, when I'm not dressed.'

She had finished her seeing of him by repeating the intimacy of holding his shoulders as though in an embrace, then releasing him without moving away. 'I really know what you look like now,' she said. 'It's a nice face, but I don't think that I'd feel very safe had I done something awful and you were after me.'

'You embarrass me, madam,' he said lightly. 'It's the face I wear when I'm working. The other one's even worse.'

He followed her from the room – the physically blind leading the brain-disabled, he told himself sardonically – back along the short corridor to the hall. There, unlocking and opening an inner door, she led him into the larger hall of the main house, switching on a light for him as they entered. Sombrely tiled in shiny brown, it contained in it the back of the double doors that hadn't been opened to his knocking, a partly opened door to an unlit room, a tall carved-wood cabinet and a wide staircase with a mahogany banister rising to the upper floor. She climbed the stairs as though she could see where she was going, light-footed enough to make Rogers, following her, feel sluggish.

There were eight doors in the L-shaped corridor at the top. Opening the first of them and feeling inside for the light switch, she said, 'This one is occupied by Mr Whitaker.'

Not in keeping with the heavy Victoriana of the house, it could have been the bedroom of a three-star hotel. It was furnished with two single beds with quilted headboards, a built-in wardrobe, a wash-basin, bedside tables and reading lamps and a triple-mirrored dressing-table. There were none of the carelessly strewn bits and pieces of a man's occupation visible and he noted the abnormality. While she stood in the doorway, he walked around it. There were no signs of scattered

48

pellet holes and if any blood had soaked into either of the bed mattresses or the unpatterned fawn carpeting, it had since been cleaned to invisibility.

Checking similarly in the other identically furnished rooms – she named their occupants as they entered them – was a repetition of his finding no evidence that the dead woman had been shot in any one of them. It was a blight on his expectations, although not a disintegration of them, for there remained one further small indication of a departure from normality. He had noticed in Miss Foxton's room that her dressing-table top had been clear of any of the bottles, tubes and jars of cosmetics he had seen in the two other rooms occupied by women. It still wasn't much, but it was something.

'A clean bill of health, I think, Mrs Haggar,' he said as they descended the stairs. 'Certainly nobody's been shot in any of your bedrooms.'

'And if they had, I would have heard it, wouldn't I?' She was gently reproving.

'Yes, I'm sure that you would,' he agreed, wondering if this was the point at which she would begin to think him to be a blundering nosy-parkering nuisance and react with unfriendliness. 'Now could I trouble you further and see the guns?'

'Of course,' she said. 'They're kept in the hall.'

Standing at the cabinet, she reached and retrieved a key from its top, unlocking and swinging open the door. Two double-barrelled shotguns were held upright in clamps against the back wall. Hammerless, with under-and-over barrels showing the dullness of long use, they were years from being new. Three boxes of cartridges lay on a shelf, one open and showing its red-cased contents. A spouted tin of oil, a brass cleaning rod, a roll of flannelette and a small tin cash box were with them. A square of card pinned to the edge of the shelf was printed *Shooting only between 10 and 12 for the consideration of other guests. Please clean guns after use.* On the floor were two open boxes of black clay saucers. In the smaller of the boxes the top saucer had three equidistant coin-sized holes near its rim and Rogers made a mental note to find out why.

'Would they all know where the key is kept?' he asked her.

'Naturally.' She looked mildly amused as if she were

49

humouring a man struggling for certainties. 'These *are* for their use.'

'Do they come to you for permission to use them?'

'No. They have no need to. They use them as they wish and put the money for the cartridges and clays they've shot in the cash box.'

A woman, he considered, with a misguided trust in the honesty of her fellow-men. He closed the door, locked it and withdrew the key. 'I'd be grateful if you'd let me keep the key until I've satisfied myself about your guests,' he said. 'And that should be very soon.'

She inclined her head. 'I wouldn't think anybody would want to go clay shooting at night,' she said drily.

Not clays only, he told himself, remembering Lingard's pessimistic warning, but also the admittedly remote prospect of an already wounded detective superintendent being used as a target. And, although he decided against telling her, he might want the guns checked for fingerprints.

'Mentioning your guests,' he said. 'Do you keep a visitors' book? I'd like to know their full names.' Her agreeable docility to his demands was beginning to puzzle him. There were no signs of anxiety in her face and that could mean that she had little doubt that he was chasing an illusory fancy.

She went to a small table near the inner door that led to what appeared to be a sittingroom and opened its drawer, handing him a green-covered book. 'They should be in there,' she said, 'but I do have to rely on other people making sure that it's done.'

He opened it and read the recent entries written in it: Leslie Gough, Michael Whitaker, Arnold and Eva Tolliver, Angela Foxton, Sebastian Quennell, Luther Player and Catherine Horn. With the exception of the Tollivers, who had given a South Wirral address, they all had addresses in Abbotsburn.

He closed the book and returned it to the drawer. 'I'm grateful for your help, Mrs Haggar,' he said, 'and I'm sorry that I've taken up so much of your time. I'd like to see your guests when they return, but I'll wait outside.' He had noticed that she was courteous enough not to show the relief she must have felt.

'They won't be back until about ten or ten-thirty, and I'm

perfectly happy that you should wait inside.' She sounded as though she meant it. 'I'll make coffee if you wish.'

'I'm grateful again,' he said, 'but if I may, I think that while I'm here I should have a look at the cove. Do you mind?' He knew that in a sense he was running away from a woman who was proving to be unsettling to the emotionless consideration he should be giving to his investigation.

'Of course not, if you must. You'll have to be very careful though, it can be dangerous in the dark.'

'And you think I shall be wasting my time?' He put a smile into his voice.

'If you are, I assure you that you haven't been wasting mine,' she said.

Letting himself out into the darkness he knew that, given any encouragement by her, he could be envious of the man with whom she had spent her years, even jealous of the beautiful doe-eyed Emily who took so understandably a large share of her affection. With it went the hope that it was all a temporary aberration of his glands or whatever and unlikely to interfere with his accountability to the dead woman whose presence seemed still to be insistently with him.

10

Sitting in the van and smoking the meerschaum he had forborne using because of Phaedra Haggar's sensitive nose, Rogers used the radio transmitter to call Headquarters Control, asking the operator to find out if Lingard was in the building and to call him back immediately.

Something could have happened, something useful could have been discovered, to convince him that he wasn't mistaken in believing that the death of the unknown woman had occurred in Catteshead House. His enquiries had, so far, produced little to support it. Whitaker's seemingly unoccupied room might have an explanation in that he was an exceedingly tidy man, but the absence of cosmetics from the dressing-table in Angela

Foxton's room had a significance that he could not overlook. He could recall no past instance, in his occasional frequenting of different bedrooms, of a woman keeping her packaged fragrances and paints under cover and not cluttering up a dressing-table with them.

Other things similarly cluttered up his thinking. Where had he spent those unremembered hours after leaving Lewis in Thurnholme Bay? Six of them, not counting whatever relatively short time he had been out of his skull and lying in Ridge Clump. Logically, it should have a connection with the event that terminated with his being hit on the head. Reminded, he touched the lump it had produced with his fingers. Still there, not too far above his shirt collar, still sore and feeling as large as it ever had been. And that familiar-looking female stranger who had stared at him so arrogantly on the breakwater; who in the hell was she? Was she the woman who had said the snatch of words . . . *and I think you should go* . . . that had risen unsought in his mind?

Flogging a lost memory was, he thought, much like trying to grasp handfuls of swirling mist, grateful for the radio that broke into his thinking when it transmitted his name and needed his attention. The information that Lingard was nowhere in the building was both satisfying in that he must be out doing something hopefully useful, and irritating in that he wasn't available when wanted. Switching off the radio and checking the time – it was 9.20 – he took a handlamp from a fitted equipment case and climbed from the van. A van, he decided, that he would be rid of as soon as he could, feeling irrationally that its use made him appear to be a greengrocer's delivery man and against the interests of his amour-propre. Climbing from it hadn't done him all that good either. It was as if he had stepped out and left all his vitality on the seat. Mind over matter, he told himself without too much conviction. He wasn't tired, he wasn't clapped-out and if his head ached it was only in his imagination.

With the moon fully risen in a cloudless starlit sky, the night glowed a phosphorescent greenish-blue with inky shadows; quiet and with a left-over warmth from the day. The saffron suffusion of Thurnholme Bay's street lamps showed from behind the darkness of trees and Rogers could just distinguish a square of reddish light from the foliage-shrouded cottage at the entrance to the drive. From far away, he heard the barking of a lonely dog.

His shoes crunched loudly on the gravel before he reached the grass, walking then in comparative soundlessness towards the path leading to the cove. As he passed the side of the house he saw her, a darker form against the luminescence of the conservatory glass. He muttered 'Damn!' to himself and re-traced his steps. 'Just on my way to the cove, Mrs Haggar,' he said. 'Did you want me?'

'Yes,' she replied. 'I heard you and I'm worried about you going there. It's very dangerous in the dark, and you don't know it as I do.' In the moonlight her hair and eyes were black against the paleness of her face, her mouth glistening.

'I've a lamp in my hand and I really am used to getting around at night,' he said easily. 'If I do fall over the edge or drown, it won't be because you haven't already warned me.' He wasn't too pleased that his physical capabilities were, in effect, being downgraded; neither did he wish to explain that he wanted to see the cove at night because it was most likely then that the woman's body had been launched into the water.

'May I come with you? I know it so well.' She hadn't shown him her amused smile and there was an underlying insistence in her words.

He hesitated, not certain whether she actually was worried and wanted to be with him, or that she was more concerned about what he did or saw. And, with his being on her property by sufferance, it wasn't anything to which he could justifiably object. 'Of course,' he said quickly before she could notice his reluctance. 'I'd be happy to have you with me. Won't you need Emily?' If *she* didn't, he thought facetiously, *he* might.

'No.' She was smiling now that she had got her own way. 'Not if I have you for the awkward bits.' She moved to him and held out her hand. 'You, instead of Emily.'

Surprised, he took it, warm in his bigger hand like a soft curled-up mouse. In all innocence she was doing the worst thing she could; the intimacy of her touch, the headiness of her scent so close to him and the eroticism of her mature femininity disorganizing his concentration. Nothing in the seminars he had attended at the Police College had given him a defence against it. 'I won't bark any more than I have to,' he said solemnly.

Not needing to use his handlamp, he walked with her along the flagstones embedded in the turf and leading to the cove. Not given to small talk, he searched his brain for something useful to his investigation. 'Is this from where your people shoot at clay pigeons, Mrs Haggar?' he asked her.

'Not quite,' she said. 'The trap's much nearer the edge where it's safer. For other people, I mean. I'll show it to you before we go down.' She pulled at his hand with her own. 'Bear left over the grass. Can you see the fencing around it?'

'Yes, I can,' he replied. It was nearly a hundred yards away, close to a spread of small trees and shrubbery and silhouetted clearly against the gleaming sea. 'Is it the only place they shoot from?'

'It has to be. The trap's a fixture there.'

'Mrs Haggar,' he said. 'Why is . . .'

She interrupted him, turning her head to him. 'Call me Phaedra,' she commanded him. 'Everybody does. You're making me feel dreadfully archaic.'

'I don't think anybody could do that,' he said gallantly, as he was obviously meant to and meaning it. He started again. 'Phaedra, is it likely . . .'

She chopped him short once more. 'And I can't go on calling you Mr Rogers, can I?' Her fingers, which had been lax, pressed against the palm of his hand and he could make what he wished of that.

'George,' he said, and he thought that his name had never sounded so bloody ordinary as he heard himself say it. 'A lot of murderers have been called that.'

She laughed, her teeth very white in the moonlight. 'Also lots of kings and one dragon-slaying saint.'

They had reached the fencing panels screening the shooting trap and Rogers guided her around them, releasing her hand. They were about eight yards from the unrailed lip of the cliff and he said, 'You will stand still, won't you? The edge is pretty close.'

54

'Of course I shall.' She was humouring him. 'I really do know exactly where I am.'

The two interwoven wood panels, each six feet high, were staked into the ground in the shape of a V with the opening facing the sea. Within it, covered by thick orange plastic sheeting which Rogers removed, stood a metal contraption; a crouching miniature ballista operated by a heavy coil spring and looking dangerously powerful.

'Can this be operated by the person shooting?' He peered at its clamps and levers, not being clear about how it would work. 'I mean, need he have someone with him to do it?'

'No. It is tiresome loading and cocking it oneself, I suppose, but it's done. After which the trigger release arm can be kicked off from the firing ready position.'

Rogers replaced the plastic, his main interest in the trap having been that anybody under six feet in height using it would certainly be hidden from the house by the panels; and, covered a possible eventuality, realizing that a woman crossing careless-ly and soundlessly on the grass in front of the firing stand could very easily be shot accidently by an equally careless somebody intent on releasing his clay and blasting at it.

'Seen and understood,' he assured her. 'Now I want to look over the edge, so don't follow me.' She made no reply, only bent her head and he was once more finding it frustrating not to be able to read what might be in her eyes.

Even in the shadowed darkness, his feet necessarily too close to what appeared to be a fast-eroding cliff top, his peering over did unpleasant things to his acrophobia. Only a few degrees from being vertical, there was an unbroken fall of what he estimated to be sixty feet or more to jagged crenellations and slabs of shiny black rock through which the quiet sea lapped and made pools. Behind them, the base of the cliff, curving out into deep water to enclose the cove, was gashed and riven into crevices. To his far right where he could see the handrail of the steps, the face of the cliff shallowed in an incline to a small shingled beach bounded by off-shore rock ridges that showed only their peaks at what he knew to be low water. It was a microcosmic lunar world of naked and hostile rock that could hurt and, Rogers decided, while not a place likely to attract holidaying sunbathers and coloured beach umbrellas, it would have a supposed usefulness for a hard-pressed killer needing to dispose of a body. With a receding tide, it could have been expected that it would be swept out to sea and not seen again until the fish and crabs had eaten it to an unidentifiable skeleton.

She had not moved and he reached and took her hand. Not, he admitted to himself, the most distasteful task he had had to do that day. 'I'd like to go down below now,' he said, adding 'Phaedra' as an afterthought, deciding that he had best get used to the familiarity if he wanted her co-operation.

The steps leading down to the beach had been fashioned from wide slabs of outgrowth rock, filled in and made level with rough cement. Out of the moonlight, Rogers used his handlamp and she followed him unfaltering down the steep zigzagging route, only occasionally using the handrail. Although there weren't too many steps, the climb down made his calf-muscles ache, the jolting of his feet on hard rock putting some of the soreness back into his head. Apart from the agreeableness of having a self-appointed consultant on the topography of the cove with him, he could think of better places to be; bed – on his own – being one of them.

'Would you mind waiting here?' he said when they had reached the bottom. 'I want to do the whole beach and I'll probably be clambering over rocks and things.'

'If you happen to see my husband, I'd be grateful if you'd tell me,' she said calmly.

'Your husband?' Rogers felt bemused, glad at least that she couldn't see what he thought must be goggling idiocy written in his features.

'Yes. When he wasn't shooting at clays he was down here fishing for bass. At all hours.' There was a just-discernible edge of disparagement in her voice. 'I suppose it was quite appropriate that he died down here as well with a dead fish on the end of his line. Poor Hubert,' she said in a gentler tone, 'but it was probably how he wanted to go.'

'I'm sorry.' It was banal but what else, he thought, could be said. Hubert and Phaedra. They certainly didn't sound as though they had been a twentieth century Abelard and Heloise,

56

which was perhaps why she had as good as told him that she had been neglected. 'I'll tell you if I do see him,' he promised her gravely.

'Do you ever see spirits of the dead?' She had lowered herself to sit on the bottom step and was schoolgirlishly hugging her knees.

'Not that I can recall. But I imagine there's always a first time for everything, if it happens at all.' Not that he was certain in his scepticism, for two years of night beat patrolling as a probationer PC – shaking hands with door handles, it was called – had never rid him of the lurking disquiet that he might, as most newly recruited probationers were, be ordered one night to check that no headstones had been stolen from the local cemetery and churchyards.

'Don't be too unbelieving,' she said banteringly. 'You never know when you might.'

Moving along the beach with the night air on his face like damp tissue paper, the shingle shifting under his shoes, he was conscious of the inevitability of her knowing by the sounds he made of exactly where he went and what he did. Which wasn't at all what he wanted, and he tried to confine his passage to outcrops of rock, although all of them were slippery with a bladdery seaweed and risky with the possibility of further damage to his head.

Seen now at its own level, the flatness of the sea had only been apparent. Rhythmically breaking waves fringed the beach and rocks with their white froth, the sloping shingle moving sibilantly under the gently heaving retreat of a tidal ebb. With the cliff face above him casting its shadow on the beach, Rogers needed to use his handlamp, its yellow beam throwing more shadows; shadows that scurried and vanished disconcertingly, suggesting furtive watchers. He cursed Phaedra Haggar's mention of ghosts, recalling unwillingly the short story *Oh, Whistle and I'll Come to You, My Lad* in which a white and horrible something had flitted menacingly behind rocks on a similar beach. Even she looked bleached to bloodlessness in her white dress and seen only dimly in the distance, suggesting a something not quite comfortable.

When the handlamp's beam picked out the low rectangular

shape of a shed, it was to return his mind to what would be, were it daylight, the prosaic ordinariness of a man-made structure in what was, anyway, a commonplace cove. Of unpainted weather-scoured wood, it had a wide padlocked door with a single-pane window on its leeside. Shining the beam through glass green with algae, he could see a grey inflatable boat with yellow oars fixed in its rowlocks. By placing the side of his face flat against the glass, he made out the hanging folds of a black rubbery material next to the window, but otherwise out of his view. If the temporary concealment of the woman's body became an issue, the use of the boat-house was a possibility he would bear in mind.

The shingle beach extended beyond the boat-house for twenty yards or so before losing itself in a ridge of broken rock that, in its turn, merged with the base of the cliff. With its conformation suggesting that an exit from the cove could be made there, Rogers walked to its end. Deciding that it could, although only by an agile rock-face climber equipped with suction pads, he turned to go back. The beam of his handlamp, showing his way over the shore's-edge rocks, attracted his attention to what appeared to be a stubby rod standing upright in them. Reaching it – having in his scrambling plunged his foot ankle-deep in a rock pool and saying 'Buggering hell!' incautiously loud enough for even the distant Phaedra Haggar to have heard him – he crouched over it. It was an ordinary enough length of steel tubing that had been hammered into a crevice in the rock. But for a collar of clean metal where a double twist of rope had protected it, it was lightly rusted. In Rogers's strictly non-seafaring opinion, as a mooring for a boat it was in the wrong place, for submerged rocks were visible where the missing rope would have reached the water. It also occurred to him that the rope tied to it must have been in position for some days to have prevented the rusting, and that ropes carried in boats were usually only tied temporarily to mooring points.

Fretting on the tubing's possible use and wondering whether he was being mentally thick about what was obviously a non-significant triviality, he heard the sound of a car's engine, faint but clear in the quietness, coming from the direction of the house. When it stopped, he knew that there had been a return from eating in Thurnholme Bay and that he would soon discover whether or not he had been wasting his time in blundering around in the dark like a myopic mountain goat.

With his left shoe and sock making sucking noises as he walked, he returned to where Phaedra Haggar was waiting. Still on the step where he had left her, although now with her hands resting on her lap, she stood as he approached. 'Did you find what you were looking for?' she asked him, apparently un-worried that he might have.

'I wasn't looking for anything in particular,' he prevaricated. 'I certainly didn't see your husband.'

She gave him an oblique smile. 'No, you wouldn't. He'd never fish for bass on an outgoing tide.'

'Shall we go back now?' he said, still not certain whether she was being serious about the possibility of her dead husband's nocturnal appearances. 'I'll be behind you.'

'To catch me should I fall?' she could read his mind in large print.

'I'd do my best.' It wouldn't be anything but a pleasant experience for him to have her in his arms, although he felt that he wouldn't be able to do it without his knees collapsing.

He followed her as she mounted the steps and, in looking upwards from what until then had been an unnecessarily lengthy scrutiny of her body from behind, saw momentarily movement on the cliff's top. Silhouetted darkly against the moonlit sky, it had given him the impression of a sudden withdrawal of the head and shoulders of someone peering down at them.

'I see that you have an inflatable in the boat-house,' he said, keeping his voice low and hoping that she would not notice and ask why. 'Is it the replacement for your stolen dinghy?'

'You know about that?' She sounded surprised. 'No, it belongs to Mr Player. He brought it with him.'

'He fishes as well?' What could be easier, he thought, than to conceal a body in the well of a boat and row out to sea before pushing it overboard?

'Snorkel swimming, I believe, but they don't tell me every-thing they do while they're here. And so long as nobody steals the silver I don't really mind.'

'The boathouse is locked. Who holds the key?' he asked.

'There should be two, and they're kept in the drawer with the visitors' book.'

He saved further breath for the climb, suspecting from the aching of his leg muscles and his nearly exhausted lungs that some agency had maliciously added to the number and steepness of the steps during their stay on the beach. In truth, he was beginning to feel like an old, old man attempting to climb the north face of the Eiger. At the top and on the path to the house, now in full moonlight and with no signs of the watcher – if, indeed, there had been one – he took her hand again, releasing it only when they reached her door.

'I heard a car, so somebody's back,' he said, 'and I think I can manage now. I'll let you know what happens.'

'I won't be able to sleep until I know, and I hope that you're wrong,' she replied.

'I often am,' he said wryly, 'if that gives you any comfort.'

With her back to a door she was making no effort to enter, she looked up at him, the moon reflecting small discs of light in her dead eyes. Juvenile memories of doorstep goodnights to girls not too long away from school came into his mind and, but for the banging in his sore head, his wet shoe and sock and the rather pressing matter of a murdered woman, he thought that he might have regressed to his adolescent sexual initiatives.

Her sightless stare was fixed on him. 'You wouldn't believe me an over-imaginative woman would you, George?'

'No, I wouldn't think so,' he said cautiously, not knowing anyway. 'Why?'

She bit at her lower lip in indecision. 'It doesn't . . . no, I wasn't intending telling you, but I think I must. While we were down on the beach I had a very strong feeling that there was somebody else . . . somebody watching me, I think. Then, just now when we were walking over here, I heard somebody moving away from us in the bushes.'

'Could it have been an animal? A bird?' He knew that it wasn't going to be.

She shook her head. 'I thought you'd know by now.'

'I'm sorry, of course I should. Thank you for telling me, I didn't hear it myself. It's probably nosiness on somebody's part.' He smiled for her benefit although his face found it a hard thing to do. 'About you and me being together, I mean.' Holding hands in the moonlight, seeking solitude on the beach; it could have added up to the whetting of a voyeur's appetite. Except that he didn't believe it for one moment. 'It doesn't bother you, does it?'

'Of course not. I just thought that you should know.' She turned, put her hand out and felt for the door handle. 'I shall see you later?'

His imagination was reading something more than a conventional question in her words, then deciding that its owner was a bloody idiot who should be keeping his mind more firmly directed towards his investigation. Wasn't it Samson or some other character, he thought, who had his mind taken off the tearing down of temples by his unwanted attraction towards a beautiful woman?

'Yes,' he said, deciding that because his imagination might not be wholly untrustworthy, he could, at least, keep his options open.

I I

A white Ford Sierra with a roof-rack had been parked alongside the Cavalier and Mini at the front of the house, its windows open and the ignition key left in the switch; a carelessness that offended against Rogers's standards of security.

One side of the double door was ajar and he pushed it further open and entered the hall. Light and the flat sounds of angry male voices shouting at each other came from the room he had so far seen only in darkness. Through the gap in the door he could see an expanse of green wallpaper with gold fleur-de-lis in a latticework design, a high black-leather wing chair and part of another, a section of a filled bookcase and some well-worn carpeting.

Inside, the chair he had seen only partly was occupied by a man, the voices coming from a television set he was watching.

He turned his head at Rogers's entry, nodded briefly, registered what the detective accepted as disinterest and refocused his attention on what was obviously a more appealing coloured picture. Patently dismissed as being no concern of his, Rogers profiled him into his memory. Slumped in the chair and stocky in build, his height was difficult to judge. About forty years old with thinning brown hair and eyes the colour of moist chocolate, his full mouth and heavy jowls suggested him to be a man who both liked and possessed the plushiness available to those with enough money. His clothing, although crumpled, supported it. He wore a pinkish-fawn linen suit of holiday flamboyance, a pink shirt and tie, and a silk handkerchief that flopped from his breast pocket. A half-full bottle of vodka and its mixer that looked like blood-tinged water stood on a spindly table at his side. He held an empty tumbler in the hand resting on the arm of the chair.

Rogers moved closer to him and said 'Good evening', reasonably amiable and loud enough to be heard over the squealing of car tyres coming from the television set. 'Could I have a few words with you?'

The man pressed a button on the remote control handset he was holding and the sound vanished. 'It's rubbish, anyway,' he said agreeably enough. 'The late-night films usually are. Say on.'

'Detective Superintendent Rogers,' the detective said. 'You are?'

'Sebastian Somerset Ayscough Quennell.' He reached and tipped vodka into the tumbler, then added a minimum of the mixer. 'You were trotting around here this morning?'

'More or less.' Rogers pulled the spare wing chair closer to Quennell and sat in it.

'I warn you, friend, I'm not in a very chatty mood, having just drunk a half-gallon or so of restaurant plonk and now trying to kill it with this. Is it really me you want to speak to? I'm only a guest here.'

'And the only one I've seen so far. Are the others about?' Rogers was guessing, but he thought that Quennell was part way into an alcoholic high. His articulation was over-precise and his eyes had an abnormal shine.

'They're probably in bed,' he said. 'Except . . . well, if they've returned, that is.'

Rogers thought him to be evasive. 'Who, Mr Quennell?'

'The Tollivers.' He drank generously from the tumbler. 'They went in their own car.'

'And who went with you?'

Quennell held the tumbler up and squinted at it. 'It's awfully good for you,' he said earnestly. 'It's a prophylactic against leprosy. It must be, because it's certainly kept it away from me.' He drank some of it and then smiled at the detective.

A mind-your-own-bloody-business remark, Rogers accepted. Deliberately off-putting and intending that it should show. 'I think that giving me your medical information might be misplaced,' he said mildly. 'I'm here to see if I can identify a dead woman taken from the harbour at Thurnholme Bay today.'

There was surprise in his face certainly, but thunderstruck by the information he wasn't. 'Ah! My profound apologies. I suppose that makes a difference. It accounts for all the hoo-hah going on there this evening. We could see the inquisitive *hoi polloi* milling around from the Hog's Nose.'

Rogers knew of the Hog's Nose Eating House. It commanded a lofty view of the harbour and, despite its unappetizing name, it was linen-tablecloth expensive and served the best food in Thurnholme Bay.

'Who's "we", Mr Quennell?'

'Luther Player, Leslie Gough, Cathy Horn and myself.' He hadn't turned his head to speak, but glanced at Rogers from the corners of his eyes, giving him a guarded look. 'What's this woman to do with us?'

'That's what I'm trying to find out. Is there anyone missing from here?'

'Not missing, no.' He had hesitated before answering and there was a qualification in the way he said it. 'Gone off, you could say.'

'Gone off? He frowned. 'Do you mean Miss Foxton?'

'O sweet Judas!' he protested. His head had swivelled full-face to Rogers. 'You can't be suggesting it was Angela? I'm not going to believe you because I know she's with Michael Whitaker.'

'She is? Where, Mr Quennell?' Rogers insisted.

'How would I know? They went off together on Wednesday.'

'You saw them go?'

'Not exactly. But I wasn't surprised when they did.' His words had a faint slurring and he was speaking more slowly.

'Why weren't you?'

'I don't like telling tales out of school, but I know that Michael was cocking his leg over her on the quiet. It'd be understandable that they'd want to go off where they could carry on without interruption.'

'Why on the quiet? Why without interruption? She's un-married, isn't she, and it's not yet a crime?'

'Ah!' Quennell seemed doubtful that he should be saying it. 'I imagine you'll find out anyway, but she was Leslie Gough's little pigeon. He brought her here and I suppose it could be embarrassing if he caught them *in flagrante delicto*, so to speak. And Mrs Haggar wouldn't like it either.' He poured out another large vodka, tincturing it only faintly with the mixer and drinking most of it. 'I'm not a boozer, if that's what you're thinking,' he giggled. 'Just frightened of catching leprosy.'

'I've read somewhere that it's confined largely to the tropics,' Rogers said drily. 'I didn't know it had reached us.' Quennell appeared to be making a determined effort towards drunkenness.

'Sarcasm wasted,' Quennell said, unoffended. 'I've no doubt you're a nice bloke in yourself, but you're still a copper.' He belched. 'Sorry, that's too much spaghetti alla carbonara.'

Quennell having mentioned food, Rogers was reminded that he hadn't eaten since midday and what he had then had only been a couple of sandwiches. It might be that it was the cause of his not feeling so good himself. His eyes had done their thing again when, for a second or two, he had seen Quennell with an overlapping ghostly face.

'Tell me what Miss Foxton looks like,' he said. 'Describe her.'

Quennell shrugged elaborately. 'Why not? I have nothing

that isn't of the most admiring.' He looked at the flickering soundless picture on the screen that had been irritating Rogers. 'A M-Modiglianiesque figure, stretched out and slender. Black hair she wears long, a nice little nose and you'd say she was pretty. Not beautiful, but pretty.' He had returned to watching Rogers's face and his expression was suddenly sad with all downturned lines. 'You're going to say that it's her, aren't you?' His acceptance of her identification seemed to have sobered his speech a little.

'I hadn't any doubts about it since you told me that she was missing. She wore gold chain bracelets?'

'Yes,' he said reluctantly. 'On both wrists.'

Rogers waited until he had finished drinking his vodka, which was the whole of what was left in the tumbler. 'I obviously want to know more about both of them, so tell me about Whitaker. He's a friend of yours?'

'We belong to the same . . . well, you could say that we're averagely matey.'

'What does he do for a living?'

'Electronic systems. Clever stuff I wouldn't understand.' He leaned towards Rogers, bizarrely earnest, his face paler than it had been. 'You haven't told me, was Angela drowned?'

'No. She was shot.' Rogers watched the mouth gaping in surprise, possibly shock, but nothing to suggest that he might have already known.

'Poor, poor Angela, she didn't deserve that.' He bit at his lip and thought hard before saying, 'Not by Michael.' He shook his head hard, hiccuping as he did it. 'You'll never make me believe that.'

'Apart from the fact that I haven't suggested it, why not?'

'Because.' He was trying to hold the detective's stare with unsteady eyes, looking a man whose drinking had suddenly caught up with him. 'He isn't that sort of a bloke. Angela laid it on for him, not the other way round. You know? Difficult to refuse a lady an' all that. Which he didn't.' He was almost mumbling it. 'Why would he shoot her when he went away with her?'

'When did you last see either of them?' Rogers thought that rational communication would shortly finish.

Quennell's forehead creased and his lips moved soundlessly. Then he said, 'Bloody days . . . all the same on holiday. Wednesday? That's it, Wednesday. I saw Michael . . . coming out of bathroom when I got up. Can't remember whether later. Don't always eat together until evening. Then he wasn't with us . . . nor Angela. Tha's when we wondered where they were . . . not in bed that night. W-we had a look . . . worried, you know.' He stretched his arm for the vodka bottle. ''Nother drink,' he mumbled and, wildly misjudging, knocked the bottle over, the remaining liquid in it running from the table on to the carpet. Staring stupidly at the emptied bottle, he said, 'It's a north-country shithouse of a world, d-don't you think?'

Rogers, who had started instinctively in his chair to help in the mishap and who hadn't got nearly enough information from Quennell, said equably, 'I've always thought so. You were telling me about Miss Foxton?'

Quennell grasped both arms of his chair and began levering himself upright. 'N-no offence, friend,' he said in a tight-edged voice, 'but would you mind p-pissing off. I'm tired . . . bloody tired . . .' Standing without the support of the chair, much shorter than he had appeared sitting in it, he swayed as if buffeted by a strong wind and turning, his eyes staring in surprise, collapsed across the table and on to the floor.

A man bloated with food and sodden with wine and vodka, he was more difficult to heave back on his feet than Rogers expected, the smell of his breath unpleasant in his nostrils. With one arm supporting him and his fist clutching the lapels of his jacket, the detective led him on his rubbery legs from the room. Climbing the stairs with him and using the banister rail to hold him upright, he manhandled him in a series of jolting heaves, discomfiting even for a semi-conscious man who, although well anaesthetized by alcohol, still retained enough coherence to mumble, 'Sorry 'bout this . . . mus' be something I ate.'

Reaching the corridor at the top and bushed enough to feel that it should be Quennell who did the supporting, Rogers propelled him past the first door. Whitaker, Quennell, Player, Gough, was the sequence of names he remembered from his inspecting the rooms with Phaedra Haggar. Pinning him stiff-armed against the wall, he pushed open the door to his bed-room. 'Bed,' he said into his ear, steering him to it and allowing him to fall on it. With Quennell remaining in the position in which he had come to rest, his eyes staring blankly at the ceiling, he pulled off his shoes and dropped them at the side of the bed.

As he left the room, Quennell groaned and turned on his side and Rogers closed the door on the sounds of his pre-vomit urging. He guessed how he must feel and, despite his having earned it, could feel sorry for him. Should he vomit, he also felt sorry for Phaedra Haggar's carpet, for Quennell would never reach the wash-basin unaided.

12

Entering Whitaker's room next door, he searched it. Empty drawers, naked clothes-hangers in the wardrobe, and a tablet of stale soap on the wash-basin, were all that he found. But for the evidence of the soap, the room might never have been used. Locking the door with a key taken from its inside, he pocketed it.

Around the corner of the corridor there were four doors; the first to the bathroom, then Angela Foxton's room before Catherine Horn's, with the Tollivers' immediately opposite. He opened the door to Angela Foxton's room and walked in. The wardrobe and drawers were empty of her clothing, the cos-metics she had used and the suitcase or whatever in which she had brought them all. A small metal bin beneath the wash-basin contained stained globs of cotton wool, torn-up fragments of a handwritten letter and its envelope, and a screwed-up pill of printed paper. But for the persisting odour of the scent she had used – a clinging muskiness of which Rogers, in his present mood, disapproved for its purpose of arousing the satyriasis in men – and the likelihood of her fingerprints, and possibly somebody else's too, having been left, the room was a vacated nothingness.

A woman, in circumstances where she was about to be shot, didn't take her clothes and cosmetics with her and go off in her nightdress. But somebody who wanted others to believe that she had gone away would find it necessary to make it appear so. And would that be Whitaker? It possibly was, but it would be desperate last-stand stuff. At some time or another he would have to reappear, probably to explain that he had left her somewhere alive and kicking. And that assumed he had no fears of her body being found.

In the morning, he would instruct the meticulous Detective Sergeant Magnus from the Photographic and Fingerprint Department (whose claim it was that he had once found and identified a rapist's fingerprint on the purple sateen panties of his victim, now framed and exhibited in the force's Crime Museum to prove it) to use his powders and sprays to find what there was in both rooms, conscious in particular that the dead woman had yet to be unarguably identified as Angela Foxton.

Taking the metal bin with him and locking the door, he went slowly down the stairs. Retrieving the visitors' book from its drawer, he copied from it the names and addresses he needed into his pocket book, then, righting the overturned table and turning off the television set – a woman was speaking her soundless words to an empty room – he left the house for the night outside.

There was no fourth car, so the Tollivers had not yet returned. He didn't want to see them tonight, anyway. Or anyone else. Not even Phaedra, and that meant that he must be an ectoplasmic shell of his normal self. He should be vigorous, keen-eyed and investigationally competent, working through the night if necessary to the unmasking of the murderer. Instead, he felt unswitched-on, not even fit enough to be investigating the theft of milk from a doorstep, certain that his vitality was draining from him in some queer fashion through the stitched cuts in his scalp. His seawater-soaked foot, trivial in itself, wasn't helping either. Placating his conscience with the thought that it was past eleven o'clock and it seemed that everyone but him and the Tollivers had gone to bed – he couldn't imagine that a reproachful Angela Foxton would be twirling around in her refrigerated drawer should he take a few hours sleep himself – he groped in his trouser pocket for the ignition key and climbed into the van.

13

Rogers hesitated in turning the key in the ignition switch. His self-exculpatory dismissal of Angela Foxton hadn't worked, his tired imagination now putting her into the seat at his side, a personal albatross that should be carried slung around his neck. But not too tired that it couldn't visualize against his will the horror of her mutilated face and set it against the relative triviality of the discomforts he was using to excuse a continued search for the justice her death demanded. Too, he had overlooked the obligation requiring him to inform the presumably already unhappy Leslie Gough that his erstwhile girlfriend was dead, for he could claim some sort of a quasi-right to be told. That she might have relatives somewhere who would have to know was something else he needed to find out.

Removing the key from the ignition, he switched on the interior light and adjusted the rear-view mirror to peer at the reflection of the self-accepted walking-wounded Rogers. He considered that he didn't appear to be all that traumatized. Slightly hangdog and a bit on the yellow side, but that might be the effect of the sickly light from a 7-watt bulb. They weren't the features of a grown-up man intending to go to bed just because of a couple of bruises and the onset of fatigue. Unshaven and filthy as he felt, he had still to show the durability, stubbornness and leather-skinned bloody-mindedness that went with a detective superintendent's badge of office. If, he thought sardonically, it were Whoever-it-is-up-there's intention that he was to drop dead, he would rather be remembered for doing so on the job, preferably in circumstances attracting a laudatory reference to it in the force's General Orders. It called for the narcotizing of his tobacco-starved system and he filled and lit his pipe, feeling that it could, like Quennell's absurd prophylactic against leprosy, also hold at bay his lethargy, enabling him to manage a few more hours of not-too-active investigating.

Unhooking the radio handset and pushing down the 'on' switch, he called up Headquarters Control, asking if they had contacted Detective Chief Inspector Lingard. They had. Anticipating his senior's possible impatience, Lingard had left a message to be relayed to him when he, in turn, had chosen to make his location known. His second-in-command was now in possession of possibly useful information about shotguns and the effect of distance on the pattern of pellets. Dr Twite had telephoned, indicating that he was prepared to do the post-mortem examination that night and, Rogers not being contactable, Lingard was proposing to attend in his place. If wanted, he could be located at the mortuary.

Rogers dictated a message to be passed back to Lingard. He was to be informed that the dead woman had been provisionally identified as Angela Foxton from Abbotsburn, that her fingerprints were to be taken and that he was to report at Catteshead House at the finish of the examination, bringing with him a sergeant who would be briefed to set up a Murder Investigation Room. In a separate instruction to Control, he asked for Detective Inspector Coltart, Detective Sergeant Magnus, six members of the department and a communications car to be at his disposal by first light. Switching off, he knew that he had effectively closed the door on any likelihood of sleep, for that he could never do while his subordinates worked on the same investigation. The only thing he could think of was a more meticulous search of the vacated bedrooms. It wasn't much, but it was something.

Entering the house and climbing the stairs again, his footfalls deadened by its carpeting, he had the feeling that while everyone there must be aware of his presence – he would certainly have been heard hefting the drunken Quennell up to his room – he was being avoided. Turning into the corridor, he surprised a man holding the handle of Quennell's open bedroom door. He turned, scowling, as Rogers approached him. Shorter than the detective, a terrier type of man, he was pink-complexioned, looked sinewy and well-muscled, and wore dark trousers with a formal shirt and tie. His pale-grey eyes were unfriendly, his mouth under a thin moustache without amiability and his hair, combed straight across his forehead, hay-coloured. On his wrist he wore an oversized watch with a midnight-blue dial. To Rogers, he looked the type of man usually photographed following in the wake of elderly actresses.

'What are you doing? Who are you?' he demanded. He spoke in an arrogant drawl with a hard edge to it.

Rogers had looked for recognition in the eyes of a man who might have the clobbering of him in a wood on his conscience, but saw none. He knew that he wasn't going to like him anyway. 'I'm a police officer,' he said. 'Detective Superintendent Rogers.'

'How do I know that? You could be anyone.' His breath, reaching the detective, smelled of peppermint.

'So I could.' He produced his warrant card and held it open for the man's inspection. While he was narrowing his eyes at it in apparent suspicion, Rogers glanced into the bedroom. Quennell was unconscious, or something very like it, and making snorting noises. He had either held back on any vomiting or had managed to reach the wash-basin. 'Satisfied?' Rogers said, closing the door and putting the warrant card back in his pocket. 'Now, who are you?'

'You're the one who brought Quennell upstairs?' There was distaste in his voice.

'We'd been talking,' Rogers said tersely. 'I asked you who you were.'

'Gough. Why do you want to know?'

'You're just the man I needed to see.' Had he imagined it, or had he seen a shadow of alarm in his eyes? He already had him classified as one of the twisted characters who hated all policemen on principle.

'I was about to go to bed.'

'So I imagine. Nevertheless, I want a few words with you about Miss Foxton. Your room will do.'

Gough had compressed his lips at the mention of her name, then shrugged. 'If you must,' he said arrogantly, 'although I can't see that she's any of your business.'

'I shall tell you that she is.' Rogers was beginning to reciprocate Gough's obvious dislike of him. Apart from his hard mouth and unfriendly eyes, his peremptory manner scratched a rawness of irritation in the detective.

Gough turned and, with Rogers close behind, entered the end room in the corridor. He stood by his bed, patently suffering unwillingly Rogers's intrusion. He folded his arms and looked out through the window at the moonlit kitchen garden. 'Get it over with, then,' he said tightly.

'You were friendly with Miss Foxton?' Rogers kept his voice neutral.

The pale eyes turned to him. 'You're a bit mealy-mouthed for a policeman, aren't you?' he sneered. 'You mean, did we sleep together?'

'If you like. Did you?'

'Yes, we did.' He was prickly about that. 'Do you want to make an issue of it?'

'Not really, it's all right now,' Rogers said mildly. 'Otherwise I wouldn't have considered it *your* business.' He felt that the sympathy he had for the victims of bereavement was going to be less than usual. 'Miss Foxton is dead. She was taken out of the harbour this evening.'

Gough stared incredulously at him, his mouth opening and closing. 'You're a bloody liar!' he got out. 'If you're trying something on . . .' He sat abruptly on the bed.

In the silence that followed, as Rogers had watched his reaction, he heard the incongruity of heavy snoring coming from the next room. 'If you say so,' he concurred, accepting the role of punchbag for a man he saw in apparent emotional shock. 'But I'm afraid she remains dead just the same. You might as well know she'd been shot.'

Gough jerked and his mouth moved soundlessly. Rogers thought he saw the words *I'll kill the bastard!* formed, but it need not have been, although it would be something that he would remember. 'Who did it?' Gough said hoarsely. 'I want to know who did it.' His fingers were clenched, his hands shaking.

Rogers stared at him, not certain whether he was exaggerating a reaction to the death of a woman who had left him for another man, but leaning towards an opinion that he was.

Nothing of what he'd done would be difficult to act. 'So do I,' he said, 'and that's why I've questions to ask you.'

Gough sat hunched as if holding himself together, silent for a few moments. 'Does it have to be now?' he asked, scowling belligerently. 'I was going to bed.'

'So you said before, and so was I,' Rogers said tersely. 'We'll suffer together. I understand that you brought Miss Foxton here with you?'

'So you know; so what?' He was persisting in unpleasantness. Rogers was patient with the man, although he saw no reason why he should be particularly polite with it. 'And your relationship was close enough for you to be jumping into her bed? At least, I imagine, until Whitaker took her over?'

Gough, his inner struggle written in his face, said, 'If you're trying to fit me up for something, Rogers, you're wasting your time. I didn't like her all that much. She wasn't anything more than a casual, and if she was stupid enough to prefer Whitaker, that was his bad luck.'

'How long had you known her?'

He held Rogers's eyes unblinkingly, the prelude to a lie, the detective thought. 'A week or two.'

'And no ill-feeling towards Whitaker?'

'To that little arsehole!' He gave a short derisive laugh. 'No, but it surprised me. I had the wrong impression about him.'

'Which was what?' Rogers had noticed that the snoring from the next bedroom had stopped.

'Just that. My opinions are my own, not for you.'

'When did you last see Miss Foxton?'

Gough stared at him, scowling – it seemed to be his most used expression – and picked at his moustache. 'You're still at it, aren't you? So I can't remember. So it might have been just before she and Whitaker shoved off.'

'Which was Wednesday?' As he was questioning Gough, Rogers was trying to identify the tie he was wearing. He thought that he had seen the grey, pink and green slanting stripes before. Not that of a public school, surely, and being worn by this mannerless lout.

'If you say so.'

'Did you speak to her?'

73

'No, I damned well didn't,' he said angrily. 'Why the hell should I have? She's dead, but that doesn't stop her having been a promiscuous bitch.'

'You obviously had to say something to her when you realized she'd chucked you for Whitaker. When was that?'

Gough cleared his throat in annoyance. 'You want to grow up, Rogers. I didn't give a damn and she knew it. We didn't have to talk about it.'

'When was the last time you were in her room?'

'You *are* a nosy sod, aren't you,' Gough sneered. 'Do you want to know how many times? And what it was like?'

'Even allowing for the circumstances, I find that you're an unpleasant bugger to talk to,' Rogers said amiably. 'Either answer the questions I ask you, or refuse to. In which case I'd want to know why. When was the last time you were in her bedroom?'

Gough glowered, warning blotches of pink on his cheeks. 'Last week, and it isn't that important that I'd write it down or try and remember it.'

'Given your opinion of Miss Foxton's promiscuity, would there be anyone else other than Whitaker who might have gone there?'

'I don't know, I don't care and I wouldn't tell you anyway. You coppers make me want to puke; always digging for filth and enjoying it.'

'Yes,' Rogers agreed ironically. 'It's a happy life we lead. When was the last time you used one of Mrs Haggar's shotguns?'

'Ah! You've got around to that, have you?' He twisted his body and swung his legs on to the bed, resting his shoulders against the pillow and folding his arms in an attitude of disassociation. 'Never,' he said. 'Go and climb another tree. I shoot wildfowl, not useless bits of clay.'

His arrogance nettled Rogers. 'Is that because they don't bleed when you hit them?' he asked expressionlessly.

'That's bloody offensive.' The warning blotches were on his face again.

'It was meant to be,' the detective said, showing his teeth. 'I'm occasionally allowed it with hostile and objectionable witnesses. Accepting that you don't shoot at clays with Mrs Haggar's guns, what do you do when you're down on the beach?'

There was a definite shadowing of caution in Gough's eyes before he looked up at the ceiling in contempt. He said sarcastically, 'I put my swimming trunks on in my bedroom – they're navy-blue with a dolphin logo, if you have to know – and I walk down there carrying a towel. Then I go into the water and swim around for as long as I want to. When I think that I've had enough I . . .'

Rogers cut him off short. 'Tomorrow, I'd be grateful if you'd let me have your fingerprints taken for elimination purposes.'

Gough raised his eyebrows at that. 'I don't think so,' he said. 'Why?'

'We shall probably find them with others in Miss Foxton's bedroom and will obviously need to identify them as yours. As you've had legitimate access, they'll have no other interest for us. But any others certainly would.'

'I'm sure I don't have to give them to you, and I don't think I will.' He turned his back on the detective. 'Full stop, and make it goodnight.'

'I'd better see you again tomorrow,' Rogers said. 'We might even get to talk to one another in a civilized manner.'

Gough swivelled his head to him. 'Don't think that you're going to soft-soap me, Rogers,' he growled. 'I'm putting in a complaint about your offensiveness to your Chief Constable.'

'Do so.' Rogers smiled, knowing it would irritate him further. 'It's all very childish, but when you do I shall be given the opportunity to quote the remarks provoking what you call offensiveness. And I doubt that you'll welcome that.'

Outside the bedroom and closing the door on him, Rogers stood silently in the corridor, staring as if interested aesthetically at the art nouveau leaded window at its end. After a brief period of waiting, he heard the muffled thumping of what he imagined to be fists beating at a pillow. At that, he thought, it was better than throwing things, which was probably what he himself would do in the same circumstances.

75

14

This time Phaedra Haggar switched on the inner light, unchaining and opening her door almost in the echo of Rogers's knocking on it. Probably waiting on his arrival, she could have recognized his footfalls on the gravel. 'I'm sorry,' he said. 'It's late, but I do have to see you.'

She wore what he thought to be a housecoat; cream-coloured with small green long-tailed birds embroidered on it. Her hair was untied, reaching to her shoulders and making her look different, more feminine. He had always thought that a woman letting her hair down meant something by it, but as he could smell no freshly-applied scent he accepted – regretfully, he had to admit, although in no condition to do anything about it – that any prospect of his seduction had been in his imagination only.

'I know,' she said as he followed her into the sittingroom. 'It's in your voice.'

The phosphorescent rectangles of moonlight flooding through the windows gave the room the shadowed tranquillity he felt he needed, its quietness promising a soothing of the raggedness of his malaise. Emily, slapping her tail against the wickerwork of her basket at his entry, made him welcome to it.

When she reached for the light switch, he said, 'You needn't, you know. The moon's bright and I can see quite well. You don't mind?'

She hesitated, then withdrew her hand. 'Of course not, but please not on my account.'

'I've a thumping headache,' he was led into admitting, 'and I think no light might help.'

'Would you take some paracetamol? With coffee?' she asked him. 'And do please sit down.'

'I'd be grateful,' he said, sitting as she had ordered him and feeling it an emollient in itself to be cared for by a woman.

She quirked her mouth. 'Is it from being hit on the head in Ridge Clump, George?'

'You knew?' She had surprised him.

'It could hardly be otherwise,' she rebuked him gently. 'You were smelling like a pharmacy when you called this morning. And you aren't so dreadfully subtle, you know.' She turned and opened a door into what was obviously her kitchen.

Listening to her moving things, near enough for her to hear him without a raised voice, he said, 'I've some bad news for you, I'm afraid. The dead woman is one of your guests.'

There were a few moments of silence in which he could only hear the breathing of the sleeping dog. Then she said, 'I knew it. I mean, that you had bad news. I could feel it coming from you and I think I've known all day.' Her words sounded strained.

'Miss Foxton,' he said. 'She's been identified.'

There was another silence, broken only by the bubbling of percolating coffee. He wondered why he had started this disembodied conversation when he was unable to see the reaction to it in her expression. Was it, he thought, that he didn't wish to because it might tell the non-police part of his mind something that he wouldn't want to know? Self-analysis of his emotions wasn't likely to convince him either way and he let the thought drift into nothingness as he heard her sigh.

'I'm sorry,' she said at last in a low, sad voice. 'I didn't really know her, but it's a terrible thing to happen.'

He left it at that until she brought in two cups of coffee on a tray – very preoccupied, he considered – and, feeling for its location with one hand, laid it on the table at the side of her chair. She sat without speaking and he took the cup with the two white tablets in its saucer. He put them in his mouth, where they stuck in his throat like gobbets of wire wool, and washed them down with the coffee, conscious that to her sensitive hearing he must sound like a thirsty horse drinking at a trough. Her own coffee was apparently only a gesture of hospitality, for she made no move to touch it.

'I've been told,' he said carefully, 'that Miss Foxton and Mr Whitaker left here together on Wednesday, taking their luggage with them. Today being Friday,' he added unnecessarily, but needing to emphasize the time elapsed.

Her surprise showed clearly, followed by bewilderment. 'I didn't know,' she said. 'Why wasn't I told?'

'I'm as much in the dark as you are,' he said, then wincing at the inappropriateness of his words. *If there's anything into which I can put my bloody foot*, he thought savagely, *I put it*. 'I think you'll find that the others knew.'

'Please,' she said. 'Let me take it all in. It's so much . . .' She held one hand in the other, kneading it, turning her head towards the window and staring sightlessly at it, her face illuminated in the moonlight. The detective had never felt more pity for her in her vulnerability, but knowing that he shouldn't express it.

When she turned her head back to him, he said gently, 'I do have questions to ask you, Phaedra.'

She essayed a little lightness. 'I thought that's what you'd been doing ever since we met.' She was serious again. 'Was it Mr Whitaker?'

'I've only just started,' he equivocated. 'I'd like to ask you first how two of your guests could leave here without your being told. Wouldn't your cleaning woman have noticed that their rooms were empty?'

She shrugged helplessly. 'I would have thought so. But if the beds were already made – some guests do make their own – she might do no more than look in. I don't eat with them ever and if I don't speak to any of them for a day or two, that isn't unusual. After all, they aren't here to keep me company.' She bit at her bottom lip. 'What I don't understand is why Luther never told me.'

'Why him?' He wondered at her familiarity with Player's name.

'They're his friends. Not the Tollivers, but the others are. He's stayed with us several times and he occasionally brings somebody with him. Or recommends that they stay here.' She was relaxing in her chair, kicking off the soft shoes she wore and tucking her legs beneath her.

'I haven't met him. Do you know what he does?'

'An entrepreneur, I think. Something to do with building construction machinery.'

'Would you have noticed had there been any friction between any of them?'

'I haven't and I don't think I would, being with them so little.'

'You've spoken to Whitaker?' Although nothing of it showed in her face, he thought there was a reluctance to talk too freely about her guests. It would be natural, he supposed.

'Once,' she said. 'When he arrived and was introduced to me by Luther. We shook hands and I said I hoped he would enjoy his stay here. He said that he was sure he would.' As if she had seen his expression, she added, 'As I do that with every guest, it can't be of much help, can it?'

'It might,' he said. 'A very small pin can puncture a very large balloon.' The excruciating banality of his philosophy, he told himself and then heard the sound of tyres on gravel approaching the house. No engine noise, but silence and then the slamming of a car's door, followed by another. Her head had turned as she heard it too. 'The Tollivers,' he said, his watch showing the time to be twelve-forty and the beginning of Saturday. 'Do they usually return as late as this?'

'Occasionally,' she replied. 'I think they go to discos.' Something, he read into her expression, that she equated with eating babies. It pleased him that she should reflect his own views.

'Do you know who owns the cars I've seen outside?' he asked.

'I'm almost sure, although I don't know which is which. Luther has one, Mr Gough and Mr Quennell have and, of course, Mr Tolliver.'

'Not Whitaker, Phaedra?' He was adding her name occasionally to soften the possible terseness of his questions, not wishing her to regard them wholly as bloodless officialese. 'I'm thinking about his leaving here, supposedly with Miss Foxton and all their luggage. Would you have known if a taxi called on Wednesday?'

'I needn't have known, and I don't. But possibly one of the others might.'

79

'There's the matter of the payment of their bills,' he pointed out. 'As you didn't know they'd gone, they obviously left without settling with you.'

'Basil looks after that side of it. I'm sure he would have told me if he'd known. The poor girl's dead and I can't worry about it. I'm afraid I'm not too businesslike and he's always scolding me about it.'

'You mean Mr Grice?' She was stroking her bare leg with an unsettling, if unintended, sensuousness and he wished that she wouldn't.

'Yes, I do.'

'You've told me that Player's been here before; have any of the others?'

'Only the Tollivers. Once, last year.'

He paused in his speaking. The paracetamols hadn't done him much good and he was trying in his drowsiness to flog his yawning brain into supplying significant questions he could ask. Looking away from her and through the window at the conservatory plants silhouetted darkly against a gleaming sea didn't help either. Phaedra's blindness, her apparent lack of close contact with her guests – and, having met two of them, he could understand why – while understandable, was frustrating. On hearing them return, he had been tempted to intercept the Tollivers before they bedded down, even to the digging out of Player and Catherine Horn from their rooms, but then accepted that, so far, he had too little information to ask the right questions. And that apart from a marked disinclination to ever move from his chair.

'Phaedra,' he said. 'Could we go back to the subject of your not hearing a shot at night? Is it possible that you might not have heard it because you were sleeping?'

She shook her head slowly. 'I've thought about it since, and I really can't imagine that I wouldn't. On the other hand, I can't be positive. Who could be, George? Are you sure it was at night?'

'She was wearing her nightdress when she was shot. And as I'm told it was raining, I have to assume that she was somewhere in the house when it happened, even though I haven't yet found any evidence to support it.'

She wrinkled her forehead. 'I do hear odd noises at night, but a shotgun being fired isn't one of them.'

'What noises, Phaedra?' He leaned forward in his eagerness to hear at last something of use to him.

'Oh, none of importance. An engine running continuously somewhere. I've heard it several times lately. Once or twice in the daytime, but more often late at night.'

'Coming from where?'

'From the sea, I think. Or the cove, if not. It's difficult to say precisely because sounds seem to bounce from different directions.'

Rogers was disappointed. 'A boat's engine, probably?'

'No, not a boat's engine, George. I've heard too many of them to be mistaken. Not a car engine, either. This has a sort of . . . well, a puttering noise. *And* it wasn't moving.'

'How long would it run?'

She frowned, thinking about it. 'Half-an-hour at least and anything up to an hour.'

'You said "noises",' he reminded her.

'I was really emphasizing that I usually do hear any unusual sounds made at night.' She was being patient with his questioning. 'Such as there's a difference between hearing somebody walking normally on the grass outside and hearing them walking on it when they don't wish it to be known.'

'And you've heard that?' It could, he guessed, have been Whitaker and Angela Foxton creeping from the house to indulge in whatever it was between them free from being surprised by Gough. But Phaedra wouldn't know that.

'Several times. It's why I keep the door bolted and chained.'

'Were they like those you heard this evening when we were coming back from the cove?'

'Something like them,' she said, and smiled. 'But I had you with me then.'

And a hell of a lot of good I'd have been, he told himself. *Bushed and almost walking on my chinstrap.* He said, 'Coming or going?'

She looked puzzled for a second or two. 'Oh,' she said, 'I see what you mean. Both, I suppose, and always at the back of the house.'

Which, he knew, faced on to Ridge Clump, which should be

81

making sense to him, but wasn't. 'Would it be any of your guests?' he asked her.

'Why should it be? They can walk around here as much as they wish. And they do, of course.'

He yawned behind closed teeth and it reminded him that she, too, must be tired. 'I'm keeping you up, Phaedra, and my being here must be a nuisance to you. Unfortunately, I'm going to be forced into being an even bigger nuisance in the morning. You're going to be swarming with inquisitive policemen looking for things, which is the usual drill when somebody's been murdered. It's a necessary imposition,' he said earnestly.

'I've managed to bear with it so far,' she said, her mouth lifting in a wry smile. 'And there isn't any option, is there?'

'There is, but I don't imagine you'd like it any better. Could I impose on you further? It would help me considerably if there's a room in the house I could use as a temporary office.'

She rose from her chair – how gracefully she did it, he thought – and said, 'My husband's study. It's not been used since his death and I'm sure he won't mind.'

It puzzled him that she spoke of him always as though he were still hanging around the place. He stood, certain that the creaking of his body in doing so was audible and, waiting until she had retrieved a key from a drawer in the wall cabinet, followed her from the room to the door in the hall. She held out her hand and said, 'Do you mind? They sometimes leave chairs and things in the way.' Through the door holding her hand, lax and with no tactile messages in it, he followed her along the passage to a door halfway along its length. Releasing his hand, she ran her index finger down from the door handle to find the keyhole, then unlocked the door and walked in, pressing down the wall light switch. 'Is it on?' she asked him. 'Nobody's been in here for five years.' Her face showed nothing of what she might have felt at opening up a room that should hold old memories for her.

'Yes, it is, thank you,' he said. The room was small, panelled in dark wood, smelled musty like a subterranean vault and dust lay grey on its furniture. Spiders' webs hung in loops from the ceiling and from dusty green velvet curtains drawn over a tall window. A large desk with nothing on it but a few small discs of pale mould on the leather top stood near the window and, drawn up to it, a chair upholstered in pig-hide and brass studs. A capacious stone fireplace had long-dead wood ash in its iron basket, the book shelves on either side of it empty. On the walls were framed photographs, a faded sepia now, of topee'd, twill-uniformed soldiers regimented in groups, sitting on small horses and posed against rocky landscapes with rifles and pack-mules.

Rogers fancied that he could feel the old soldier's personality still in it. 'It's fine,' he said to Phaedra who had been standing silent by his side, 'and I'm most grateful.'

With the key of it in his pocket and back in her moonlit sittingroom – she had not asked for his hand on returning – he said, 'I've finished now and you must be tired; I'll wait outside for my troops.'

'I'm going to make myself a coffee,' she said, 'so stay if you'd like another.' Her expression, he thought, had shown the faintest sign of anxiety.

'I'd love one.' Better, he admitted, than sitting outside in that outrageous van.

'Has your headache gone?' she asked.

'Yes,' he lied, hating to admit to even the most minor of disabilities, and grateful that he hadn't mentioned the cuts in his scalp. 'Completely.'

She was suddenly very close to him. 'Would you let me see what happened to you?'

'It's only a smallish lump on the back,' he protested. 'There's nothing much to see.'

With her eyelids closed – he wondered why? – she reached and put her fingers to his face, sliding them beneath his ear and on to the back of his neck, near enough for him to smell her hair and feel the warmth of her body. Then her fingers touched gently on the swelling and drew away as she raised herself on her toes, her lips brushing lightly on his cheek, then moving quickly away from him and dissolving into the dark shadows of the kitchen. Her body had not touched his and she had withdrawn too quickly for him to respond in any way his surprised mind might have decided.

It had been a moth's wing of a kiss, one that could have been given him by an affectionate sister, and it was impossible for him to decide whether it had been intended as a promise of things to come. And, about that, he had doubts. Her fine-boned elegance and unaffected grace made it difficult for him to imagine her in the often ungainly and ridiculous postures of sexual coition. Fitting himself back in his chair, having decided against an immediate impulse to follow her, he started, as a dislocation of his mind from her, to list mentally the tasks that would confront him once his Murder Room had been set up and there was a staff he could direct to them. Phaedra was saying something to him from the kitchen – he was never able to recall what it was – when his brain decided finally that enough was enough and, without his knowing it, closed his consciousness down in sleep.

15

The words 'George! George!', reaching him in his darkness, brought him to a stupefied awareness that he had slept. Until he saw her leaning over him, he was without any sense of where he was. Then he jerked as though leaping into some sort of action, pushing himself from the chair as she stood back from him.

'Sorry about that,' he mumbled. 'It was unforgivable. I've kept you up.' He was struggling against his brain's disorientation as it gave room to his mortification. At least in her sightlessness she hadn't seen him in what could have been a gross caricature of sleep, his unshaven chin dropped in an open-mouthed gape, his clothing rumpled and altogether an affront to his masculine vanity. He hoped to God he hadn't snored, for there would have been no concealing that from her.

'A car's arrived,' she said with her amused smile as if she had sensed his discomfiture, 'and there's a man been knocking at the doors.'

'It must be Chief Inspector Lingard.' His mind was clearing. 'Did it have a loud exhaust?'

'The car? Yes, it did. Like a big motor launch.'

'It's him,' he assured her. 'I'm expecting him and that was his Bentley.' He looked at his watch, seeing that he had slept for over an hour. 'I'll leave you now,' he said, 'and I really am sorry.'

'Don't be.' Her blank eyes seemed directed at the centre of his forehead. 'Will I see you in the morning?'

'Almost certainly.' Because he might be misreading her earlier gesture in kissing him, and her intent, he added, 'I'll make sure that none of us gets too much under your feet.'

Outside, Lingard was standing at the angle of the house where he could view both doors. Rogers ignored the quizzical eyebrow lifted at his finding his senior coming from a darkened part of the house after an overlong delay in answering his knocking; and, no doubt, looking as though he had been doing some hard breathing. Explaining would only worsen it. 'You've brought the Murder Room sergeant with you, David?' he asked as they fell into step. His headache had calmed down and he felt a little less close to being comatose after his brief sleep. It helped him put briskness into his words. He was, he told himself, even getting used to suffering a wet foot.

'She's in the car,' Lingard said. Rogers could smell the mortuary's formalin on his clothing.

He had parked his green Bentley at the side of a large shooting wagon which, Rogers accepted, was the Tollivers'. Its canvas hood was down and Sergeant Millier, owner of the departmentally disruptive mouth, sat in the passenger seat. Carrying the wooden murder box and climbing out when she saw Rogers's approach, she went fittingly, he conceded, with the Bentley's long raciness and thoroughbred lines.

He led them both in through the double doors and into the late brigadier's study, unlocking it and switching on the light to its neglect. 'This, sergeant,' he told Millier, 'will be from where we'll operate. It needs dusting, which I don't suppose you'll mind doing. When you've settled in, you'll find a bin in the van. It has a torn-up letter in it. Fit it together so that I can read it later. And also tell me about the other bits and pieces when you've sorted them out. The troops won't be here until first light, so you've plenty of time.'

The unsettlingly beautiful mouth smiled 'Yes, sir,' at him

and he suspected that his second-in-command had selected the attractive Millier against the team of available male sergeants in the department for whatever reasons other than suitability he might have. He was going to be disappointed if he thought that he would be working with her. 'You come with me, David,' Rogers said. 'We're doing a recce of the landscape and a filling in of information.'

Crossing the grass together, with himself lighting his meerschaum and Lingard feeding snuff into his nose, Rogers gave him the information, sparse enough, that he had obtained. They had halted and looked back at the house when Rogers referred to it, as if again to take in its substance. In the livid moonlight its walls were a shimmering crimson, the roof slates glistening gun-metal. A light mist hung in swathes around it at lower window level, giving the building a Gothic mysteriousness in its setting of funereal cypresses.

'You don't sound too bloodhoundish about Whitaker, George,' Lingard said.

'Only because I'm not,' Rogers answered him, 'although we'll gazette him as wanted for questioning to cover ourselves. Up to a point it all seems reasonably logical. He and Angela Foxton having it off more or less under Gough's nose, and although I'm not sure he did, he would be moronic not to suspect what was going on. Whitaker, for God knows what reason, takes a shotgun from the gun cupboard, shoots her in her nightgown, presumably in the house because it was raining that night and because I can't imagine a woman wandering about in it without putting something else on. Then he decides to bury her in Ridge Clump which, incidentally, is a fair old drag uphill if you happen to be carrying a body as well as a spade. While he's up there, although not necessarily with the body, he's unexpectedly confronted at three o'clock or thereabouts with a nosy passerby. Banging him on the head and sending him off in his car helps, but doesn't solve the problem about getting rid of the body. Time must have been getting short, because he eventually does it by unloading it into the sea, which wasn't very intelligent of him. Perhaps he was in a cold sweat and panicking by then, what with daylight coming on soon and another job to do. So, that was to remove his stuff –

and hers – from their rooms to suggest to the rest that they'd gone away together, presumably like a couple of born-again lovebirds. Which means in its turn that he had to smuggle out two suitcases and either take them with him, or to somehow dispose of hers before he left. You've got the picture, David?' He turned and recommenced walking with Lingard following him.

'Yes, and it's not impressing me at all,' Lingard said. He seemed as much concerned about his hand-sewn shoes darkening in the damp grass.

'Not only you,' Rogers said. 'Why should Whitaker go away at all? When the body was found – as it was likely to be when put into the sea – he would be the immediate suspect with a hell of a lot of awkward questions to answer. It would have been more sensible of him to have stayed put and argued his way out of any suspicion we might have had about him. Suspicion,' he added drily, 'never put anyone in jail.'

'You said he could have panicked,' Lingard pointed out. 'Panic and sensible thinking don't always go together.'

'No, they don't,' Rogers agreed. 'It's probably the only fact that keeps him in the frame. When we get back, I want you to check on his home address – it's in the Visitors' Book – and bring him in if he's daft enough to be there. Failing that, call at Angela Foxton's address – that's in there as well – and if there's a relative or friend who should know, break the news to them. In any event, dig in for background information.'

'I'm not too happy about your not finding any evidence of the shooting,' Lingard said. He wasn't doubting, but remarking; one of his responsibilities being to jog his senior's thinking processes. 'She must have bled a torrent, and a few of the pellets should have gone wide and into something or other.'

'I haven't searched all the rooms, David. Magnus can do that in the morning. But for starters, she could have bled on a rug that was taken away; she could have been shot in front of an open window with any stray pellets finishing up outside. And if that's how it so conveniently was,' he said sardonically, 'then I'm a bloody Dutchman.'

They were approaching the panel fencing shielding the shooting trap, near to its neighbouring shrubbery and close

87

enough to the cliff's edge for them to hear the stirring of shingle below as the incoming sea broke on it, its smell dank in their nostrils.

'This,' Rogers said, 'is where they blast away at the clays, and . . .' He stopped abruptly, holding Lingard's arm and cautioning him to silence with an upraised finger. 'Stay here,' he whispered. 'I heard something moving.' He left him with fast strides, entering the shrubbery.

With most of it as tall as himself, heavily foliaged and uncomfortably damp with mist, he pushed into it until reaching a narrow grass-grown path, knowing anyway that his own bull-elephant crashing through would have blotted out any sounds of another's movements. He stood silent and listened, hearing nothing but the hissing of blood in his ears. His neck hairs had bristled in an involuntary aggression, for to be secretly watched was a threat to him. Whoever it was, if there had been somebody incautious enough to rustle leaves in watching him, he had only now to stand motionless and his chances of being found in the darkness would be minimal. Glancing along the path, he made out a solid rectangle in the shadowed bushiness, patches of moonlit sea showing through the leaves at its sides. Going to it, he recognized it as a summerhouse with a rampant creeper smothering its roof and sides, making it virtually indistinguishable from its surrounding foliage. Its front, only yards from the cliff edge, was glassed in for a view of the sea, only partly obstructed by hanging tendrils of creeper. Although deeply shadowed inside, it was not too dark to prevent his seeing that no skulking watcher hid inside.

'I don't know,' he grunted on returning to Lingard. 'I'm possibly imagining things, or it could have been a rabbit or a hedgehog.' He recalled Phaedra's dismissal of a similar suggestion, convincing him that it hadn't been. 'If it was somebody, he's damned sight quieter than I am at moving around in wet bushes.'

'It was probably chummy trying to get in a second bang to your head,' Lingard said unhelpfully.

'You're so comforting, David.' He knew it to be an unlikely happening and dismissed the thought. 'You've seen the shooting stand, so now the cove.' He turned along the cliff towards the steps leading down to the beach. 'Tell me what we've got from the post-mortem.'

Lingard, refilling his nostrils with snuff and flapping away loose grains with a red and green silk handkerchief, said, 'Our chubby friend has had his nose put out of joint over something. Which was why, I'm certain, he obliged us tonight.'

'He'd been eating out with one of his girlfriends,' Rogers told him. 'It was probably as simple as her not liking the smell of garlic and saying "No". What did he find?'

'Nothing we couldn't reasonably expect. No evidence of drowning and she died from cerebral lacerations caused by a shotgun wound. No exit wound, the pellets all finished up in the brain tissue and the back of the skull. Twite estimates that the shot was fired at an angle of about fifteen degrees from the line of her body. Which would indicate that she was lying on her back when she was shot, or – and you'll agree that it's unlikely – she was standing and was shot by somebody lying on the floor below her. Distance?' Lingard shrugged. 'A guess at twelve to fifteen feet, but depending very much on the choke of the barrel, of which more later. The shape of the entry wound – no further comment and no guesses at what caused it either. Something interesting though. Post-mortem staining and contact lividity initially on the back, indicating that her body was on it for several hours. Then, secondary staining in the legs due, Twite says, to a later liquefying of the blood and its gravitation while she was in a standing position.'

Rogers was frowning his perplexity. 'That's odd. He's sure?'

'Yes, and so am I. I saw it. But more, George. Apart from the abrasions you saw, there were indentations on the sides of her arms, buttocks and thighs. All caused after death when her skin had lost its elasticity. Much as if,' he said, 'she'd been resting for some time on sharp stones.'

'Shingle on the beach?' Rogers was theorizing, imagining her, a pale body on a dark beach, as visible as a stranded mermaid. He shook his head, arguing with himself. 'No. The shingle's nearly all smooth pebbles and she'd be too easily seen down there, even among the rocks, and he wouldn't risk it. Nor could it happen while she was in the water and drifting in the current.' He frowned again. 'Nor could the abrasions. If she'd

89

scraped along the bottom they'd surely have been made on parts
of the body other than the thighs and arms. Were they?'

'No, they weren't, and yes, they would have,' Lingard
agreed. 'And there's something else. Twite found a sizeable
splinter of wood pushed into the back of her left thigh. Post-
death, he's certain.'

Rogers smiled wryly. 'You and he aren't making things easy
for me, are you? A body lying down, standing up; lying on
stones and picking up wood splinters. I take it we've got the
time of death within a day or two?'

'Being in the sea has done for exactness as far as he's
concerned,' Lingard said. 'He estimated between fifty and
seventy hours, and crossed himself when he said it. But it'll be
narrowed down when he does some laboratory work on it.'

Rogers did a mental calculation, not easy for him at two
o'clock on a fatiguing night. 'Early morning to late at night on
Wednesday,' he muttered. 'It's a hell of a gap, but at least it
fits.'

They had reached the top of the steps and Rogers leaned
gratefully against the iron handrail. The moon had moved in its
orbit to where it now illuminated in detail the face of the cliff
and the beach. 'Take it in from up here, David,' he said. 'I'm
not going down again tonight. You'd have to carry me back.'

'One of the penalties of being ancient,' Lingard murmured,
being all of six years younger. He was examining the scene
below, fitting it in with what Rogers had told him. 'It's not
exactly a Riviera *plage*, is it?' he said disparagingly. 'Do people
actually go down there for pleasure?'

'That's what I've to find out.' Rogers had his back to the cove
and, without being obvious about it, watched the shrubbery for
any movement as he refilled his pipe and lit it. 'I've a feeling
there's something peculiar going on down there that I should
know about.'

'Such as throwing dead women into the sea?' Lingard said
banteringly. 'Which reminds me. I took her fingerprints and
just as well I did. Friend Twite's made an even worse mess of
her face in digging things out. It's pretty bloody and I don't
think we should encourage a visual identification.'

'Approved, but make sure that Magnus has the prints early to

90

check with her bedroom. I've gone out on a limb about her identification and I don't want to have to enlist in the French Foreign Legion if I'm found to be wrong.'

'One other thing,' Lingard said, ignoring his senior's put-on pessimism. 'At the other end, Twite says that she was well habituated to sexual intercourse.'

Rogers, unsurprised about that, growled, 'Other than me, mention somebody over fourteen who isn't. We'll go back now, I've things to do and so have you.' Walking towards the house, he said, 'You've some information about shotguns?'

'Nothing that's likely to make you run amok.' Lingard was having difficulty in keeping up with the long strides of a hurrying Rogers. 'I spoke to Bagnell the gunsmith, yanked the poor chap out of bed actually. It's much as you already know,' he said diplomatically. 'The spread of shot depends on the distance from which it's fired and any choking of the gun's barrel. And that can be anything from no choke at all to full choke. The fuller the choke, the narrower the spread. The further away from the target you are, the wider. It has to be a laboratory job with Mrs Haggar's guns if you feel that one of them was used.'

'I know it was. But, whichever, I'm satisfied that she was shot from a few feet, well within the length of a normal room.'

Nearing the house, feeling that with the routine chores under way he could, without any further flagellation of his conscience, take an hour off to change his clothing and make himself sweet-smelling again, he saw the figure of a man standing between the pillars of the front doors. Only yards away, he loomed hulking and forbidding in the mist, looking as though he were waiting there to hit somebody.

'Bloody hell!' Rogers whispered disgustedly to Lingard, not expecting an answer. 'Stand by for flying glass! I suspect I'm not about to have my hand shaken.'

16

Standing on the steps in the cone of light from the lamp above his head, his legs apart and his arms folded, the man appeared even bigger than he was. Taller than Rogers by inches, with the sloping shoulders and thick neck of a pugilist, he was dressed only in a shirt and trousers, his feet in leather sandals. With a thrusting nose, eye sockets shadowed under prominent brow ridges, coarse tow-coloured hair and a thick beard, there was something primeval about him.

'What's going on here?' he demanded abruptly in the voice of a man accustomed to being listened to, and acting as if he owned the place. 'Who are you?'

'I imagine you already know,' Rogers growled. The man was big enough to allow him to bristle his own masculinity. He held out his warrant card, returning it to his pocket when it was not looked at. 'More to the point, who are you?'

He hesitated, then said, 'Player. Why wasn't I told?'

'If you hadn't been in bed asleep,' Rogers said sharply, 'you might have been. I'd no particular obligation or time to go round telling everybody in the house.' He was conscious of Lingard standing behind him and probably enjoying the small fracas. 'I presume Gough woke you up and told you?'

'I still want to know what's going on.' His deep-set eyes narrowed and he showed his big square teeth as he said it, plainly intent on brow-beating the detective into an answer.

Unearned aggression, and having to look up at the man, made Rogers bloody-minded. He was damned if he was going to be pushed into anything by this hulking throwback to *Pithecanthropus erectus*. He made his voice authoritative. 'All you need know at the moment is that I'm investigating the murder of Miss Foxton, and that when I get around to it I shall be asking what *you* know about what's going on.' Then he smiled, not too genially, and said 'Goodnight to you,' leaving him saying words that were, in the crunching of his and Lingard's shoes on the gravel, largely unintelligible.

Driving out on to the road and turning towards Abbotsburn, Rogers regretted that he had allowed Player to irritate him, and that irritated him further. Yet, for all the big man's aggressiveness, he thought that he had sensed an element of uncertainty in him; as though, despite his appearance and words, bellicosity wasn't in his temperament at all. He had also noticed that his sandals were discoloured, as if he had been walking on damp grass. Phaedra, he told himself, had some damned odd guests.

Heavy-eyed, with his vitality supposedly at its lowest in the dead hours of the morning, his body stale and his underclothing feeling like sandpaper, he thought that he could justify his departure from Player without asking the questions he had held in waiting for him. Unlike the detectives he had seen acted on television, rarely needing sleep, shot or beaten up, their bones splintered and their flesh mangled in collisions with other cars, and then up bright and active and wearing clean shirts in an hour or so, Rogers felt that he could sleep for days as he was, dirty and rumpled, on up-ended razor-blades. They also, he reflected with some envy, seemed always to find the time and inclination to throw an untired leg over the occasional woman they met in their endeavours.

Rounding the bend in the road where he had earlier gone over the top, the hotted-up engine pulling him faster than he had intended it to, his tyres hammered on the central cats's-eyes and, with his heart thumping his alarm, he wrenched at the steering wheel to get himself back to the nearside again. To be found in a wrecked car – inexcusably this time – on the second occasion in three nights would have confirmed the Traffic Department's suspicions, were he still alive to have cared. It underlined his need to do something to overcome his brain's intent on closing down for the night.

Having called in at Headquarters on his way and collected a conventionally deep-blue car, undistinguished in itself, but better than the banana-coloured excrescence he left in its place, he parked it in his drive, unlocking the door to his dark and wifeless home. Before doing anything else, he climbed slowly

93

up the stairs to the bathroom. Opening the medicine cabinet, he took out a tiny bottle. It contained benzedrine-based capsules, the few survivors of those his wife had left behind when she left; mute reminders, he had always held, that on her leaving him she would no longer need them against that for which they had been prescribed. He took one of them, knowing that it would hold his need for sleep at bay and – only God knew why, but it worked – put a bomb under whatever it was that could produce a period of unflagging activity.

In the kitchen, needing no reminding that his system needed caffeine and that he was hungry, he filled and put on the coffee percolator. Then he toasted slices of bread to sandwich what he called ham when buying it, but could not help thinking of as chemically-cured slices of an unfortunate pig's buttock when eating it. As he prepared his meal, he took off his clothing – like bark being stripped from a tree, it seemed to him – and piled it in a corner, the still-wet shoe and sock being the first to go.

It was the first time he had eaten a meal sitting naked in the kitchen and, with his stomach satisfied, he returned to the bathroom. Mowing the emergent stubble from his chin and jowls, satisfied that underneath them he hadn't aged noticeably, he felt the beginnings of bird-quickness in his brain, something a little better than sluggishness energizing his body.

'Benzedrine,' he misquoted badly, but gratefully, to nobody in particular, 'thy name is Virtue.'

Under the shower, cautiously keeping his damaged head away from the spray of hot water, he looked at himself in the steamy full-length mirror; not egotistically, but critically. Swarthy features that could be called hawkish, he supposed, with a little too sharp a nose that Phaedra Haggar could have inwardly frowned over when she had traced its shape. The bruise on his chest was now a blotchy mauve and there was a small cut on his shoulder which he hadn't known was there. Middling normal in all other respects but for his legs, they being more hairy than the average. They had often given rise to fanciful thoughts that a way-back ancestress could have been overly friendly with a shaggy satyr, he passing on through his genes his hair and instincts to a descendant who wanted neither.

His eyes went back to the cut on his shoulder, a thought

nudging him that it could be important but which he couldn't bring into focus or relate it to . . . It was then that he stiffened, bath-brush held poised in his hand, as a picture superimposed itself on his mind in a momentary flash and vanished before he could grasp at it. A man's face, a face not too clearly defined and one that he hadn't seen before. Rigidly angry, its mouth was saying unheard words to him while he, conscious of a woman at his side, said words back. There was a clear sense of baffled outrage in him and it was directed at the unknown woman.

A dream I've had, he told himself, and it's just coming back to me. It had to be, it had better be, for he had never yet had another man showing anger to him over a woman. But he was thoughtful about it as he rubbed himself dry with a towel and then put on fresh clothing.

17

Apart from a niggling ache in his leg muscles and the dull feeling that a nail had been hammered into his skull and left there to rust, Rogers was a regenerated man, his brain slippery with activity. He could at a pinch, he considered, push over fairly large dustbins.

When he braked to a halt outside a mist-shrouded and darkened Catteshead House, he saw that Lingard's Bentley had gone, which was to be expected, and, which was not, there was an empty space where Gough's car had been. With Player occupying his attention when he had earlier approached the front of the house, he couldn't be certain that it had been there then. Gough's apparent departure wasn't a good start for his reactivated sense of purpose but, while as unwanted as it was suspicious, it was nothing he could have prevented even if he had known beforehand of his intent. So far as Roger's powers to prevent him were concerned, he could depart, stay away or return as he wished. Also, given an extension of credulity, he could be a man who liked to go out at four-thirty in the morning to visit friends, or just to view the dawn breaking. Thinking these implausibilities did nothing to pacify an extremely irritated detective.

Pushing through a door no longer obstructed by an aggressive Player, he stalked silently up the dark stairs and into the upper corridor. Opening the door of Gough's bedroom and sensing immediately that it was unoccupied, he switched on the light. The disorderliness of a man's use of a bedroom, which he had seen there before, had gone. The wardrobe had nothing in it but clothes-hangers. 'Bugger and bloody damn!' he swore softly as he left the room, turning the key on its emptiness and taking it with him. He would at this rate, he thought, soon have every room in the house locked up.

Descending the stairs as quietly as he had mounted them, he walked along the passage to where a light shone from the open door of the brigadier's study. Sergeant Millier stood from the desk as he entered. She had laid out on it the registers, forms and files he would need and had shown initiative in finding a desk lamp from somewhere, and in bringing with her a portable typewriter. There was more to her, he conceded to an absent Lingard, than blue eyes, a beautiful mouth and a very feminine body beneath the neat grey suit.

'When you arrived, sergeant,' he asked, 'did you happen to notice the number of the blue Cavalier outside?'

She was surprised. 'No, sir, I'm afraid I didn't. Should I have?'

'I suppose not.' There must have been irritation in his voice, for she had looked apprehensive in admitting it. 'Don't worry, I've walked past the damned thing myself half-a-dozen times and all I remember is that the number plate had a W year-letter on it. Anyway, it's gone,' he said. 'Did you hear it go?'

'Yes, I did.' She looked at her watch. 'About three-quarters of an hour ago. I'm sorry, was there something I should have done?'

'There was nothing you could, sergeant. It belongs to a man called Gough. Did you hear him going out?'

'No. The only noise I heard was the car being started and then driven away.'

'Doing a moonlight flit he'd naturally creep out, so you wouldn't. Has there been anything else?' he asked smiling, coming off his boil. 'No huge anthropoid wanting to tear off my arms? No banging of doors or quarrelling noises from upstairs?'

'Do you mean the man I heard you talking to outside?' She looked puzzled, obviously not having seen Player.

'Yes, I do. Did you hear him go outside beforehand?' he was remembering the damp sandals.

'No, I didn't. But I think I must have heard him coming in, although that was over an hour later. If it wasn't somebody else, of course,' she qualified.

'It could have been,' he agreed, but not believing it. 'Anything else of interest?'

'There was somebody moving about upstairs, and I heard men's voices. I can't say whether they were quarrelling, I could only just hear them.' She looked concerned. 'I'm sorry, should I have made notes at the time?'

'Not really, sergeant,' he said. 'Perhaps I should have asked you to, but it is a sort of free-for-all guesthouse and they can run around much as they please. But make a note of it when we've finished, and anything else you hear or see.'

'I've a message, sir,' she said. 'Mrs Haggar came in to see if you were here.' Her forehead wrinkled. 'It was awfully embarrassing. I didn't realize that she was blind, I'm afraid.'

'I don't think she'd particularly want you to, sergeant. Don't let it make any difference to how you treat her,' he cautioned her. 'She's perfectly capable on her own ground and she'd resent it. What was the message?'

'Would you go in and see her on your return. She has some information she thinks you should know.'

'She's being a bit of a damned nuisance,' he growled, the words disguising what he actually felt. 'Doesn't she ever sleep?'

'She said that she would be waiting up, sir.' There was a touch of reproof in the sergeant's voice. She was definitely pro-Mrs Haggar. 'And I thought that she looked a little nervous.'

'Of course I'll see her. Have you sorted out that letter?'

'And the envelope,' she said. 'There were pieces missing, but they're ready for you.'

He took them from her and sat in the brigadier's hide chair she had kept warm for him. It groaned under his weight in a complaining way as he did so. 'Don't stay on your feet, sergeant,' he said. 'There are plenty of chairs. Bring one over and have your notebook ready.'

The letter, written in large schoolgirlish italics and pasted together on a blank statement form, read *Darling Angie, What a rubbishy   ng to be so frightfully myste   bout. I couldn't even buy anyt   I tried, so the   isn't on. Are you going to m   a penda   Do let me know,   ounds exciting   ant wait. In a hurry. Love, J*

The envelope, not so fragmented as the letter, was addressed to Miss Angela Foxton, c/o Catteshead House, Abbotsburn Road, Thurnholme Bay. The postmark cancelling the stamp was smudged, but partially decipherable as *Alle . . . 10 Aug . . .*

'Posted from Allerton, I'd guess,' Rogers said, 'and with no address, a lot of help in a population of ten thousand.'

Millier reached and passed him a paper slip. 'It's on there,' she said. 'It's a registered letter receipt.'

This had been the screwed-up pill of paper he had recovered with the bin. It was a Certificate of Posting with the addressee shown as *J. Foxton, Old Mill Cottage, Kinniston*, date-stamped *Thurnholme Bay PO. 8 Aug* and endorsed that a fee of £1.10p had been paid.

'Um,' he said thoughtfully, 'we've a new dimension to worry over. What about the rest?'

'The balls of cotton wool, sir? They'd been used with a skin lotion, I think. Or a cleansing cream. I've packaged them ready for the laboratory, if that's what you wanted.'

Sitting near him, her hair a lustrous deep-gold in the illumination of the desk lamp, she was an unsettling factor for a man believing that an occasional ice-cold shower was needed to be able to work impersonally with her. Needed because, as a subordinate policewoman, she was as debarred from any non-professional intimacy with him as would be a cloistered nun.

'Yes, I did.' She was doing all the right things, and he approved. 'I'd better see what Mrs Haggar wants,' he said. He stood and fished in his pocket for keys, putting them on the desk. 'Use the radio in the car I've left outside and call up HQ. Say that I want Mr Coltart to bring a dictionary with him.'

Seeing her look of incomprehension, he added genially, 'There's a two-volume Oxford Shorter on my office desk if he doesn't happen to carry one around with him, and he need only bring the M to Z one. It'd be helpful to know how many words there are beginning with "penda", don't you think?'

'Yes, sir.' She made a note of it, clearly working that one out for herself.

'I shouldn't be long,' he said, 'but if Mr Lingard returns and I'm still next door, let me know immediately.' And if that, he thought, wasn't an insurance against his succumbing to a goatish weakness, then nothing was.

18

When Phaedra admitted him in answer to his knocking, he noticed that she was still wearing the cream housecoat with the green birds on it, not apparently having been to bed. She led him through into the sittingroom and, although invited to sit – she sat herself – he remained standing. She had not switched on the light but, with a misted moon shining through the windows, it was enough for him to see that she was unsmiling, that there was no lightness in her demeanour.

'You've a problem, Phaedra?' he asked, being now wholly Rogers-on-the-job.

'Not a problem.' Her voice was subdued and she looked small and lost in her easy chair. 'Luther came in to talk to me.'

'I see,' he said, although he didn't. 'When was this?'

'Just after I heard the cars leaving.'

'That was after I'd spoken to him. What did he want?'

She was biting her lip. 'He was angry. I don't think particularly with me, but something had upset him. He asked me how long you'd been here and where you'd been; who you'd spoken to . . . that sort of thing.'

'And you told him?' He could imagine the anthropoidal Player bulldozing questions at her.

'Yes. I had no reason not to. He asked me had you been down

to the beach and when I told him that I'd gone with you, he said that I had been most unwise. Then he asked me what you'd done down there. I told him I didn't know – which I don't – and that you hadn't told me. He wasn't very pleased about that.'

'And my looking around the house?'

'I said that you'd looked in the bedrooms, that's all. I didn't mention the guns. He sounded dreadfully annoyed about that, and with letting you use the study. He said it was an intolerable imposition when they were here on holiday.'

'I agree,' he said mildly. 'And it was intolerably thoughtless of Miss Foxton to get herself murdered in the middle of it. Did he say anything about Whitaker?'

'Only that it was obviously something to do with him because he'd gone off with her in the first place, that you should be looking for him instead of questioning people who knew nothing at all about it.'

'Or questioning people who might?' That didn't require an answer and he said, 'Did he say anything else?'

'Why don't you sit down?' she asked him.

'I think I'd seize up if I did,' he excused himself. 'Did he?'

'He told me that I must be careful of what I said to the police about anything.' She hesitated, her fingers twining. 'He said that the police didn't mind who they got, just so long as they got somebody. I know that's not true, George.'

That wasn't worth defending. He said, 'Player sounds to me like one of those characters who believe we started World War Two in between operating a sort of Spanish Inquisition. Just accept that he's embittered over something or other. You're not worried about what he's been saying, are you?' He searched her face for the answer.

She managed a tremulous smile. 'Of course not. And it was so unlike him. It's what happened afterwards that worries me.'

'Oh?' He frowned. 'What was that?'

'When Luther left me, I made myself a cup of coffee and then went out with Emily. She always has a free run before I go to bed. As soon as I was outside, I heard somebody walking on the grass from the back of the house towards the beach. I wouldn't have been in full view because I was standing around the corner of the conservatory, but if he looked for me I suppose I could have been seen through it. He could see Emily, of course, who was out there.' She paused for a moment, her forehead creasing as though reliving what had happened. The suffocatingly frightening darkness of the blind, he thought, as he waited. 'The footsteps stopped,' she continued, 'and that was what frightened me; his not saying anything. People do usually, knowing I can't see them. He just stood there, hoping, I imagine, that I hadn't heard anything.

'He mightn't have know who you were,' he said, not thinking it for a moment. 'He could have been a stranger.' And that, he swore to himself, had been the wrong thing to say, worrying her even more.

She shook her head. 'No. Emily knew him. I heard her go over to him, heard him stroking and patting her, I suppose to keep her quiet. I'm sure she would have growled at a stranger, certainly not have gone to him. Knowing that, I called out "Who is it?' and not getting an answer made it worse. I could *feel* him watching me until I heard him walking away, hurrying almost. I called Emily and came indoors, trembling a little, I'm afraid, because it did frighten me.'

He could visualize it as a tableau; the woman standing sightless and vulnerable in the bright moonlight, uncertain of what was to happen in a silence that she could have felt menacing, the unknown figure frozen into immobility by her unexpected appearance, knowing that although she couldn't see him, he had been heard. The dog, unwitting of the woman's alarm, going to him because she recognized him, and then his silent departure.

'It must have,' he commiserated with her. He was trying to work out why anybody from the house should be so secretive about who he was, and why he should be going towards the cove in the middle of the night. 'Are you certain it was a man?' he asked.

'I took it to be.' Her face wasn't turned in his direction, her head bowed as though she were looking at her hands.

'Could the sounds have been made by a woman?'

She thought about that, her forehead furrowed again. 'Yes,' she agreed hesitantly. 'I thought not at the time, but when you can't see there isn't really any gender to shoes on grass.'

'Only in a policeman's size elevens,' he said amiably. 'Assuming it to have been a man, could he have been Player?'

Her folded hands tightened and she was slow in answering him. 'Why do you ask that? Surely you don't think he had anything to do with it?'

'I'm asking about the man you heard tonight, Phaedra.' He didn't say, but thought it, that with the bomb of a violent death exploding in a group of people, there would always be somebody scurrying to cover up matters which, although embarrassing if discovered, might be entirely disassociated from it. 'He was up and about. It's as likely to have been him as anyone else. Could it have been?' he persisted.

'Yes,' she said simply, 'it could.'

'But only could? Not was?'

'I'd hate to swear to it, and the more I think about it the less certain I feel.'

'You said he came from around the back of the house. Is there a rear door?'

'No, but there is a side door that goes out into the kitchen garden. And that has a back gate to it, although it's seldom used.'

'Is there anything else you have to tell me?' he asked gently.

'I don't think so.' She shivered and, in the bleaching light from the window, her face looked bloodless and fragile-boned. 'It's suddenly come to me and I'm frightened. There's somebody that's been here who's killed a woman . . . he could be back. Do you think it was Mr Whitaker?'

'I don't know, Phaedra.' He wanted to go, unable to give her much comfort without lying. 'Whether it was or not, he won't come back here.'

'Only, if it isn't him,' she said quietly, 'it's someone who's still here and I feel awfully defenceless.'

'You've no reason to,' he assured her. 'Even were there to be, why should anyone wish to harm you?'

She rose from her chair and came to him. 'Stay with me, George.' She reached out her hand and, when he took it in his, held it tightly with warm fingers. 'Please,' she said. 'At least until it's daylight.'

He felt her pulling him towards her, gently but insistently

and, although there was nothing of eroticism in her expression, it was impossible not to recognize her intent. At its worst – which he resisted believing – she was offering herself for the security of his presence. At its best – and he couldn't believe it at five in the morning – because he was a lovable, unputdownable masculine desirability. With either, his above-the-waist thinking was doing its priggishly ascetic rejection of what its below-the-waist reckless, but warmer brother knew it wanted.

He made his voice regretful, and it was how he felt. 'I have to be terribly stuffy, Phaedra, but I am on duty and I've things to do now. Honestly, you'll be quite safe, and I'm only next door if you want me.'

Standing there silent, she had the look of the woman who stared always into darkness of night and he felt that he could bay at the moon in the frustration of his ambivalence towards her.

'My men will be here at any moment,' he blundered on when she didn't speak, 'and they'll be wanting to be told what to do.'

'Yes,' she said softly, but not all that nicely. 'I do understand, and I'm sorry I asked.'

He took her hand as a gesture of affection or comfort – he wasn't sure which – but, when it remained folded and unresponsive in his, he released it and left her in silence. She had made him feel an insensitive and graceless clod, accepting that she might never forgive him for being it.

19

Outside, there was an early morning freshness in the air, the moon papery in a paling sky. Streaks of first light threw into dark silhouette the bulk of the distant moor. Layers of milky mist, soon to be burned up by the rising sun, hugged the ground. It was a time when Rogers should feel that it was good to be up and doing, only he didn't quite; a time to savour the smell of frying bacon, only there was none and, for him, unlikely to be. Because there was no yardstick by which he could measure how long he would be held upright and able to think by the benzedrine he had taken, he needed to discharge his commitment to the dead Angela Foxton before it failed him.

The study – he couldn't yet think of it as a Murder Room – still smelled of dust and dead air. Sergeant Millier, sitting at the desk in a cone of yellow light that left the walls in shadow, stood as he entered.

'You've done it once tonight, sergeant,' he said, 'and you don't need to do it every time I come in. Has anything happened?'

'Somebody upstairs flushed a lavatory, sir.' She smiled, having given even that ordinariness a something special. 'I made a note of it. Would you like some coffee?'

He saw a vacuum flask and two cups on the desk. 'I would indeed,' he told her, surprised. 'Where did that come from?'

'I brought the coffee with me and borrowed the cups from the kitchen. You don't think anyone will mind?'

'You've the makings in you of being the first woman Chief Constable, sergeant,' he said. 'Pour it out and let me take my chair.'

Shutting out Millier from his awareness while he drank his coffee, he began trying to put into a manageable coherency the bagful of facts, suspected lies and evasions his brain had assimilated. It left him with a concept – half a concept, he qualified cautiously – that was as difficult to hold fast to as the incidents recalled so randomly from his absent-without-leave memory. It centred all too waveringly on the broken pattern of pellets that had shattered Angela Foxton's face and an unre-membered something which had passed through his mind and suggested an explanation for it. It would return eventually, he knew, but, as with most of the needful things in life, he wanted it now.

He thought also about the unknown somebody who had been skulking in his and Phaedra's footsteps; whom he had seen from the beach and whose movements she had heard on their return from it. Hearing a car approaching the house ten minutes or so before his seeing the head and shoulders of the watcher on the top of the cliff could eliminate Player, Quennell, Gough and Mrs Horn. With the Tollivers out of the picture because they had returned much later, it left nobody from the house he could brood over. Other than – he smiled at the preposterous thought – Emily and the ghost of the late Brigadier Haggar which Phaedra had said wouldn't anyway be fishing on the beach in an ebbing tide.

The caffeine was already filtering into his veins to join forces with the benzedrine and the nicotine from his pipe tobacco when he heard the rumbling of Lingard's Bentley approaching along the drive. When he entered the study, it gave Rogers a touch of unworthy satisfaction to see that his second-in-command's face showed definite signs of weariness, his jowls rough with a blond stubble and his shirt collar curled and creased. 'Good morning, David,' he said cheerfully, holding himself erect in his chair. 'Take a seat. You've things to tell me, I hope?'

Lingard raised a languid hand to Millier and pulled a chair over to the desk. Sitting, he took out his tiny ivory box and inhaled his powdered tobacco, the scent of attar of roses reaching Rogers's nostrils. 'I'll tell you one thing,' he said, flicking loose grains away from his upper lip with his silk handkerchief, 'and that is, nobody seems to like being hauled out of bed in the witching hours and asked what they think are a lot of damned silly questions.'

He opened his pocket book and laid it on the desk. 'Virtue and hard slog rewarded,' he said jauntily. 'I think we're on to something solid with Whitaker. Did he come here in a car?'

'Not so far as I've been told,' Rogers replied. 'Should he have?'

'No. It's just that it happens to be missing from the garage where he's supposed to have left it.'

Rogers frowned, looking not too happy about it as he might be expected. 'With no transport, returning and collecting it after he'd killed Angela Foxton? Taking off in it to parts unknown? Knowing, as he would, that a car is the possession most easily identifiable? With her supposedly alive and loving in his company and needing to be accounted for if she hadn't been found in the meantime?' He wagged his head in disbelief. 'Nobody but a fool would believe that you can put a body in the sea off-shore and not expect it to be washed up and identified sooner or later. And I know that if I ever get around to throttling a woman, the last thing I'd do would be to let it be assumed that we'd gone off together. Subject to whatever background stuff you've got, I'm inclined to put a missing car alongside the missing suitcases and clothing – a cover-up.' He grimaced. 'It smells, David, as I told you before. And you were agreeing with me.'

'I also mentioned,' Lingard said ruefully, not so jaunty now, 'that panic and sensible thinking don't make for good bed-fellows. It's a reasonable probability that he did it and lost his cool. But if you're right and he didn't, where is he?'

'If I knew, or could guess, I'd be a damned sight happier than I am now. But don't let me put you off, because I'm not saying Whitaker couldn't have done it.' He was standing Lingard back on his feet. 'It's just that I can't convince myself that he did when I really think about it. What about all the creeping about and watching we've been having? I've had it; Mrs Haggar's had it. There's something murky happening here that makes me wonder whether we've the slightest idea of what's been going on, or what is now.' He frowned again. 'Let's get on to facts, which are our only salvation. What did you find out about Whitaker?'

'Not all that much,' Lingard said. 'His full name is Michael Anthony John Whitaker. Thirty years approximately, brown eyes, mousy brown hair, one of those repulsive gun-fighter's moustaches, wears half-cleric spectacles for reading and such-like, five feet eight inches or thereabouts of desiccated meat with apparently no hips to speak of. He's an electronics egg-head employed by Omblatts Software, which I've never heard of. He's been in his rented apartment at De Vaux Close for about six months, isn't overly friendly and if he has a thing going for the ladies, it isn't known; those visitors seen ringing his door bell being male and apparently friends in his line of business. All that from his upstairs neighbour. A chap who didn't believe that helping the police with their enquiries included an innocent quantity surveyor with a very irritable wife being rousted out of bed at four in the morning. Whitaker's not been back since he left on holiday twelve days ago, and until I checked his lock-up garage – it was unlocked, by the way – it was believed that his car was still there.'

'Why?'

'Because the neighbour saw him leave in another car, a small car, a topside view from his window of Whitaker tottering to it carrying a suitcase and a hold-all. He's absolutely no recollection of its colour or make and is only sure that it wasn't a Rolls-Royce Silver Shadow. How do you . . .'

Rogers held a finger up for silence. 'I think I hear one of them moving about upstairs,' he said. 'Floorboards creaking. I expect we'll soon be having heavy-breathing company. Friend Player, I'd guess, wanting to come out for the second round.' When no more sounds were heard, he nodded for Lingard to continue.

Lingard said, 'I was about to ask how do you want him circulated? Whereabouts sought for interrogation? Arrest on suspicion of?'

Rogers frowned his indecision. 'I think it's a waste of effort and only a going through the motions, but do an Arrest on Suspicion of Murder circulation.' Seeing Lingard's lifted eyebrows, he said, 'Dammit, David, whatever I think I've still to play it by the book. You've something about Angela Foxton?'

Lingard turned a page of his pocket book. 'Angela Foxton it is now that all the excitement's over,' he said ironically. He had recovered his jaunty aplomb. 'She was in lodgings until three weeks ago at the address she gave here. She left without giving the landlady – a stout party, by the way, who wears her hair curlers in bed – any reason for doing so and not leaving a forwarding address. She sounded peeved about it, so what she said, and there wasn't much of it, might be biased. Angela left nothing identifiable as hers in her rooms and these have since been re-let to another young lady, making them definitely unavailable for a nocturnal examination by anything male. The landlady understood that Angela was a secretary employed by Lampitters the betting office people, and nobody there's available yet for checking. She's alleged to have been in the habit of cantering around her bedroom more or less starkers with the curtains undrawn. Thank the Lord our policewomen don't stoop to such lewd practices.' He parodied a leer at Millier who poked out the tip of her tongue at him.

'Anyway,' he continued, 'it appears to have annoyed the

landlady, even if it gave pleasure to passers-by. All in all, she was obviously a bit of a lass for us men – the landlady said she was man-mad – apparently had quite a few hangers-on calling for her, but didn't have them inside and wouldn't have been allowed to. She also hinted, although she wouldn't say outright, that she was light-fingered. She didn't own a car and went to work by bus. She had her own key and invariably came back late at night, being dropped outside, which left the landlady unable to say who any of them were. She believes she has a sister somewhere, not too far away.'

'Kinniston,' Rogers interposed. 'You'll be going there as soon as we've finished.'

'Fabulous, by gad!' Lingard said with mock enthusiasm. 'For one horrible moment I thought you were going to send me home to bed. So that's about it for poor Angela, I fear. At least until it's bookmakers' opening time. I think that she'd have to tell them her new address.'

'I'm certain she would,' Rogers said. 'Before then, fill in by doing a bit of speculating about Gough. He fled the coop tonight as soon as you and I left for other parts. There's not a lot you can do about it, but call at his address and find out what's what and why. If the circumstances fit, narrow your eyes at him and point out that he won't get off the hook so easily as that, and that I want him back here.'

He reached for the envelope and letter and passed them to Lingard. 'Kinniston; the chore I'm unloading on you,' he said benignly. 'This was obviously written by the sister you mentioned. See her, find out what she's on about. I think she's referring to making a pendant and I want to know what's so mysterious about that. She'll not know about her sister's death, so you'll have that to do as well. In between, find out if she knows anything about her sister's goings-on with Gough and Whitaker.'

He stood, hearing from outside the sounds of vehicles arriving at the front of the house. He smiled his humorous intent and said, 'I suggest you take half-an-hour off beforehand for a shower, a shave and some breakfast, David. I wouldn't want the department's best-dressed man interviewing a young woman looking emaciated and smelling of old socks.'

20

With Lingard gone and having given Detective Sergeant Magnus instructions where in the house – he had excluded Mrs Haggar's annex – to use his fingerprint powders and lifting tapes, Rogers turned his attention to Inspector Coltart.

Coltart was a thick meaty man whose brown suit hung on his bulk like a badly-made tent, his orange-coloured shirt and blue woollen tie clashing distastefully enough to ensure that Lingard would wince should he see them. His hair was sandy, short and plastered to his skull, his small green eyes that rarely showed humour in a pasty freckled face. A rabid non-smoker, he was a great chewer of wooden toothpicks. He was a misogynist, disapproving of women in general and, because he so obviously did, was dubbed the Abbotsburn Rapist behind his back. Pointedly ignoring Sergeant Millier, he handed Rogers the dictionary he had asked for.

A man of few words – those he did speak rumbling out in a subterranean growl – he complained to his understanding senior that he should have been called out at the beginning of the investigation and not left to sleep in ignorance of it in bed. It could, in a way, be considered a disregard of his usefulness, and Rogers had to disarm him by explaining his need to have at least one of his lieutenants able to do things with bright eyes and an unfatigued mind. Coltart listened impassively to Rogers's summary of what had happened and to the detailing of his instructions. He and his men were to search the grounds and outhouses for a suitcase or travelling bag, female clothing and cosmetics, a recently used spade – preferably with traces of leaf-mould on it – a 12-bore cartridge case, disturbed soil and signs of pellet holes and shed blood; anything, indeed, that could be considered as being even remotely connected with Angela Foxton's death and Whitaker's departure. 'Leave the boathouse to me,' Rogers said finally, because Coltart was quite capable of forcing an entry into it with all the subtlety of an armoured vehicle, 'it's locked anyway.'

With the ineluctible routine of a murder investigation under way, his staff busy ferreting for the detritus of violent death, the confidence of a fully-equipped mind seemed to be back with him. He was drawing back the curtains to the brightening daylight, saying 'We're now open and in business,' to a tired looking Millier, when the door opened and Player entered. Still hulking, dressed in what appeared to be his uniform of a shirt, trousers and sandals, he seemed to have swallowed most of the aggression and arrogance previously directed at the detective.

Rogers arranged his features to geniality. 'Good morning. You're about early?'

'I couldn't sleep,' he said. 'Not knowing about Angela . . . being worried.'

'You probably know already as much as I can tell you,' Rogers answered him. 'She was shot dead on Wednesday and put into the sea, taken from it at six-thirty last evening and I'm here to find out who did it.'

Player thought about that, his expression showing dissatisfaction. 'That isn't much,' he said. 'What about Whitaker?'

'I'm not a news agency, Mr Player,' Rogers explained patiently. 'I've necessarily to be discreet in my opinions and careful with my facts. If you take a seat we'll probably get around to him, and I do have questions to ask you.'

Rogers saw a reaction to that in Player's eyes before he moved to the chair placed in front of the desk and sat. Rogers jerked his head at Millier and she retreated to the rear of the room, having been told beforehand to take her notes from behind those interviewed. Visible notekeeping was an inhibiting factor even to the garrulous, and Player wasn't promising to be one of them.

Seating himself, Rogers's role adapted itself to his necessarily impersonal authority and he studied Player expressionlessly before asking his first question. Seated, he topped the detective by half a head and, seen in daylight, looked even more a primitive wearing incongruously civilized clothing and talking with an educated tongue. His features were riven with crevices running down into the forest of his moustache and beard, his eyebrows overhangs to a thrusting ridge of a nose. Hair grew over his cheekbones; his pale blue, deep-set eyes, when he stared, had a built-in balefulness that didn't quite make it. Rogers assessed him provisionally as a probably conventional man who worked hard at keeping up with his bigness.

'You're a friend of Whitaker's, I understand?' he commenced.

'I'd like to say first that I'm sorry I lost my temper last night,' Player said. Close to, his conciliatory words came sterilized in the smell of medicated mouthwash. 'I was shocked at hearing about Angela, and your not telling me, that's all.'

Surprised, but not convinced, Rogers nodded. 'I understand, and there was no offence taken. You and Whitaker?'

'He isn't what you'd call a close friend,' he said. 'Particularly not since he left here. He's more a friend of Quennell's. You've met him?'

'Yes.' Rogers was further surprised at Player's apparent readiness to answer his questions. 'He is one of your group, isn't he?'

'It isn't exactly a group.' That hadn't come so easily. 'We're like-minded people who wanted a holiday away from crowds.'

'But you all know each other?' Rogers noticed that Player had the odd habit of turning his head sideways when listening.

'Yes, but some more than others.' There had been a just-discernible reluctance in his voice. Not the fastest thinker in the world, the creases in his forehead seemed well-worn.

'I know that you arrived in your separate cars because I've seen them, but who came with whom?' Rogers had sensed the distinct unease in the big man when he had lumped them altogether.

Player licked his lips, apparently considering what had to be well known to him. 'Angela came with Leslie Gough, Whitaker with Seb Quennell, and Mrs Horn with me. She's divorced,' he said, apparently feeling required to explain.

'And you're a friend of Mrs Haggar's? Having been here before and recommending it to your friends, in effect?'

'That's so. It's a quiet, friendly place.' He combed thick hairy fingers through his beard, frowning over something.

'I get the impression,' Rogers said with deliberation, his expression stern, 'that you aren't being completely open with me. Is there something about the reason for your group's visit which isn't what you say it is?'

That brought a dull flush over his cheekbones and more unease in the deep-set eyes, but his reply was hostile. 'That's a bloody stupid thing to say! Why?'

'I said that I get that impression,' Rogers said urbanely, having achieved his intended effect. 'If it's any comfort to you, from others as well.'

Player grunted. 'You said you were here to find out who killed Angela, and I should think that's sticking out a mile.' His voice was suddenly harsh and minatory. 'How I spend my holiday and what I do with it isn't any of your damned business.' He rose to his feet, towering over the seated detective. 'If that's all you've got to ask me, I've things to do.'

'Sit down,' Rogers said authoritatively, undisturbed by the man's aggression, although his eyes had darkened. 'I haven't asked about your using a shotgun yet. And a shotgun *is* connected with Miss Foxton's murder, isn't it?'

Player hesitated, then slowly lowered his big frame back on to the chair. It had been a gesture that the detective had recognized as such. 'That doesn't worry me either,' he said, his manner suggesting that he was prepared to tolerate patiently more stupid questions.

'I'm glad,' Rogers told him straightfaced. Player had accepted the guess he had made about using a gun. 'So tell me when was the last time you used one of them?'

His forehead creased. 'This week. I think Tuesday or Wednesday. Whoever told you might know for sure,' he added with sarcasm.

'So they might,' Rogers agreed, 'and perhaps they have. Who else do you know who's used them? For shooting at clay pigeons, naturally.'

'Quennell, Whitaker, Cathy . . . Mrs Horn, that is, and Angela,' he said quite readily with no unease now in him. 'Cathy and Angela usually together, but only on two or three occasions.'

'Not Gough?' He had decided that Player should discover Gough's absence for himself. If he didn't already know, it could provoke an informative reaction.

Player shook his head. 'Not so that I've seen him.'

'The Tollivers?'

He shook his head again. 'Not while I've been here. But then, I'm not here all the time.' He showed his square teeth in disparagement. 'If you want to know of everybody, aren't you going to ask me about Mrs Haggar as well?'

Rogers concealed his surprise. 'I was. So tell me.'

'No you weren't,' he contradicted him, almost sneering it. 'You didn't know. She shoots too.'

As Rogers stared at him, so his mind recalled the perforated clays he had seen in the cupboard, which he had meant to find out about and hadn't. Clays with holes that would, when spinning through the air, probably make some sort of a whistling sound for the remarkably sensitive hearing of Phaedra to orientate to and aim at.

'I do know,' he said, not willing to give Player any satisfaction in having told him. 'I've seen the clays. You've loaded the thrower for her?'

'No. Uriah Heep does that.' Something like a smile showed in his beard, but there was derision in his voice.

'Give me his name,' Rogers said. 'I'm not in the mood for guessing games.'

'Grice. Mrs Haggar's boyfriend.' He was searching Rogers's face. 'Is that something else you don't know?' he said mockingly.

Rogers felt a glow of anger at that. The man was deliberately needling him as though he knew of, or suspected, his interest in Phaedra. And Millier was hearing it as she scratched away with her pen, screwing her eyes in the half-light that reached the far wall. He wasn't prepared to remain the butt of Player's attempts to belittle him; not with her writing it down.

'What I know or don't know isn't your concern,' he said sharply, allowing his anger to show. 'It's what you know, or think you know, that matters. If you stop trying to score something off me, we'll get on a lot better. When did you last see Miss Foxton?'

Player had blinked at the words, but nothing more. 'I *think* Wednesday morning, and I *think* I saw her walking towards the beach.' He was being sarcastic. 'If somebody has said differently, I wouldn't argue about it.'

'And Whitaker?'

He grimaced his unknowingness. 'It might have been Wednesday morning, it might have been the day before. One day here's much like another.' Now sitting lax in his chair, he didn't appear a man who might have the shooting of a woman to death on his conscience.

'But you knew when he'd gone?'

'By Wednesday evening, yes. But only because he and Angela weren't here to eat with us in Thurnholme.'

'It surprised you?'

'Of course it didn't, they weren't required to. We all knew what was going on between them, and who would care a damn?'

'Gough might,' Rogers said. On that subject, he was studying Player, trying to fathom what attraction he could have for Catherine Horn should she be to him what could reasonably be assumed. Even the affectionate act of kissing him would be like plunging naked into a thicket of thorn bushes, and there was very little in him suggesting gentleness.

'He didn't act as if he did,' he replied positively. 'I don't think there was anything very serious in it from the beginning.'

'Why didn't you tell Mrs Haggar they'd left?'

'Because I didn't wish to worry her, and I thought they'd be back after a couple of days.'

'Although they'd cleared their rooms?'

'I didn't know.'

That was unbelievable, but Rogers didn't press it. 'Have you ever been in her bedroom? Quite innocently, of course,' he added blandly, seeing the flush back over his cheekbones.

'I think you'd better be careful,' Player growled. 'There's such a thing as slander.'

'Yes, there is. Had you?'

'Only with Cathy when she spoke to her on one occasion.' His eyes were challenging the detective to say differently. 'She'll confirm that.'

'Then you'd have no objection to elimination fingerprints being taken?'

'No,' he agreed without any hesitation. 'I've nothing to hide.'

'Did you like Miss Foxton?' Rogers asked, almost casually.

'You want me to say I didn't, I suppose?' That hadn't pleased him. 'Well, I did. She was a very friendly girl. Everybody liked her.'

'Accepted,' Rogers said. 'Other than, possibly, the one who shot her. Where do you moor your inflatable when it isn't in the boathouse?'

The sudden change of subject made Player frown and brought unease back to his eyes. He hesitated before saying carefully, 'I don't moor it anywhere. When I'm not using it, it's kept in the boathouse.'

Rogers held his hand out across the desk. 'Which reminds me,' he said. 'I'd like the key to it, please.'

'It's Mrs Haggar's property. I'd better give it to her.' He was, in his way, as bloody-minded as Rogers could often be.

'It's not yours and you'll give it to me.' Rogers's voice was hard and he held his stare, willing him to submission. 'And I won't ask again.' He was aware of Millier watching them, smiling in the background at what she must think of as two aggressive bulls butting at each other with their heads.

Player scowled and dug into his trouser pocket. Ignoring the detective's outstretched hand, he held the key between finger and thumb before dropping it contemptuously on the desk.

'Thank you,' Rogers said, leaving the key where it had been dropped. 'What do you use the inflatable for?'

Player made a noise in his throat. 'Messing about, like you do with boats. Sometimes fishing, sometimes swimming, but usually minding my own business.'

Opening the dictionary that Coltart had delivered to him, Rogers said, 'How many words beginning p-e-n-d-a can you think of, Mr Player?'

His astonishment was completely unforced as he stared at the book and then at Rogers. 'What the hell are you on about?' he spluttered, pushing his bearded chin forward. 'Are you mad? How would I know, and what's it to do with me anyway?'

'I don't know.' Rogers was being irritatingly polite. 'But would you believe it, there's only one word in the dictionary it can possibly be. *Pendant*,' he said, emphasizing it. 'The only word with that sequence of letters.' He was watching Player's eyes, seeing nothing in them that told him anything. When it was apparent that he was to get no comment on that, he said, 'I'm asking you because one of your party has written a letter indicating that a something from here was possibly going to be made into a pendant. No doubt that will . . .'

He stopped. Player looked as though Rogers had leaned across the desk and hit him in the face. In the taut silence that followed he struggled to re-form his features from the demoralization they had shown.

'You're lying,' he got out at last. 'Who wrote it?'

'That's twice I've been accused of that,' Rogers told him calmly. 'All right, you think I'm lying, but it doesn't quite go with your "Who wrote it?" does it? So tell me why you're so upset about somebody making a pendant.'

Player shook his head. 'It's nothing to do with Angela's murder,' he said dully. 'Nothing . . . believe me.' He closed his mouth and looked away from the detective, plainly determined on saying nothing further.

After staring at him for long moments, muted sounds from outside the only intrusion into the quietness, Rogers picked up his meerschaum and began filling it, being all for leaving an uncommunicative Player dangling on the hook of his own making. 'Thank you,' he said, his expression unreadable. 'I shall want to see you again later. I'd be obliged if you didn't leave the house or grounds without letting me know.' He snapped his lighter at his pipe, clearly dismissing Player from his further consideration.

Of one thing he was certain. He didn't much like Player. That he was a man clearly disorganized, walking from the study as if in anticipation of the roof falling in on his head, gave the detective just a little unprofessional satisfaction.

21

To Rogers, it was obvious that each of the men he had so far interviewed had managed to find a reason for chopping his interrogation off short; Quennell by collapsing on him, Gough from sheer nastiness and now Player because of his refusal to expose the sensitive nerve of whatever guilt he was suffering. It implied a conspiracy between them to be silent about something. Not that he felt frustrated by their defensive dodging and ducking. Apart from Gough perhaps, there would be time and opportunity for further probing, all the more useful when his armoury of facts had been added to. And that meant, among other things and before doing anything else, a visit to the cove in daylight. Moonlight and the company of a disturbing woman had been no aids to a clarity of vision or thought.

Allowing Player time to remove himself from the vicinity, he left the study. The kitchen door at the end of the passage was open and from it, overlaid with the perfume of percolating coffee, came the almost unbearable smell of frying mushrooms and bacon. For a hungry Rogers, at seven-thirty in the morning, it was more heady than a scent on an attractive woman's body and he went to it.

The woman standing at an Aga range and doing things to a frying pan, while possibly not heavy enough to crack floor-tiles, could reasonably be called hefty. She wore a loose green dress that did little to conceal intimidating breasts and the sturdy stockingless legs that ended in woven straw sandals. Her brown hair, parted precisely, hung unfussily straight to the lobes of her ears, her features neat, good-looking with a hot red poppy of a mouth, her skin flawless and glossy with good health. About his own age, she made the detective feel physically delicate and in poor condition.

She turned her head at his entering the door, her sharp brown eyes taking him in, evaluating him down to his shoelaces until she finally decided on a pleasant smile. 'I can guess who *you* are,' she said.

'Detective Superintendent Rogers,' he acknowledged, smiling back and deciding that he liked her. 'And you're Mrs Tolliver.'

She nodded, returning to tending her frying pan. 'My father was a policeman,' she said. 'An inspector in the old Blackpool Borough. He's on pension now, of course.'

'A happy man,' he said amiably. 'So you'll know the form; that I shall be asking you questions about Miss Foxton. You do know about her?'

'That she's been murdered? Yes, I do, poor girl.' She pushed absently at strips of bacon with a fork, making Rogers avert eyes he suspected must reflect his stomach's hunger. 'Mind, I'm not too surprised the way she was acting up.'

'With one or two of the men, you mean?' A gift from the gods who sometimes looked after CID officers, he told himself. A potentially gabby woman who probably wouldn't need pushing or shoving into answering questions.

'Well, obviously not with me,' she said drily. 'And not now, if you don't mind. I've a short-tempered and hungry husband who'll soon be down yelling for his breakfast.' She didn't sound as if it worried her.

Drawn back to eyeing the frying pan, his provoked hunger was magnifying the mushrooms and bacon in it to enough to feed a houseful of guests. 'Of course,' he said, turning to leave, 'later would suit me fine.'

'Before you go there's something else,' she told him. 'I don't know whether it's the accoustics or what, but I could hear you and that Player man shouting at one another. Perhaps others could too.'

'I'm grateful,' he said. 'Obviously some of your father's attributes have rubbed off on to you.'

'I hope they have.' Then she frowned and said, 'Damn! I'm forgetting myself. You must be hungry. When I've finished feeding Arnold I'll fry up something for you and the policewoman.'

'I'd ask you to marry me if you didn't have a husband already,' he smiled at her. 'I'd be happy if you could feed Miss

Millier and leave mine until I get back from the cove. I've no objection at all to its being cold.' That wasn't true, but he couldn't justify waiting around and being idle until her exceptionally fortunate husband had been fed.

Outside, with the sun well up in a cloudless sky, the mist had already been dissipated by the warming air. In the bright light, the house now looked anything but Gothic, the cypresses less funereal, and there were even two brilliantly blue butterflies dancing intricate patterns over the grass. Before descending the steps, Rogers filled and lit his meerschaum; a poor substitute, he had to admit, for a refused breakfast, but something.

About to pass Quennell's Mini, parked behind the Tollivers' shooting wagon, he saw through the rear window the head and shoulders of its owner. Bending and peering through the open side window, he said, 'Good morning. Remember me?'

Quennell, his eyes pink-jellied and red-rimmed, his chin and jowls dark with unshaved stubble, looked as though he had just been resurrected from a two-days' death. His linen suit in which he had undoubtedly slept his drunken sleep was creased and rumpled, with damp stains down its front. He held in a visibly shaking hand an old leather-covered hip-flask with a silver cap from which he had been drinking. 'God,' he muttered, 'but I certainly do. Was I so bloody awful?'

'Bad enough, but not too bad for a man fighting off leprosy,' Rogers said. Sympathy was the last thing a hangover needed. 'You're going somewhere?'

'Nirvana, if I can achieve it.' He was screwing the cap back on the flask. 'I don't suppose you'd care to shoot me?'

'If it'd help I would.' Rogers moved his head back from Quennell's pungent breath. 'But first we have an interrupted conversation to continue. I'm going down to the cove, so possibly you'd walk part way with me.' It wasn't what he wanted, but with a murder room that leaked words to an occupied kitchen he had little choice.

Unexpectedly compliant, he said, 'Always willing to oblige a copper.' He gave Rogers a sour smile. 'The cliff'll do as well as anything else.' Pushing the flask into his jacket pocket, he climbed from the car.

With the squat and unlovely Quennell walking at his side and passing on to the turf, he saw Phaedra standing among the flowers in the conservatory. With her hair back in its ponytail and wearing her dark glasses she was facing in his direction and, without thought, he waved an arm in greeting.

'Damn,' he muttered, 'but it takes some getting used to.'

'She probably heard us,' Quennell said. 'Personally the woman gives me the willies.'

Already a man with something about his persona that repelled Rogers, his opinion of him dropped even lower. 'I know you live in Abbotsburn, Mr Quennell,' he said, not showing his displeasure, although what had been said could sharpen his questioning, 'but I don't know what you do for a living.'

'I deal in antiques. Shouldn't you know that too?'

'Not unless you'd been under suspicion of receiving stolen property,' Rogers replied in a tone of voice that left the possibility open to its being so. 'At your address?' He slowed his pace. The shorter, stockier man was having to take more steps to keep up with him.

'It's got Quennell's Antiques painted in ye olde world script over the shop window, so I think I do.'

Rogers sighed. Quennell seemed about to be another difficult bugger; another odd-ball in a shoal of them, all unable or unwilling to give a straight answer. 'You live there with your wife?' he asked.

'I don't have a wife,' he said, bristling resentment. 'At least, not living with me. Why ask me that?'

'Only because you came on your own. Because you came without one or a girlfriend.' Quennell's mood had changed with that question; unwitting nerve-end touching again, Rogers thought.

'I didn't come on my own,' he said. 'I brought Michael Whitaker with me.'

'I see. What did you come here for anyway?'

Quennell's fleshy face tightened momentarily and he swallowed. Then he gave a short laugh that sounded forced. 'For Christ's sake!' he said. 'What do you think? I'm here on a holiday.'

'I wondered, that's all,' Rogers said mildly. 'You don't seem to be enjoying it.' Quennell had, he considered, a more relaxed wordiness when drunk. At the moment he seemed to be straining for equivocation.

'We don't always, do we?' He managed a smile with no humour in it. 'Especially when we've had Angela shot and you lot turning the place upside-down.'

'A nuisance,' Rogers said as if agreeing with him. 'Did you ever by any chance visit her room?'

'My God, but you're a dirty-minded sod!' He said that as a denial and it rang true. There was no animosity in the way it was spoken.

'I imagine I am,' Rogers said affably. 'It's to do with the people I have to mix with. I'm asking you, were you interested in Miss Foxton yourself?'

'Don't be too bloody clever, old chum,' he said. 'No, I wasn't, and even if she had been in me, which is unlikely, it wasn't on. I know I'm a fool to say it, but I didn't like her.'

'But your friend Whitaker apparently did.'

'I told you, she chucked herself at him.'

'You sound as though you didn't approve.'

'A matter of indifference, actually. But we came together, so I certainly didn't approve of him going off with her.'

'Why didn't you like her?'

'I don't know. Probably because I'd a good idea she didn't like me. And if you're about to ask me why she didn't, I don't know that either. Probably the shape of my nose or the colour of my hair.'

'What kind of a man is Whitaker?'

'I'm sorry, but that's not a fair question. He's my friend. I've already told you he wouldn't have done anything to Angela.'

'So you did,' Rogers said as if that settled the question. 'Did Gough ever speak to you about what Whitaker was doing with his girlfriend?'

'Not one word. He isn't the sort to cry on somebody's shoulder.'

'Other than Player, did Mrs Haggar know any of you from previous visits?'

'She wouldn't know me.' There was a definite wariness in his answer.

'You can take it from me that she didn't know the others

either. So why should Gough and Miss Foxton, both unknown to her, choose to occupy separate rooms?' To Rogers this was, as with Player and Mrs Horn, an overly prissy regard to appearances that seemed unfashionable, out of character and astonishingly unnecessary to any holiday hotel or guesthouse proprietor.

Quennell said, 'I don't think that Mrs Haggar would have liked it otherwise.'

'Come off it,' Rogers said, heavily sardonic. 'You mean to say it would be against their religion or something to book in as Mr and Mrs Gough?'

'It might be. You should ask Gough.'

They were approaching the panel screen concealing the clay-pigeon thrower and Rogers halted. The sun, higher in the sky now, was hot on his back and with no cooling sea breeze coming in over the cliff's edge as it should he was already beginning to feel the dampness of sweat beneath his shirt. The sea, running against the beach below in smooth rollers, reflected a bright glare that was manifestly painful to Quennell's bloodshot eyes. He was turning his head away and blinking an unhappy hangover's discomfort to it. Rogers allowed himself a driblet of sympathy for him; a couple of hours back he had felt like it himself, if not for the same reason.

'You've shot clays from here?' he asked, his eyes steady on Quennell's.

'Quite often.' He gave a lopsided self-deprecatory grin. 'Actually, I'm rather good at it.'

'When was the last time?'

'Wednesday.' He took the flask from his pocket and began pouring a drink into the silver cap. 'Excuse me,' he said, 'but I haven't achieved well-being yet.' He drank it in one gulp, screwed on the cap and put it back into his pocket.

'Were you on your own?' Rogers was tempted, but withheld it, to ask him if he had ever hit a clay with anything but a blast of vodka-smelling breath.

'Yes, but not always. Gough sometimes loaded the thrower for me.'

'On Wednesday?'

'No, he wasn't here.'

'Did he ever shoot clays himself?'

'Not that I knew of.'

'Was there anyone else here when you were?' Rogers could hear the sounds of activity and see the movement of bushes as Coltart's searchers quartered the thick shrubbery away from them. If Quennell heard, he gave no sign of it.

He hesitated, then shrugged and said, 'I think Luther Player followed me.'

'You saw him?'

'Later, when I was back in the house. I think it was him because I could see the back of his head above the screen.'

'You heard shots?'

'I imagine so.' He was staring with brighter-looking eyes at the bleached slats of the panel near him. 'I remember now. Before I left the house I heard somebody firing from here. And when I collected my gun from the cupboard it was the only one there.'

'And you saw who it was?'

He shook his head. 'No, I didn't.'

'But you'd pass whoever it was coming back,' Rogers pointed out. It would be normal for anyone returning to the house from the shooting point to cross the open expanse of turf.

'I should, but I didn't.'

'That didn't surprise you?'

'I never thought about it. Why should I?'

'And when you put your gun back?'

'It was still not there.'

There seemed to be a significance about that which Rogers couldn't yet grasp. 'Player could have taken it, of course?'

'He could. And he could also have taken mine. He began shooting long after I'd returned the gun.' Quennell was moving his feet restlessly and there was a film of sweat on his forehead. 'Have you finished? I hate to be unco-operative, but I *am* hungry and I'd like to get into a change of clothing. I think I must have slept in these.'

'You did, and I've nearly finished,' Rogers said. 'After you've done what you need to do, I'd like to have your fingerprints taken for elimination purposes on the gun you used.'

Quennell grimaced. 'Am I obliged to?'

'No, but only somebody with something to hide could raise any objection to it.'

'Then I'm tempted to tell you to shove it,' he said. 'I'll think about it when I haven't got you leaning on me. Can I go now?'

'Before you do, I'd like you to look down at the beach.' Rogers moved across the grass to the edge of the cliff and Quennell, looking perplexed, followed him.

Being on the top of the loftiest and steepest face of the cliff and not having eliminated Quennell as a possible murderer or the man who had banged him on the head, Rogers stood a yard away from him as, still puzzled, he screwed his eyes to view the beach below him. The tide was in and the cove empty of life but for a solitary detective picking his way through outcrops of rock; not, Rogers thought, very enthusiastically, and understandably so, for there was little there for him to find but shingle, washed-ashore seaweed and shells and the padlocked boathouse.

'Do you mean that man down there?' Quennell asked after his silent contemplation of the nothing much.

'No, he's one of mine,' Rogers said. He sharpened his voice, forcing Quennell to meet his challenging stare. 'I want to know from you what's been going on down there that everyone seems so anxious I shouldn't be told.'

Expecting it or not, Quennell was fractionally slow in concealing the sudden look of alarm in his eyes. With his expression now one of ingenuous perplexity, he said, 'I don't know what you're talking about. Who's keeping what from you?'

'I'm asking *you*.'

'If there's anything going on down there that could interest you, then I know nothing about it.' He held Rogers's hard stare far too long to be telling the truth.

Rogers let him see the patient disbelief in his face. Quennell was a poor liar, but promising clearly to be a stubborn one. 'You'll come, Quennell, for whatever it is,' he said tersely, hoping that he wasn't going to have to eat his words. 'Don't make any mistake about that.'

Where another man would have shown resentment, Quennell, holding back whatever he felt, said, 'May I go now?'

Without waiting for an answer, he turned from the detective and left him.

Rogers watched him thoughtfully as he moved towards the house. A scruffy five-star drunk, he was convinced, who had things to hide behind that jowly unshaven face of his. 'I'm not doing so bloody well, am I?' he said aloud to the phantasmagoric and reproachful Angela Foxton he imagined to be standing at his side; not wholly believing that she could be, but not prepared to disbelieve it either.

22

Waiting for Quennell to move out of sight before descending to the beach, Rogers stood at the top of the steps and took in a daylight view of the cove. Frustratingly, it didn't tell him much more than he had learned by moonlight.

A quite small bite out of the land with curving crescent arms, its off-shore outcrops of rock could be seen as underwater streaks of foam. Entry to it would be dangerous for any but shallow-draught boats. The enclosing cliffs of the crescent were riven with fissures and vertical crevices; the waves, rolling in with a measured cadence, breaking into them with a hollow slapping of streaming spume. A few seagulls drifted airborne over the water and two shags, looking like old women in black mourning clothes, perched side by side on an exposed stack of rock. It was, Rogers thought, despite the growing heat, a more suitable habitat for penguins and basking seals. Far out and soundlessly, a cargo boat muddied its part of the sky with brown smoke.

Moving down the steps brought his earlier descent to mind, and Phaedra – so desirable in retrospect – who had accompanied him. Distanced from her by the passage of two hours or so, he was wishing that he hadn't so insufferably and priggishly withdrawn from her overtures of intimacy. Perhaps, he excused himself, the benzedrine capsule he had taken produced an initially dampening effect on a body's need to go through the motions of procreation. But, with it, was the certain knowledge that if there had been an *après*-Phaedra situation he would probably be regretting it, self-inflicted doubts squirming inside him like unhappy worms. And this was qualified by the equally certain knowledge that one day he would have grey hair, shrivelled parts and a despairing mildewed regret that he had too often side-stepped the possible.

Seeing the beach-searching detective start climbing the steps towards him returned his mind to what he was going down there for. Nearer, Rogers recognized him as DPC Foreman, accepted into the department partly for his invaluable usefulness in not looking like a policeman in plain clothes. He held what appeared to be a white sandal in one hand.

Rogers halted and let Foreman come up to him. 'You've found something, I see,' he said.

'Washed up on the beach, sir,' Foreman said. It wasn't every day that he had a personal conference with his superintendent halfway up a cliff, or anywhere else for that matter, and his nervousness showed. 'I think it's a woman's shoe.'

'I think it must be,' Rogers agreed gravely, taking it from him and not underlining its obviousness. It was clearly a woman's flat-heeled shoe – he guessed about size 4 or 5 – in white patent leather and mostly all thin straps with a gilt fastening buckle. Any manufacturer's lettering on the inner sole had been worn away to indecipherability. It was sodden with sea-water, but otherwise undamaged and not a shoe to be worn on the beach or to be thrown away. If it had been Angela Foxton's, lost when she was put into the sea – and he would accept that it had been hers until it was proved otherwise – then her wearing of shoes could mean that she had moved from her bedroom to somewhere outside the house. There was an alternative to that which made him mutter, 'I think we've been a couple of bloody idiots,' requiring an explanation to a startled Foreman that his remark hadn't referred to him.

Leaving the DPC, he continued his descent of the steps. Although he was only working on an assumed possibility, he was irritated with himself, with Lingard and with murdered females for their tendency to make matters more difficult for working detective superintendents. It led him also to include

God for being so apparently indecisive in his ordering of the activities of himself and *Homo sapiens* in general.

Reaching the bottom and making his way to the boathouse across loose shingle, his shoes sank into the grinding pebbles, doing the polished uppers no good at all. Examining the shoe he carried in his hand and finding it free of the scuff-marks spoiling his own, he was sure that whoever had worn it could not have walked in it on the punishing stones.

The boathouse, looking elderly, weatherbeaten and salt-sprayed in the bright sun, sat on a flat shelf of rock above the spume of incoming waves nearly reaching it. Rogers found it difficult to imagine that it would not be hurled against the foot of the cliff by even a moderate gale. Although padlocked, it would certainly be laughably simple for any strong-fingered villain with a need for a boat to break into.

Unlocking the door he pulled it open, it's bottom edge scraping on the rock as he did so, and stepped into the shadowed interior. The greenish light that shone through the algae-covered glass of the window could suggest it an appropriate place in which to murder someone but not, he thought, in which to meet a lover. The inflatable boat he had glimpsed only partly by torchlight took up most of the floor space. Of a thick dark-grey rubberized fabric like elephant's hide, it was large and bulgy and looked as though it had been sailed a couple of times around Cape Horn in rough seas. In addition to the application of several red-rubber repair patches, somebody with a sense of the ridiculous had stencilled *Sea-Nymphet* on each plump side of its flotation pontoons. There were no signs of an outboard engine, of the necessary fittings for one on the boat's tail-end or of one ever having been used on it. The floor beneath the seat was dirty with grit and what appeared to be smears of a light-coloured rust which he discounted as being bloodstaining but, conceding himself to be fallible, thought that he would have checked just in case.

An ancient sea-angling rod – surely having once belonged to the dead brigadier – rested in the angle of the rear wall. Its cork butt was flaking, the large reel rusty and insecurely attached, and its hookless line bleached to a greenish-white. Slow in noticing something no longer there, he realized that the black fabric he had seen hanging in a fold at the side of the window was now gone. Three large nails hammered in a row at head height in the planking convinced him that he hadn't been hallucinating. That made whatever had been hanging from them important to somebody; that his own further visit to the boathouse had been expected and guarded against. Phaedra had known that he had visited it and had told Player. Either could have told somebody else but, refusing to speculate, they were the only two he could consider. He tried to recall Player's attitude when he had demanded the boathouse key and, apart from his contemptuous gesture in dropping it on the desk, he couldn't remember. 'Damn!' he said aloud. It acerbated his frustration that there was nothing else in what seemed a peculiarly under-equipped boathouse, and that his anticipation of finding a rope of sorts was unrealized.

With the inflatable taking up most of the floor area, logic made it highly unlikely that, given the position in which Angela Foxton was lying, she could have been shot there without one at least of the inflatable's flotation chambers being punctured by stray pellets. But, because Rogers had been misled previously by apparent logic, he examined – abortively, it proved – the walls and floorboards for bloodstaining and the tiny holes that shotgun pellets made. What he did find in the process, on a floorboard close to the wall and immediately beneath the window, was a dark patch of soaked-in engine oil. Something had bled there, if not Angela Foxton's body.

Out in the dazzling sunshine and blinking his eyes at it – as bad as the drunken Quennell, he thought – he relocked the door and moved along the shelving beach to examine again the oddly-located length of steel tubing. It wasn't where he remembered it to have been and, deciding that he couldn't be that stupid, he clambered about the rocks and searched without result for signs of its removal.

He had in a way, he considered, violated the first rule in the discovery of what might be evidence of something. And that was, irrespective of any doubts to the contrary and if physically possible, to seize it and stick an exhibit label on it. Now it was gone and his recollection of it would be proof of nothing very much. Somebody had paid him the compliment of expecting that he could discover what it had been used for. At the moment, he thought it unearned. A rope had been tied to the missing tubing and all he could think of for its use was mooring a boat where no boat, particularly an inflatable, could safely be moored. He must, he thought, have holes in his brain. What he had seen and not seen should be telling him something about Angela Foxton's death and the disposal of her body, and it wasn't.

His climb back up the cliff steps was a lot less than mountain-goat-like and he was ready to believe that a detective superintendent's reconnoitring could best be done from the comfort of the late brigadier's study chair. Reaching the top of the cliff, his lungs and legs aching, uncomfortably damp with sweat, he saw a man standing there and only too obviously expecting his arrival. He thought of Mrs Tolliver and the mushrooms and bacon breakfast that could be waiting for him, and he groaned inside even as he composed his mouth to a semblance of amiability.

23

The man waiting for Rogers was rubbing his hands together and baring his teeth in an obsequious smile. It wasn't a good start, for the detective distrusted the smile, knowing that more often than not it was a disguise for a spiteful nature.

As tall as Rogers but rawboned and somewhere in his fifties, the man was dressed immaculately in well-creased blue twill trousers and an open-neck yellow shirt that exposed a promi-nent Adam's apple. His hair, carefully arranged in tight waves, was the colour of cigarette ash, his nose beaky in gaunt features, his eyes small and pale-grey, and the teeth he had shown so readily were china-white and too even to be natural. He carried the strong smell of an after-shave lotion about him.

'You're Mr Grice,' Rogers said, needing no introduction to identify the man Player had so derisively described as a Uriah Heep.

He bobbed his head, showing his teeth again. 'I'm pleased to meet you. You're Superintendent Rogers?'

'Yes.' Rogers made an effort to be friendly, conceding that because the man had initially got up his nose, because Player had also suggested that he was Phaedra's intimate, it did not mean that there need be anything wrong with him. 'I was going to speak to you in due course. I assume you know what's happened?'

'Indeed I do,' he said quickly, shutting off his smile. 'And what a dreadful thing it is. The poor, poor girl. Mrs Haggar told me, and I've just left her. She said I might find you here.'

Rogers couldn't think of anything to say to that, so he nodded.

'I wondered if I could be of any help,' Grice said.

'Thank you.' Rogers held, perversely, a suspicion against unsolicited offers of help, rare occurrences as they were in a police investigation. 'If you spend any time here at the cove you might. Do you?'

'No, not really. I'm working all the week and only here Saturdays and Sundays. And looking after myself at the cottage . . .' He shrugged resignedly as if it were a sadness he bore.

'So if there was anything unusual going on down there you wouldn't know?'

'I didn't know.' There was eager interest in his eyes. 'Was there?'

Rogers ignored the counter-question. 'You've heard no odd noises from your cottage? Engine noises during the evening or night?'

'Boat engines sometimes.' He seemed fascinated by the shoe Rogers held in his hand, his eyes on it more than on the detective. 'And cars going in and out. Is that what you mean?'

'Not exactly. Shotguns being fired sound loud enough; have you ever heard one being used here other than between ten and noon?'

'Never, never.' He was positive. 'If I had I'd have done something about it. Mrs Haggar is very firm about that.'

Rogers was beginning to believe that Grice's offer of help had nothing behind it. He took out his meerschaum and began filling it, not speaking but allowing the silence to work what it could. Somebody had to say something and it was Grice.

He lifted a folded hand to his mouth and gave an apologetic cough. 'Mrs Haggar doesn't like it,' he said.

'Oh? You mean the shooting?' Rogers blew smoke that drifted towards the house that showed no signs of life. All inside stuffing their faces with breakfast, he thought enviously.

'No.' Grice was definitely screwing up his resolve. 'Being continually badgered with questions . . . matters she doesn't know about . . . that sort of thing.'

Rogers took the pipe from his mouth, staring at him in amazement, uncertain whether to laugh at him or to be irritated. 'You mean by me?' he said, quietly enough for anybody not obtuse to be warned.

'She shouldn't be worried,' Grice said, looking everywhere but at Rogers. His words had a certain doggedness in them.

'She told you so?'

'Yes . . . well, not in so many words, but I knew.'

'You're not warning me off by any chance, are you?' He couldn't take the man's attitude seriously, but he hardened his voice. 'Interfering with a police investigation into a murder?'

Grice was back to rubbing his hands together and showing his teeth, but Rogers had caught a momentary glimpse of the venom in his eyes. 'I'm only thinking of her welfare . . . a lady being blind and alone. She shouldn't be worried by all this.'

'No, she shouldn't, and I don't believe she is.' Rogers was showing his annoyance now, uncertain whether it was as a detective superintendent meeting obstruction, or as a man encountering rivalry. Damn Player! he thought. Why did he have to bring out that sneer? He said, 'You consider yourself her guardian, do you?'

'I look after her business books and accounts. I see the guests in and out. I do have responsibilities towards her.'

'You wouldn't be walking around the grounds late in the evening, would you? Worrying about what trouble she might be getting into?' Grice looked as though he had just tasted lavatory cleaning fluid and pink blotches appeared over his cheekbones. They could be signs of embarrassment or anger if, Rogers thought, Uriah Heep types could ever be angry. But the answer to his question had been there.

'No, I certainly wouldn't.' His Adam's apple was convulsing his disquiet. 'Why should I? She'd be indoors.'

'It was a thought,' Rogers said as if dismissing the possibility. His annoyance had gone with the success of his chance shot, certain now that Grice had been his follower and watcher. 'At the risk of repeating myself, would you have been outside her conservatory during the night? Exercising your responsibility at about three-thirty this morning?'

'Three-thirty!' he echoed the detective, his face all astonishment. 'I've already said I haven't . . . that I wouldn't. I'd be in bed.' He was conceivably speaking the truth this time and managing with it a small show of resentment. 'Why should you think I was?'

'I don't particularly,' Rogers assured him blandly, 'but I wouldn't know for sure until I asked. You'd met Miss Foxton, of course?'

'Yes.' He seemed relieved at the change of subject. 'It was me who booked her in with Mr Gough.'

'And you've obviously seen her about the place since?'

'Yes, sunbathing with the others at the front of the house. That sort of thing.' He shook his head as if that were one of life's shamelessness. Possibly, Rogers guessed, recalling what Lingard had told him, because she had been exposing her breasts in the process.

'Anywhere else? With anyone else?' Rogers gave him an encouraging half-smile.

He hesitated, showing a sudden interest in his fingernails. 'Well . . . now that you mention it – and I tell you only because I do want to help the police – I did see her walking down here with Mr Whitaker.'

'Good,' Rogers encouraged him further. 'When was this?'

'Early in the week – Tuesday or Wednesday, I think. I think they were . . . well, you know.'

There had been a fleeting salacious look in his gaunt face. Just mentioning what he had seen had begun to turn him on. Rogers had met his type many times; destined by circumstance to be a solitary and a looker-on, satisfying an easily stimulated ruttish-

ness by watching other people practising theirs. He was prepared to apologize to him *in absentia* were he proved not to be.

'I don't know, Mr Grice,' Rogers said flatly, his encouragement gone and sternness taking its place. 'Do you mean you
thought they were intending to have sexual intercourse? Or that
you saw them actually having it?'

The Adam's apple was jerking again. 'I thought they were,
that's all.'

'From the way they were walking? Holding hands?' Rogers
couldn't quite keep the derision from his words.

'I guessed,' he said, his eyes dodging like hunted rabbits.
'Just guessed, that's all.'

'This was at night, of course.' Rogers made it a statement, not
a question.

'No . . . yes, that is . . . it was about ten. I was going to
the house to see Mrs Haggar.' It was weak, and it sounded
weak.

Rogers raised his eyebrows. 'At ten at night?'

He hesitated. 'I think it was, yes.'

Rogers bore down on him. 'But instead, you followed them.
Was it to see that they didn't do anything which might offend
Mrs Haggar?'

'Yes. She wouldn't approve of that sort of thing.' He bobbed
his head anxiously. 'But only a little way. I didn't see anything.
I wouldn't want to, I can assure you of that.'

'So where were they when you didn't see what you guessed
they were going to do?' Rogers asked ironically.

'Near the shooting stand.' He bobbed his head again. 'That's
right, I remember now, just about there.'

'And then you went back to see Mrs Haggar?' He was
encouraging him into a pitfall.

'Yes.'

'And you saw her? Spoke to her?'

To lie, or not to lie, was written clear in his face as his mouth
formed a word and then held it unspoken behind his teeth.
Finally, he said, 'No, no I didn't. She was asleep, so I didn't
want to wake her up.'

'Which was very thoughtful of you,' Rogers said, smiling
amiably and deciding not to ask the visibly demolished man

how he could know, apart from her unlikely snoring, that she was asleep. At least, not at the moment. 'Perhaps I can see you again when you've had time to remember anything else you might have seen. And thank you for your help,' he added with a straight face as Grice turned and left him. Whatever his intent had been in approaching the detective, it was plain that he hadn't enjoyed its outcome.

24

Despite the compelling attraction of the breakfast that could be awaiting him, Rogers could not yet return. What Grice had told him should be useful, although the time at which he had seen Angela Foxton and Whitaker together had no relevance to the theory he had contrived so uncertainly on being handed the shoe by DPC Foreman. He removed his awareness from the warmth and brightness of the daylight – closing his eyes when he found it difficult and hoping that nobody would see him – and sent his mind into the darkness of the night which had allowed Grice to act out his role as voyeur. In doing so, he was again retracing his walk from the house with Phaedra, adopting the intent and emotions he was assuming Whitaker to have had. And that, ignoring any lack of urgency or a pressing need for concealment, should discourage a climb down to the beach to a presumably padlocked boathouse or the unthinkability of shingle and rock. Rejecting that any coupling would be done on the open turf facing the house, he considered the panelled-in shooting stand. Even for the hard-pressed, that wouldn't do in either daylight or darkness, for the clay-pigeon thrower occupied too much of its ground space. Excluding the nearby shrubbery and the stony soil on considerations of good taste – it seemed to him a suitable venue only for a couple of mating weasels – it left the summerhouse; reasonably concealed, discreet and a place he would have chosen, given Whitaker's disposition and a willing Phaedra. That night it must have been as dark inside as when he had seen it, and it would leave Grice with only the satisfaction he could get from whatever mewings and gruntings of hurried love he could hear from where he would be standing in the bushes. It was an unpleasant thought which he dismissed quickly from his mind, opening his eyes to the glare of sunshine, feeling in himself a sense of unworthiness that he had used Phaedra as the simulacrum of a sexually orientated Angela Foxton.

The summerhouse, its greenness merging into the canopies of the tall bushes surrounding it, was virtually unnoticeable from the open turf unless looked for. Rogers reached it by passing in front of the shooting stand, pushing his way through the bushes without searching for the overgrown path leading to it. This was more convenient, but exposed his sweating skin to the thirsty attentions of disturbed insects.

In bright sunshine, the summerhouse appeared less like a tomb overgrown with foliage than when he had seen it by moonlight. Viewed from the rear its structure was smothered by a large-leafed creeper; its roof, in a Victorian baroque of once-gilded pineapple ornamentation, only just visible through it. The front, facing a panoramic view of deserted sea, had large hinged lattice windows with a glazed door at one end. Long leafy strings of the creeper hung over them, only minimally obstructing the light from entering an already shadowed interior. Much neglected as it appeared to be, it seemed attractive in its reversion to a natural wildness.

Opening the door and walking in – he had noticed that its sill was rough with splinters – he saw its melancholy decrepitude as it actually was. The blue-painted wall – and ceiling-boards were faded and flaking, riddled with woodworm holes and, in places, warped enough to show streaks of light and to allow the intrusion of tendrils of pale leaves. Spiders had colonized the angles of the ceiling with their webs and the floor beneath was littered with sucked-dry flies. A long white-enamelled slatted bench ran along the rear wall. Cushionless and promising little comfort to human flesh it was, significantly to Rogers, free of dust. The badly worn linoleum floor covering, soiled and dusty, had a lighter patch beneath one end of the bench. The summerhouse was not, he conceded, a setting he would have chosen himself, other than perhaps for an unlikely hit-and-run

135

conjunction with an unfussy woman. But he was certain that a probably more motivated Whitaker had done so.

Crouching at the end of the bench, wincing at the strain on his calf muscles, he examined the lighter patch of flooring. That it had been cleaned recently was obvious. Grimacing his distaste, he moistened the tip of a finger and smoothed it over its surface until assured that there was no reaction to spilled blood from it. From there he moved his attention to the slats of the bench and its end legs. The first sign of a pinkish suffusion on his fingertip came from behind the front leg. It wasn't much, but it was confirmation enough that Angela Foxton had met her death lying on the bench. Better as an overlooked recipient of spilled blood was the dead bluebottle fly he found lying in the angle between the leg and the floor. What had been a complex creature of shimmering metallic blue with transparent wings was now overall a dull dark-red stickiness. When he touched his moistened finger gently on to the tiny body, it came away marked with a spot of deeper pink. No longer too tiny and insignificant a creature to matter, the bluebottle could be a significant factor in bringing justice to Angela Foxton.

Examining the wall behind where her head would have been, he found that its paint had also been cleaned. Too, although not outstandingly visible because of the poor light, there were several of what appeared to be woodworm holes. Some were, but some were not. Those which were not identified themselves by showing the dull lustre of lead shotgun pellets inside. Although they were narrowly scattered, it was difficult for him to judge accurately their spread pattern, but he had no doubt at all that whoever had fired them had done so from the door at the other end of the bench.

He straightened his aching legs and stood with black discs floating across his vision. It reminded him that he was upright and more or less compos mentis only by the grace of a capsule of benzedrine which might even now be nearing the end of its effectiveness. It was time to back it up with food and, a catastrophe such as Armageddon excepted, God help anyone who tried to keep him from it.

25

The brigadier's study – too divorced from a constabulary functionalism for Rogers even now to think of it as his designated murder room – was cheerfully bright with the sun streaming through its windows. Although Sergeant Millier looked freshly scrubbed and was as lively-minded as anyone could be working at ten o'clock on a hot morning, he knew that she had to be tired after a sleepless night. The bulky Detective Inspector Coltart was with her and, contrasting with the fragrance of her scent, was smelling like a sweating horse from his recent activity.

The inspector, his sandy eyebrows lowered in his disgruntlement, did not consider the finding of a shoe and the retrieval from a tool shed of a spade with what appeared to be leaf-mould on it a satisfactory result for the four hours of his team's searching. He had, he rumbled at Rogers, sent the men round again on the basis that they had all been suffering an early-morning myopia. Never a man to be happy until he had his thick fingers locked firmly on a prisoner's collar, he was chagrined as well when Rogers told him that he had found in the summerhouse the evidence he needed to connect it with Angela Foxton's death. Thwarting Coltart's promise to metaphorically crucify the DPC who had searched that area, Rogers put his veto on it, explaining that nothing of what he had found in the shadowed interior would have been obvious unless looked for with a certainty that it must be there. Nevertheless, Rogers knew that the unfortunate DPC would be getting a longish blast of shrivelling words from the inwardly furious inspector who left the study with that intent written all over his beefy face.

Millier had made notes for Rogers, dictated by an absent Sergeant Magnus. He had identified one of the finger impressions taken from the dead woman's body with a fingerprint he had found in Angela Foxton's bedroom. Until Rogers's finding of pellet-holes and bloodstaining in the summerhouse, this was something about which he had had minor misgivings over his perhaps incautious identification of the body on the strength of a couple of gold bracelets and the colour of her hair. It could so easily have been the body of another woman altogether, with Angela Foxton and Whitaker perspiring in bed somewhere in the pursuit of a newly-found passion for each other while he, Rogers, would have been left with the most God-awful of professional blunders.

Magnus had taken the elimination prints of Player and Quennell, had lifted impressions from the bedrooms of Gough and Whitaker, and had returned to Headquarters – taking the shotguns with him – for further comparison studies and a check with the Criminal Records Office.

In answer to Rogers's queries, Millier said that the photographs taken of Angela Foxton's body had not yet arrived, nor any report from the Forensic Science Laboratory. Saying 'Bugger it!' under his breath and seating himself in his chair, Rogers reached for a sheet of paper and a pencil and sketched in a concentrated silence. When he had finished, he said, 'Come here, sergeant, and look at this,' waiting until she was standing behind him.

'Doing without any comments on my lack of artistic skills,' he said, 'this is supposed to be Angela Foxton as I saw her dead on the breakwater. Can you see from it what she was wearing? It was cotton, I think; pale-blue and came down to just below her knees.'

She peered over his shoulder, her jasmine scent disturbingly heady and her hair brushing his ear. 'A sundress?' she said.

'Could it be a nightdress?' He didn't want it to be, but at the same time he didn't wish to appear to have been completely clueless about women's clothing.

'It could be.' She looked at the drawing doubtfully. 'They can be similar, but as you've drawn it waisted I'd say a sundress.'

'Good for you,' he said, being now certain that it was and screwing the drawing into a ball before tossing it in the direction of the fireplace. 'No doubt one of the women here will have seen her wearing it.' He was both irritated that he had made originally a wrong identification of the dress, and pleased that he had made good his error – it had been Lingard's, also – before being led too far astray.

'Mrs Tolliver might,' Millier said. 'She's in the kitchen with your breakfast. I think she must have seen you coming.'

'And *now* you tell me,' he growled, lowering his eyebrows in simulated anger, then said, 'You must be all in, sergeant. I'll call in a relief and you can go home and get some sleep.'

He could always recognize when he had made a boob and, from her expression, he knew that he had now. 'No,' she said, perhaps sharper than she had intended, 'I'd rather you didn't. Certainly not if it's because I'm a woman.'

'The thought never entered my head, sergeant,' he lied straight-faced, hoping that she wasn't going to prove to be too desperately Women's Lib. 'I'm sure that if you wore a beard and had hairy legs, I'd have said the same.' He did get a smile from the lovely mouth as he turned and left her, but wondering why so many women should choose to be so bloody illogical towards a reasonably logical Rogers. And he hadn't, anyway, wanted to lose her.

26

Walking along the passage and into the kitchen, he found Eva Tolliver standing at the range tending her frying pan and looking as though she had not left it from his earlier visit. 'I don't suppose you've since considered divorcing your husband,' he said smiling, 'admirable chap although he undoubtedly is.'

She laughed, responding to his humour. 'He's gorgeous and I wouldn't dream of it. You haven't met him, have you?'

'No. Is he seven feet tall and rippling with muscle?'

'You must have seen him.' She scooped his breakfast on to a large willow-pattern plate. 'He goes in for body-building – you know? Weight-lifting and eating raw steaks.'

'Um,' he said. 'I was born a weakly coward so I think I'll just settle for the eating.' He was finding her easy to be friendly with, a contrast to most of the characters at Catteshead House.

He sat himself at the wooden table on which she had put his plate of bacon, eggs and mushrooms, together with a breakfast-cup of dark coffee, and waited for her to join him. 'If my eating doesn't disturb you,' he said, 'I'd be grateful if you'd chat away while I'm doing it, telling me what's going on here and by whom. As your father's daughter should and with no wish to mislead honest policemen. Perhaps Angela Foxton first?'

Bringing over a cup of coffee for herself, she plumped her attractive heftiness on to a chair opposite him with an air about her that made Rogers believe that she had been waiting for this and was prepared to enjoy it. 'I think I told you that Angela was acting up,' she started. 'That was a woman's shorthand for saying that any man capable of standing on his two legs was fair game to her. She even had a go at Arnold until I warned her off.' She smiled at her recollection of it as though it was an immensely satisfying one. 'To be honest, she was a nice enough girl when she hadn't designs on taking a man's trousers off, although she seemed like that most of the time. A poor dead girl now, of course, but she was what I'd call pin-brained. I rather believe that she needed to prove herself over something with anything approaching a presentable man. She came here with that arrogant Leslie Gough, took a deep breath when she met Michael Whitaker and promptly had him. I know she did because I saw him going into her bedroom one night not too long after they'd arrived.'

'And Gough wasn't objecting?' Rogers was remembering that he had mouthed something like *I'll kill the bastard!* when told of her death.

'Of course he was,' she said, her oversized breasts heaving with what could be an inner amusement. 'For a time, anyway. There were dirty looks between him and Whitaker and I heard him and Angela going at it in the lounge like a couple of squabbling jackdaws. Not that it seemed to do any good. She still stayed latched on to Whitaker. And God knows why. If ever I saw a weedy nobody, he was it. I wouldn't have thought he'd had it in him, but he seemed to. And he was oblivious of anybody but her. Whether she was playing him off against

Gough, I don't know. She could have been, but somehow I don't think so. I know they're supposed to have done a flit together only I don't believe they did. And I imagine you don't either.'

She was asking him with her questioning brown eyes and, eating, he lifted his eyebrows. She wouldn't be able to make anything out of that.

'Naturally, you wouldn't,' she said. 'You don't look like a fool. Also, I'm not so sure that he killed her. Are you?' She paused, waiting for his comment.

Despite her amiability, there was a sharpness behind the handsome and ample flesh that warned Rogers that she could chop him down should he say the wrong thing. 'Why do you think not?' he asked her.

'Because he was too wet. If anything upset him he'd be the sort to blub.' She took a king-size cigarette from a scent-box in the handbag by her side and lit it with a tiny gas lighter from the same place of concealment. 'Don't mention this to Arnold,' she said, having sucked in its smoke with an expression bordering on euphoria. 'He's one of those no-smoking fanatics and he'd tear my arms off.'

'I promise not to if you'll tell me more about Angela.' Getting involved in question and answer wasn't helping with his breakfast. All he wished to do was to listen. 'What she did, with whom and where.'

'You're worse than my father was,' she chided him; he thought, almost approvingly. 'He had a deaf ear too when it suited him. Well . . . most of the time she and Whitaker were with the others; going down to do some of that childish shooting business, sunbathing, eating out in the evening and things like that. We didn't go with them after I'd had my little say at her about making cow eyes at Arnold.' Her florid red mouth smiled again as if at some hidden thought. 'I also had a few words with her about her sunbathing. Topless on a beach is one thing, but quite another up here. Especially when it wasn't only on the lawn, but around the house too. She didn't like that either, but she covered up afterwards. Not that it . . .'

Damn! He had to ask and he interrupted her. 'What did she wear when she wasn't exposing her bosoms?' Remembering them on the shattered body and knowing that, in life, they would have justified being exposed, he suspected that Eva Tolliver could have been a mite envious of them and, accordingly, over-cautious of the straying of her body-building Arnold. 'Could it have been a sundress?'

'When it wasn't a bikini, yes, it was.'

'A blue one with shoulder straps?'

'Once or twice, yes.' She looked puzzled. 'Is that important?'

'Not really. It's just that she was wearing it when she was shot. You've seen her on her own with Whitaker?'

'I think they must have been a bit sneaky about it. If she ever went off alone with him, or with any of them if it comes to that, it must have been when we were out.'

'The beach?' Looking at her, he was finding room in his thinking to wonder why so many big women had such tiny hands and feet. And, from there, in a momentary and involuntary response to the implanted compulsion of his genes to get on with the procreating of his species, to consider what it would be like to be in bed and subject to the brawny passions of this large and solid woman. It gave him an immediate sense of guilt for his body's intrusion into his thoughts.

'I never saw her go down there,' she said, happily oblivious of what he had been thinking. 'One or two of the others, but not her. Arnold liked to go out in the afternoons, so when and if they went down I wouldn't know. We never did . . . no, just a moment, I'd forgotten and I shouldn't have. I did see her down there once. We'd been out and came back early because Arnold had a belly-ache and said he'd like to lie down for a while. I went out to sit in a deckchair and saw Angela way off and sitting at the top of the steps that go down to the beach. I don't know why – perhaps because I'm inquisitive, for I wasn't all that anxious to speak to her – but I went down to her. It did seem an odd place to just sit and do nothing. And she was facing more to the house than the sea. When she saw me coming, and I was still some distance away, she stood up and sort of waved down to the beach.' She flapped her hand to describe it and Rogers felt that it could have had in it a warning. 'When I got there, I saw that it was only Luther Player and Cathy Horn sitting in the boat. It was her waving to them that puzzled me.'

'What exactly were they doing? They wouldn't be just sitting, would they?' He pushed his empty plate away from him and began stuffing tobacco in his meerschaum. He felt beautifully replete and almost at peace with the world. If his head was aching, it was not enough to provoke him into irritation, and the benzedrine was still keeping fatigue from his brain. He thought that he might be able to last out the day.

'No, they weren't.' She wrinkled her forehead as she thought. 'He was kind of turning the boat with an oar and I think she had hold of a rope that went into the water. Like as if they were anchored there. I'm almost sure I saw a fishing rod propped over the end because I thought at the time that if it was and nobody was holding it, a big fish could pull it overboard.'

'How far out were they?'

'That's difficult.' Her forehead wrinkled again. 'Not too far. I'd say about forty to fifty yards.'

'How were they dressed?'

'In swimming costumes, although they didn't look as if they'd been in.'

'And you considered it all very odd?'

'Not at the time, only later when I thought about it. And then not anything important.'

'And Angela somehow got rid of you?' He was guessing.

She thought about that, too, pushing out her bottom lip. 'Now that you mention it, yes, she did. She said that she supposed she'd better be getting back to the house, obviously with me. When we'd gone a short way, she said that she'd forgotten to tell Cathy something and went back.' The cigarette end she dropped sizzling into the dregs in her coffee cup was smeared red with lipstick, the only thing Rogers could disapprove about her, although in his younger days he had been weak enough to acquire a taste for it. She immediately lit another and said, 'You think that's important, too?'

'It could be.' He considered for his own information that it was. 'What about Gough? Did he spend his time glowering?'

'Not really – surprising, that. Of course, he wasn't liking Whitaker so very much, but neither was he acting as if he wanted to beat him up. At least, not so you'd notice. After I heard him and Angela ragging each other, he seemed not to care a damn. They were on civilized speaking terms, even if a bit chilly, but that doesn't mean anything, does it?' She stared at him hard with wide-opened eyes that were apparently accustomed to forcing admissions from a reluctant husband. 'Particularly as he did a bunk at the first sight of you.'

She had, Rogers accepted, a very garrulous source of information in the house. 'He could have gone home for some spare shirts,' he equivocated, creasing his eyes at her. 'Can you give me anything useful about Player?'

She sighed and looked with mock resignation at the puff clouds of her cigarette smoke drifting to the ceiling, but unruffled at being put off. 'Not about his shirts, I can't,' she said sarcastically. 'He brought Cathy Horn with him and they're floppy about each other. She, I believe, is in the middle of divorcing her husband. She certainly spends more time in Luther's bedroom than she does in her own. And I should know, her room's opposite ours. He's a really nice man and kind with it. He looks and sometimes acts a toughie, but he isn't. Arnold could eat him for starters if he had a reason to. I shouldn't think you'd be interested in him. He wouldn't have given Angela a second thought and he'd have to, wouldn't he, to want to shoot her?'

He grinned at her. 'You're trying to get yourself attached to my department, I see. So who's your particular suspect?'

She shrugged her plump shoulders and smiled back at him. 'You probably know as well as I do that there's only one man who's got any reason to do it. And I think he could be nasty enough to do it. He's a clever cock, somebody with something to hide and I'd imagine a cold-blooded bugger with any woman daft enough to fall for him. And that's my father's daughter's opinion without any evidence whatsoever, superintendent.' She wrinkled her nose at him. 'Dad wouldn't have let him run off. He'd have had him in a cell by now, even if he was proved wrong later on.'

As an informant, Rogers warmed to her. No niggling questioning for reluctant answers and, right or wrong, a woman who could chew up a character like a raw steak. 'I'm the cautious type,' he said mildly, deciding to ignore the implication. 'Lots of low cunning and all that sort of stuff. What do you know about Quennell?'

'Very little. He's a queer sort of chap and he gives me the creeps. He doesn't mix much, doesn't seem interested in being friendly with anyone. He seems to have been the only man here who Angela didn't cotton on to, perhaps because of it. When he had the opportunity, he certainly wasn't interested in her bosoms. And you've probably been told that he drinks too much. He came with Whitaker and, as soon as he got here, went round the house like a bum-bailiff sorting out the furniture. That's what he talks about when he does – boring old antiques, if that means anything to you.'

'That fits him,' Rogers said, 'although he's spared me the antiques. Have you heard a whisper of whatever's going on down in the cove that nobody wants me to know about?'

That was probably something she had not and her eyes were alight with interest. 'No, I haven't. What is?'

'I don't know. That's why I'm asking.' Only a half-lie, he told himself. 'There seems to be a fair amount of movement at night, mostly outside the house and going in that direction. You've heard it?'

'I'm as good as dead when I'm asleep,' she said, 'and I probably wouldn't.'

'If you had,' he said carefully, 'might you think it could be somebody not living in the house?'

'You mean strangers?'

'Not necessarily. And I don't mean the cleaning woman.' He made it as open an inference as he could without being obvious.

She stared at him, then said, 'You *have* got a low cunning, haven't you? No names, no pack-drill and you'd deny saying it if anybody asks. I'd be guessing about him, but I don't think so. And he's another that gives me the creeps.'

'Why?'

'The way he looks at us women. And especially at Phaedra.'

'Perhaps he thinks he has a reason to. With Mrs Haggar, I mean.' He managed a look of disinterest as if it were a perfunctory doesn't-really-matter question, although it was one to which he badly needed an answer. 'Could it be necessary for him to visit her at night?'

There was a quietness for several seconds. 'I know what you mean,' she said with a slight coolness in what had been a warm voice. 'I'm a friend of Phaedra's and I have been for several years. She's not the sort and while he does odd jobs for her, that isn't one of them.'

'You don't know how pleased I am to hear it,' he said hurriedly. 'Of course, I didn't think so for one moment.' He felt deservedly squashed, that it might be a good time to finish the interview. Pushing back his chair, he stood. 'I'm more than grateful for the breakfast,' he said, 'and for the information.' He looked at his wristwatch. 'Time's pushing me and I do have to go.'

There was no mistaking that he had boobed for the second time that morning and that he had forfeited some of her amiability towards him. He prayed fervently on the way out that she wasn't so friendly with Phaedra that she would repeat to her his badly-framed and ill-advised question.

27

There was no Lingard on Rogers's return to the study, although Sergeant Millier had a message from him transmitted to the communications car. It was brief. Gough had returned to his bed-sitter, paid what he owed after telling the landlord that his brother had died suddenly and left. He was now missing with his car and the whole of his possessions to parts unknown. Lingard had done nothing further about him as he was now about to contact Jane Foxton, sister of Angela and writer of the letter to her.

And one other thing, she told him. Player had called in expecting to see him and had said that he and Mrs Horn were going to Thurnholme Bay to do some necessary shopping, and that they would be returning shortly after lunch. As soon as she had heard the car being driven away, an apprehensive Millier had run upstairs and examined their bedrooms, finding that they had not been emptied of their contents as she had belatedly feared.

Rogers, needing a period of thinking away from the disturbing blonde sergeant, told her to continue holding the fort as efficiently as she had while he went somewhere to do it. That somewhere was no further than the driving seat of his borrowed car with, from it, the not-too-inspiring view of one of the house's stone-mullioned windows.

Having tumbled a few facts and suppositions about between the black holes in his skull, he could guess now in an uninformed way what the rope missing from the beach had been used for, what the fabric he had seen hanging inside the boathouse window must have been, what the object that Angela Foxton had posted to her sister should be and, putting it all together, what it was that had been going on in the cove. Perhaps. And if it were so, it could explain the oddness of Angela Foxton and Catherine Horn having bedrooms separate from the two men, their undisputed lovers, who had arrived with them. He was also reasonably satisfied that he knew the reason for the indentations on Angela Foxton's body, and for the post-mortem staining that suggested that it had, for a few hours at least, been in a standing position. Although he could say from a fairly firm conviction who had not murdered her, he could only, in his present ignorance of a motive, suspect without conviction who had. His thinking moved on to Phaedra, trying to rationalize his earlier suspicions – held fairly lightly, it was true – that she, apparently adept at aiming at perforated clay pigeons by sound, could have shot Angela Foxton for some unfathomable reason, and that the seemingly ubiquitous Grice, a lover and accomplice, had disposed of the body. That he was now convinced, Grice's relationship with her apart, that she had not and could not have, still left him with the feeling that he had wronged her. If he could take Eva Tolliver's defence of Phaedra as a valid one – and he was inclined to – then Grice was not, as Player had been bent on telling him, her boyfriend, lover or whatever. Not, he told himself, that he would have cared one way or another if he had been. But he thought that he should see her once more so that he could apply his unobstructed thinking to other, more plausible, suspects. And not only that. He felt that he had to make some sort of unspoken apology for his unjustified suspicion.

147

After making a radio call to Headquarters, he climbed from the car, knowing exactly how many blocks of stone it had taken to build each mullion in the window, and walked between the cypresses to the side of the house. The man standing motionless on the grass in bare feet near the unoccupied deckchairs ignored his patently audible approach on the slabs of the footpath. Naked but for a pair of red bathing trunks, he stood poised as if about to throw a discus. Unmistakably Arnold Tolliver, he was barrel-chested and unhandsome, his nose too blobby and his eyes too small, his black hair balding and his sidewhiskers too long. A little taller than the detective, he was all bulging and malformed muscle, straining tendons and swelling veins. His skin, glossy with horse-liniment-smelling oil, was tanned a deep brown. Everything about him made it obvious that he was in love with his own body; a type, the detective would bet good money, with not too much going for him on top.

Rogers, moving over to the windward side of him, said a pleasant 'Good morning.'

Tolliver had rearranged his pose on his approach with his muscles inflating and deflating as if breathing a life of their own. Without turning his head or looking at Rogers, he said 'Morning' back to him and adopted another pose. With his legs wide apart, he bent his arms at right angles above his head, squinting his concentration at the jiggling of his deltoid and biceps muscles.

The detective stared at him fascinated, concealing his amusement. 'I'm Detective Superintendent Rogers, Mr Tolliver,' he said. 'Could you give yourself a rest and talk to me?'

Not looking away from the working of his arm muscles, he grunted, 'Can't. Not now. And don't need a rest. Got to finish my work-out. Be half an hour.'

'I may not be here in half-an-hour's time,' Rogers said, reasonably genially he thought. He wondered what would happen if he scowled and prodded an official finger on to the vast hairless chest, deciding – only, he assured himself, because he had to be careful of the stitches in his scalp – not to do so and find out.

'That's so?' He couldn't have been less interested. 'No sweat. Mrs Tolliver'll tell you anything you want to know.' He put his arms behind his back, one hand holding the wrist of the other, then hissed through his teeth as grotesque knots of muscle squirmed beneath the skin of his shoulders.

Rogers gave in and turned away, accepting defeat with the thought that he might not, anyway, have obtained anything useful from a man whose conversation seemed limited to words of two syllables. Too, his feeling of muscular inferiority was mitigated by Tolliver's tight-fitting trunks which showed clearly that he was not overdeveloped in all parts. More importantly, he felt that he had narrowed still further the number of possible suspects, satisfying himself that Tolliver was unlikely at the least to have been responsible for banging him on the head in Ridge Clump and bundling him into a runaway car.

28

Emily was lying on her side outside the door of the annex, getting what was apparently a guide-dog's version of a suntan. She flapped her tail at him when he reached over her and knocked on the door. Feeling a little crumpled, he thought that in calling on an attractive woman he might also need a shave, but bore himself up by remembering that she wouldn't be seeing any of the signs of his growing dishevelment.

When Phaedra appeared in the doorway, he felt an unusually warm familiarity for her. 'God!' he told himself, thinking about his earlier irresolution, 'I must have been off my bloody head.' With her eyes shielded by the dark glasses and her bronze hair tied back in its ponytail, she wore a plain rose-pink dress that complemented her milk-coffee skin, making discernible the small pointed breasts on her slight body. She was, in addition, fragrantly scented.

'It's Rogers again, Phaedra,' he said smiling, searching her features for any displeasure she might feel at hearing it. 'Could I bother you with a few more questions?'

'Of course,' she said, with nothing in her expression to show either eagerness or reluctance at the prospect. 'Do please come in.'

She stood aside for him to enter and he stepped over Emily who immediately rose and followed. In her sittingroom, dim and cool with the venetian blinds down over the windows, she remained standing, keeping on her glasses. It indicated to Rogers that his stay would be brief and probably on the chilly side, feeling that she was distancing herself from him.

'I'm trying,' he said, 'to clear up the identity of whoever it was that you heard outside earlier this morning, eliminating those it couldn't be. Could the man you heard have been Mr Grice?'

He watched her face and if anything showed in it at all, it was a faint surprise. 'Why do you say him?'

'I understand that he considers himself something of a guardian of yours.'

'Oh?' Her chin went up. 'If he is, I don't know of it. Nor would I need or wish it. I'm quite capable of caring for myself.' She sounded on the edge of being angry although her features, striped gold with sunlight coming through a venetian blind, remained unreadable to the detective.

'I've never doubted it,' Rogers said, 'but could it have been him?'

'No, it could not,' she replied with emphasis. 'Emily doesn't like him, won't have him near her, and she wouldn't allow him to handle her. And she was definitely fondled by the man I heard.'

'Which meant that she knew him?'

'Yes. She wouldn't go to a stranger.'

'Now something a little more delicate, Phaedra,' he said carefully. 'It's been suggested to me that I've been badgering and worrying you with my questions. Have I been? Am I now?'

She stiffened, clearly offended. 'Basil told you that? How dare he! I think nothing of the sort; nor have I ever said or implied it.'

'Perhaps I misunderstood him,' he told her. To himself, he said 'Like hell I did.'

'No, I don't think so. He would do that. He's always

been . . .' She jerked her head with a rare irritation. 'May we forget him?'

'Gladly. I never believed it anyway.' Nor had he, he convinced himself. 'So one more question? You told me at one time in our conversation that you occasionally go out; that last Wednesday morning you went to Thurnholme. Could I ask who you went with?' He noticed that she had yet to call him by his name and that must bode something or other that mightn't do anything for his happiness.

'Yes, I had an early dental appointment and went with Mr Gough. I mean, he dropped Emily and me there and we came back by taxi.'

'Would he have returned here?'

'I don't know. He said that he had something to do in Abbotsburn. Is he . . . ?' She shook her head. 'No, you wouldn't tell me, would you?'

He smiled. 'No, I wouldn't. But there is something that I do have to tell you. Miss Foxton was killed in your summerhouse . . . I'm sorry about that but, perhaps, better than in this house. I hope it doesn't spoil the place for you.'

She grimaced, clasping her hands over her breasts. 'I never go there. Although I told you differently, I think I should now tell you that my husband died in it. And the wife of the previous owner is said . . . is said to have committed suicide in it. I've never liked it and wished I'd had the courage to have it taken down . . .' She faltered and bit at her lip, obviously trying to make up her mind about what she was to say. 'I expect that you'll be told after all this, if you don't know already, but it was believed that Hubert did as well, although he never left anything to say so. He had a cancer and was in pain . . . took too many of his tablets and went down there during the night. I didn't know . . . we slept in separate rooms.'

'It doesn't have to be what you think,' he said gently, reaching for her hand and holding it. 'Pain can be a dreadfully unbearable thing and there's always a temptation to take more pain-killers than you should to get rid of it. Did he have the bottle or whatever they were in with him?'

'No, it was left in his room.' She made no effort to remove her hand from his.

151

'He could have gone out for a walk to make sure that he didn't fall asleep on them. He needn't have had killing himself in mind at all. Especially an old soldier.' That didn't mean a thing, for he had dealt with a few old soldiers who at different times had blown their heads off or taken enough tablets of one sort or another to invite oblivion. 'Was there an inquest?'

She nodded. 'Yes, with an open verdict. I think that the coroner was being kind, but I always had the thought in my mind . . . I'm sorry,' she said. 'That was selfish of me. It was all seven years ago and I don't feel too sad about it any more.'

'If it's any comfort to you, I do think that your suspicions are unjustified.' He felt an immense sympathy for her; blind, bereaved and, despite what she said, probably reliving often the agony her husband's death had caused her. 'I've had similar instances,' he lied, 'and been quite satisfied that they were accidental. However, after we've finished here, and if I were you, I'd certainly have the summerhouse dismantled and sold. Unhappiness hangs around in some buildings and I felt it in that one.'

There was a warmth of feeling between them now and it provoked a frisson of unwanted eroticism in him, his below-the-waist recklessness taking over from his cautious and constabulary-disciplined mind. And with that mind making no real opposition, he thought that for a short sweet while he could disregard his commitments to the police authority, to the tax-paying public and to the dead Angela Foxton. He pulled at her hand and she came into his arms without resistance, taking off her dark glasses with the gesture of acquiescence another woman might show in removing her bra. If she felt any roughness from the stubble of his emerging whiskers when he kissed her, she gave no sign of it in the fervour with which it was returned.

It had always mystified him how two minds could move in parallel with a single unspoken intent, knowing with certainty that his own intent, although taking over at an unconventional eleven o'clock on a sunny morning, was hers too. He flattened his hands and smoothed them down her back, then pressed her body hard against his own, unmistakable in its meaning.

152

'Not in front of Emily,' she whispered against his cheek and, for one nonplussed moment, until she took his hands and moved towards the bedroom door, he thought that he had met a familiar female evasion tactic. When she opened the door and he saw in the curtain-drawn twilight the single narrow bed against the wall, his still just-surviving commitment to Angela Foxton made him hope that they could avoid any kind of a thundering passion, preferring the gentleness of an affection that would not accelerate too much the diminishment of whatever benzedrine was left in his blood.

29

Rogers had left Phaedra sleeping. Mentally he felt fine, with nothing of the aftermath of guilt at what his conscience insisted on dictating was profligacy, and with none of his usual feelings that he had tom-catted his way through the majority of the ten commandments and all sixteen offences under the *Police (Discipline) Regulations*. Not unsettlingly rhapsodical, it had been as if he had strolled with her through a garden of dreamy summer flowers. But of one therapeutic fact he was certain; it had done nothing for his retrograde amnesia.

The mass of uncommunicative muscle that had been Tolliver was gone, for which he was grateful, needing no speculations by Eva Tolliver about his hour-long absence from visible activity. Returning to the front of the house, he saw Lingard's Bentley parked in the shadow of the cedar of Lebanon. Feeling the warmth of its radiator, he decided that its owner had not been waiting for him all that long. He filled his meerschaum and lit it. He had need of it for he had considered that, unlike a cigarette, any post-coital smoking of a pipe in bed would not have been wholly appreciated.

In the study, Lingard sat sprawled in the brigadier's chair with his eyes closed. On Rogers entering he opened them, pushing himself upright. 'A misleading impression, George,' he murmured. 'I was thinking – just thinking about things.'

'The Lord loveth a cheerful liar,' Rogers said smiling. 'What have you done with Sergeant Millier?'

'She's doing necessary female things up in Mrs Tolliver's pad. I said I'd look after the shop while she did them.'

'Out of my chair, David, and tell me what you've got.' He moved on to the warmed hide of it and relaxed as if he had returned from an exceptionally fatiguing spell of activity. Which, in a sense, he supposed he had. 'You've seen the sister?'

Lingard sat in the not-so-comfortable chair opposite him. Not wearing his usual colourful waistcoat, he had changed into a hound's-tooth check suit which did much for his dandyism if nothing for the bagginess of fatigue showing under his eyes. 'I had difficulties,' he said. 'She works in a boutique in Abbots-burn.' He shook his head, a grimace on his narrow face. 'Don't do that to me too often, George. Not with nice young vulnerable women. She took Angela's death hard and I had to run her back to her home. But co-operative, although I had it all in between tears. We're a pushy lot of bastards when we need information, aren't we?' He shook his head again, charging his patrician nose with snuff and inhaling it elegantly, although without his customary relish. 'She'd mislaid Angela's letter,' he continued, 'but it was to the effect that would she hold on to the enclosed, not to show it or mention it to a living soul, which she hadn't, and that she – Angela, that is – would explain it all in due course. That started her off weeping again when she realized that there'd be no "in due course". When we got back to it, she told me that she didn't know Angela had been here until she received the letter and that she'd never heard of either Gough or Whitaker. Nor any of the others, if it comes to that, so no help there.'

'She gave you the coin?' The straight-faced Rogers chanced that his guessing would be right, then weakened and hedged. 'Or was it a medallion?'

'Bugger it!' Lingard showed his surprise. 'You don't tell me anything, do you? You knew?'

'Of course I didn't. Not then.' He tried not to look smug. 'Let me see it.'

Lingard produced a brown envelope from his pocket and took from it a blackened coin, rough with what appeared to be a coating of dark cement. Passing it over the desk to Rogers, he said, 'I've been told that the gubbage on it means that it's been underwater for donkey's years and that it's called concretion.'

'Looted from a wreck, David.' Rogers held the coin in his fingers, examining it. One side was wholly covered by the concretion. Covering half of the surface on its other side, it left exposed two truncated legs clothed in padded breeches. One leg had the figures 16 near its knee; the other, the figures 53. Below them was a part inscription, A.RES.PARVA. 'A piece of eight from a stately galleon of the Spanish Armada?' he asked, risking another guess. 'They look like Spanish legs to me.'

'If my memory's up to scratch,' Lingard said drily, 'that was in the 1580s and hardly likely. I called in at the Coin and Medal Centre on the way back to have it identified. They didn't know all that much, but their catalogue says that it's a double-ducat minted in Holland. Seventeenth-century, of course, and more than likely carried in a Dutch East Indiaman ship, several of which, I'm told, have been wrecked around our then not so hospitable shores and lie still undiscovered. It's gold and worth your month's untaxed salary at least. Bless my greedy soul, George, but just imagine finding a sackful of them.'

'They probably have for all we know.' Rogers was impressed. 'I've already sent for a team from the Underwater Search Branch so we'll know soon enough. They're all in it with the exception of the Tollivers and without Mrs Haggar knowing anything about it. No wonder they were so damned cagey about what was going on. And another thing. It worried me for a while why two couples who had undoubtedly been having it off elsewhere should be so coy as to book separate rooms. And that was obviously because, doing what they were doing, they wanted to monopolize the place as much as they could with no danger of being overlooked by other guests. As it was, the Tollivers appear to have booked earlier for the period that they themselves wanted, and them they had to put up with.' He pulled a face. 'Nothing of which, to get my priorities right, seems to tie in with Angela's killing.'

'For hanging on to the double-ducat? Likely to cause a spilling of beans?' Lingard looked doubtful. 'But that'd be a bit of overkill, wouldn't it?'

Rogers was inclined to agree with him, and said, 'I'd think it would be, although we've known it for lesser reasons, haven't we? But not, I think . . .'

He paused as the door opened and Sergeant Millier came in. Although looking freshly-scrubbed and tidied-up, she was manifestly weary, her eyes and the beautiful mouth struggling hard to show alertness. Rogers, having already made up his mind about her, said, 'Just the one I wanted to see, sergeant. Mr Lingard and I are leaving here in a few minutes. Go and find Inspector Coltart – he'll be still grubbing around somewhere in the grounds – and give him my instructions. He's to dismiss his search party and return to take over from you. None of the people here are to be allowed to leave before we return, and that includes Player and Mrs Horn once they get back. If anything calamitous occurs, we can be contacted at my home, at the Saracen's Head Inn or – make a note of it – at 37 Sandleheath Road, Westgate. You've got that?'

'Yes, sir,' she replied. Her expression had lost some of the smiling sweetness it had shown on her entry. 'You said Mr Coltart was to take over from me?'

'Yes, I did.' Women's Lib and sex discrimination be damned, he thought, seeing clearly that despite the freshening-up process she couldn't be far from falling flat on her face. 'When you've done what I've asked you to do, you'll book off duty and go home. And that, sergeant, is an order,' he said firmly when she was about to protest. 'I'm grateful for what you've done, but enough's enough.'

He wished he could have read the odd look in her eyes – it hadn't been, he thought, just resentment – as she turned and left the study. And she had been too disciplined to slam the door as most women would. He rose from his chair and stretched stiffness from his arms and legs, the soft cracking noises from the joints warning him, he fancied ruefully, that he was either tiring or entering into a premature old age.

'There's nothing more we can do here until the afternoon, David,' he said, 'and I feel as though I've been living here for weeks. I need to go home for a quick shower, a shave and then a visit to the Saracen's Head for a meal and a couple of drinks. You too, and we'll use your car. In between we'll

156

call and have a chat with a man I know from the Scubaqua Club.'

Having climbed into the Bentley, not slamming the door but closing it gently in deference to Lingard's hypermania about it, he belted himself in the passenger seat. He knew that he could sleep comfortably on its soft leather upholstery and, given half an opportunity, probably would, suspecting now that his body's metabolism was running short of benzedrine. Lingard, with his own refuelling system to worry about, charged his nose copiously with snuff before using the starting handle on the engine.

Out of the drive and exposed to the bright heat of the late morning, the Bentley's massive engine made light work of the climb towards Abbotsburn. Rogers, thinking of his dismissal of Sergeant Millier and of the help she had given him, said, as if idly, 'When was the last time you saw a woman wearing a nightdress, David?'

'God forbid that I ever should,' Lingard replied. 'Would that be rather overdressed? You've a reason for asking?'

They were passing Ridge Clump and, seeing it, Rogers realized that he had never visited it at night as he had intended and that it was too late to do so now. He said, 'When we were at the breakwater, you mentioned that Angela was wearing one and I accepted it. She wasn't, it was a sundress.'

'Bloody hell!' Lingard said wryly. 'Excusable ignorance because I don't normally wear one myself.' He was obviously taking his mind back to the finding of the body. 'No knickers and no shoes meant to my innocence that she'd been in bed. Ergo, I had to assume that bit of stuff she wore was a nightdress. Sorry, George. It put us out, didn't it?'

'Yes.' Rogers had to raise his voice against the rumble of the engine and the rush of warm wind over the two small and inadequate windscreens. 'I wasted a lot of time in thinking that she'd been shot during the night, and we both need kicking. She was shot in her sundress between ten and twelve o'clock on Wednesday. Location, the old summerhouse down near the clay-pigeon thrower. Not only. I'm almost certain that Whitaker was with her. If he was, they were making love on the bench in there.'

'Thus the absence of knickers?'

'Yes, I believe they are taken off for that,' Rogers said ironically. 'But something more. That interruption to the pattern of shot in her face. I may be running wild on this, but I think it was caused by Whitaker's shoulder being in the way.' He was certainly not intending to say that, being never wholly off-duty, this had finally occurred to him when his own shoulder had been in a similar position an hour or so earlier. 'If it was – and you've probably guessed it yourself by now – then he's dead too.'

'You were never very bloodthirsty about having him looked for.' Lingard wasn't disclosing what he himself thought. 'But being shot in the shoulder wouldn't necessarily kill him.'

'Not unless it hit the side of his neck too and took out an artery. If it didn't, he could have been finished off with the second barrel.'

'I suppose there are one or two more embarrassing situations than dying *in situ*,' Lingard said with an unusual cynicism, 'although I can't think of them at the moment. But, at least, they'd go out on a high note. So where is he? Still in the sea? Are you thinking he might be down in the wreck, if there is one?'

'It occurred to me, but if we assume they've been diving it since that's not too likely. If I'm wrong about where I think he is, he's out of our reach; either rolling about on the sea-bed or floating in the general direction of Ireland. But dead and dumped in it I'm certain he is.'

'And if you're not wrong?' Lingard felt it to be a wasted question, for he knew that his senior rarely revealed an opinion unless certain that it was unlikely to be discredited.

'You of all people should know even more than I do,' Rogers said blandly, annoyingly enigmatic. 'You only have to think about Angela, Twite, hypostasis and the inelasticity of dead skin, and then put them all together.'

He closed his eyes, signalling his wish to end a conversation that needed effort in raising his voice above the buffeting of wind and the noise of the Bentley's engine. For the moment, he was tired of explaining, weary with listening and even too lethargic to fill and light his pipe. His brain needed a sleep which he could not and must not have, and the rusty nail he imagined to be buried in his skull seemed to have been joined by a couple more . . . he didn't know that he had fallen asleep until an amused Lingard had shaken him awake on their arrival at his house. And then he said what Lingard had said earlier; that he had only been thinking about things with his eyes closed.

30

Showered and shaved, with two unwise whiskies and a tuna fish salad inside him, a second reluctantly-taken benzedrine capsule was giving Rogers's brain a febrile activity. None of it had removed the rusty nail from his skull or the weariness from his body, but it did allow him to bear both with a near equanimity.

In between servicing their failing bodies, he and Lingard had been briefed on long-sunken wrecks, the highly profitable looting to which they were subject when found, and how it was done. It had required a snatched visit to Headquarters and a reading by Rogers of unfamiliar pages in his *Archbold Criminal Pleading* relating to it, although conscious that it was unlikely to be directly relevant to Angela Foxton's killing. Having got his logistics in the right order of importance, he had brought back with him a fresh 50-gram pack of tobacco, a second pipe, swimming trunks and a large bath towel.

It was later in the afternoon than Rogers had anticipated when Lingard braked the Bentley to a halt in the shade of the cedar of Lebanon and he saw Player's white Sierra parked between the cars of Quennell and the Tollivers. The search party's van had left, having taken in it, Rogers hoped, the reluctant and potentially rebellious Sergeant Millier.

Coltart was alone in the study, chewing morosely on his wooden toothpick. He had had, he told Rogers, a minor problem with that bleeder Quennell. Before Player's return, Quennell had come from the lounge where he had been watching television. He was, in the inspector's looking-down-his-nose opinion, sloshed to the eyebrows and, if not actually staggering, unsteady on his feet. Coltart, following him out, saw him go to his car and open the driver's door. When he asked him what he was proposing to do, Quennell had said that he was going to Thurnholme for his lunch, which he'd damned well done daily since being in the house and would Coltart get out of his way as he was sick and tired of the smell of policemen hanging around the bloody place. Coltart, a respecter of orders if not of another's hunger, had taken the car keys from him – after a bit of a tussle, he said, which Rogers guessed to be an understatement – on the grounds that he was unfit to drive. He had given no further trouble and was now asleep in a chair in the lounge.

Player, Coltart continued, had called in the study an hour or so earlier, said he was back and then went upstairs with Mrs Horn, where they still were. Before his problem with Quennell, on one of his visits outside to check that none of the cars had been driven away, he had glimpsed a man skulking in the far shrubbery as if watching the house. As he had apparently ducked to cover on Coltart's appearance, he couldn't describe him any better than that he was tall, grey-haired and wore a yellow shirt.

'That was Grice from the cottage,' Rogers told him. 'He's Mrs Haggar's unwanted watchdog and a voyeur to boot. Even for that, he seems a mite too curious to know what's going on here and it might be worth while checking him against records. Before you do, I want you to see Player, tell him that I'd like words with him and ask him to oblige me by coming down now. Then I want you to wait outside for the arrival of the frogmen I've sent for. Take them down to the cove where they can kit up and wait for my instructions.'

31

With Coltart gone, Rogers took the brigadier's chair, hoping that, now he had more or less taken over his widow as well, the brigadier would, wherever he was, be understanding about it. Placing the envelope containing the double-ducat in front of him, he said to Lingard, 'Sit over there by the wall, David. I'm having a go at him, so take notes and watch him for twitches. I don't think he'll prove too difficult, but he might start off trying to be.'

When Player entered the study he was with the only woman Rogers had not yet met and who must be Catherine Horn. She was excessively slender against Player's bigness, wearing tight-fitting violet trousers and a white T-shirt that stretched tautly over her bra-less breasts. Felinely pretty rather than attractive, she gave off waves of hostility. Her stridently yellow hair was short and freakishly spiky, her eyelids painted a livid blue and her unsmiling mouth lipsticked a startling opaline white against the suntanned brown of her face.

Rogers stood as they approached his desk. This needed tact, one of his principles being to avoid where possible the inter-viewing of two or more suspects together where supportive lying was difficult to counter. 'Good afternoon,' he said amiably. 'You're Mrs Horn?'

'Yes.' That had *What of it?* in it, and she was definitely not returning his amiability.

'I was intending having words with you,' he said, readying himself for a rebuff, 'but after I'd spoken to Mr Player. Do you mind?'

The rebuff came from Player, his beard thrust forward. 'I don't know what you want me for,' he growled, 'but whatever it is she stays, or we both go.' The aggressive bright-red shirt he wore probably helped him to live up to the hard image he seemed to need.

Rogers stared at the two of them. They had obviously accepted already that he meant trouble for them and that, for him, was an advantage. If he needed it, it gave him reason for counter-aggression. 'As you wish,' he said, keeping his amiability going. 'It'll probably be more convenient. Bring up another chair and sit down.'

With both opposite him, the sunshine flooding in from the window behind the desk ready to illuminate with burning gold the truth or otherwise in their features, Rogers reseated him-self. When he spoke it was in a friendly conversational tone of voice. 'You both know,' he said, 'that I'm making enquiries in connection with the murder of Angela Foxton. I've already spoken to you about it, Mr Player, and you've said that you'd no knowledge of it. Does that still stand?'

'Yes.' He looked unconcerned. 'I said what I knew and there's nothing more.'

'Mrs Horn?' Rogers smiled, raising his eyebrows at her. 'Is there anything you know about it?'

She conceded nothing to his friendliness, her grey eyes only just short of being baleful. 'If I had, I would have told you before now.' Her voice, expropriated Roedean School-and-a-half, was sharp and incisive.

'Yes, I'm sure you would,' he agreed, not believing it for one moment and wondering if it were he whom she appeared to dislike so intensely, or the job he was doing. She was definitely the dominating female type, likely to use sharp cat's teeth on unsubmitting males; likely to finish up being strangled for doing it.

He leaned back in his chair as if relaxing in satisfaction with her answer. Speaking to Player and ignoring her, he said, 'Let me tell you something that you probably already know. During the sixteenth and seventeenth centuries in particular, large numbers of ships came to grief around our shores by storm or combat with us rather pugnacious English. Some were ours, of course, but more than a few were Spanish or Dutch and, I imagine, other nationalities as well. The locations of some of these wrecks are known, some are not. Some were broken up and covered on the sea bed, some either were not or have since been uncovered by tidal or current water movement.' He gazed at Player blandly, not showing his awareness that they had both stiffened at his first words and were now trying to look as if they had never known.

'It must be common knowledge,' he went on, 'that a tidy number of these ancient ships carried ingots and plate of precious metals and chests of gold and silver coinage. Not a few paltry handfuls but masses of them, and now all down there at the bottom of the sea waiting to be found. You might say – although I somehow don't think that you will – that finders are keepers.' He shook his head solemnly, watching the two set faces in front of him. 'They are not. Especially not where a ship has foundered offshore in territorial waters. If it isn't still owned by the country that lost it, it belongs to the Crown. And there's an official Receiver of Wrecks who assumes responsibility for it.' He paused for a moment, stared elaborately at his wristwatch as if the time mattered, then said politely, 'I take it that you're familiar with what I'm saying?'

Catherine Horn snapped, 'No, we're not!' simultaneously with Player hawking a noise in his throat, jerking his head sharply to look at her and turning back to Rogers to say, 'No. That is, I've read about it.'

'Belonging to the Scubaqua Club you would, wouldn't you?' Assuming the expression of a man suddenly remembering something, he reached for the envelope and opened it, taking out the coin and laying it on the desk. He said nothing, allowing the following silence to drag on as they both stared hypnotically at it. Player's mouth had an adenoidal gape and he seemed to have shrunk in his chair. Catherine Horn had clamped her lips tight, her antagonism towards the somebody or something clear in her face.

Rogers's amiability had given way to a dark frown and he tapped the coin with his fingernail. 'You're thieves,' he said sternly, 'whichever way you look at it. And this is part of what you've been stealing. Before I do what the law requires me to, is there anything you wish to say? You aren't obliged to, but anything you do will be taken down and may be used in evidence.'

Player's expression was that of a non-swimmer in a sinking boat suddenly realizing that he had no life-jacket. 'I thought . . .' he said, his beard wagging his agitation, 'I thought we could . . . because I found it. I was going to tell . . .'

Catherine Horn rounded on him, her face bony with sudden fury. 'Shut up, you fool!' she hissed. 'You stupid brainless bastard!'

Player's face reddened and he goggled at her, showing his big teeth. 'Don't talk to me like that,' he ground out, almost incoherently. 'Interrupting me . . . who the hell do you think you are?'

Ignoring the glowering Player, she spoke to Rogers, her words curt. 'We don't know what you're talking about and we aren't saying anything.'

Rogers rose from his chair. 'Mr Lingard,' he said brusquely. 'Take Mrs Horn out and see that she stays out.' Perversely, while he would prefer cohabiting with a female alligator rather than with her, he viewed the defiant woman with a greater respect than he had for the more pliant man. To Player, he said, 'Where are your car keys?'

Player hesitated, glanced angrily at the woman and then muttered, 'In my room – on the dressing table.'

'Get them, please,' Rogers told Lingard, 'and bring them back here.'

Lingard, standing behind the seated Catherine Horn, touched her on her shoulder. 'Madam,' he murmured, 'it's a time to go walkies, believe me.'

She stared up into his eyes, seeing something in them that decided her that it was. She stood, toppling her chair to the floor and leaving it there. 'Only because I want to,' she said contemptuously in Player's direction, then rounding on him with a final 'I haven't done anything, so don't drag me into the mess you're talking yourself into,' before stalking from the room with Lingard hurrying after her.

Resuming his seat and ready to keep Player off balance, Rogers said, 'Don't forget for one moment that my primary interest is the murder of Miss Foxton. Cold-blooded murder with one of the guns you yourself used on the day she was shot. She was one of your party and before she died she was in possession of this coin. So I want to know everything about it with no lies, no evasions. Did you give it to her? Was it her share?'

Player's shakiness showed in the twitching of his mouth. 'As God's my judge,' he said earnestly, 'I had nothing to do with Angela's death. I didn't even know about it until last night. Leslie Gough, he'll tell you.'

'If he were here, he might. Or might not.' Rogers tapped the coin again. 'This. Did you give it to her?'

Player shook his head desperately. 'No. One of the others must have. It could've been Whitaker, or Gough. I just don't know; she was thick with both of them.'

'Why not you?'

'Because I didn't.'

'But you had it originally. It and others taken from the wreck.'

Player made no reply to that, although his hag-ridden expression said it for him.

'It's accepted then,' Rogers pressed him, 'that you found a wreck in the cove and that you've all been unloading it?' He knew that a man would invariably, almost gladly, admit to a lesser offence in order to disassociate himself from a far more serious one.

'If you put it like that, yes.' Player's eyes were searching the detective's unresponsive face. 'But I've had nothing to do with Angela or with giving her that coin. One of the others must have.'

Rogers began filling his meerschaum, then lighting it, taking on an air of sympathetic reasonableness. It was his *modus operandi*, intended to suggest to an interrogated suspect that baring his conscience of his misdoings to him would be no bad thing. 'Now that we've established what you've been doing here without arguing about it,' he said between puffs of smoke, 'wouldn't it be easier for you if you told me from the beginning as if I knew nothing? That part of it is a lot less serious than you might imagine and, provided we get back whatever you stole, I shouldn't think you'd be anything but fined.'

If that, he told himself. He had been reminded in his research that until a discovered wreck had been designated of historical, archaeological or artistic importance by the Secretary of State, there was doubt as to whether taking property from it was a criminal offence. But he felt it no part of his duty to decide on that, or to explain it to a man who had obviously accepted it as theft by his concealment of it.

Before Player could speak, the door opened and Lingard came in. Behind the big man's back he held up a set of car keys in each hand and pulled a face, Rogers taking it to mean that Catherine Horn had had a set as well. It was something he should have considered, and hadn't. He returned his regard to Player. 'You were about to say?'

'Have I your word on it?' Player had taken on a less unhappy expression.

'No, you haven't.' Rogers was feeling slightly irritated at his oversight about the keys. 'I don't know the full facts yet. Most of them,' he exaggerated, 'but not all. It's an opinion on a matter of secondary importance to me, if not to you.'

Player shrugged. He was now a heavily whiskered mildness, not so easy to regard as a primitive. 'Fair enough, that'll do for me. What do you want to know?'

'How you found the wreck, what you've taken from it, who did what – that sort of thing.' Rogers was putting down a smokescreen of sorts to conceal the information he wanted of a different kind.

'There isn't much to tell,' Player said, doing his own minimizing. 'I found what you call the wreck when I was here last year. I was diving with a friend of mine who doesn't know anything about this. He was interested in marine biology and I was only in it for the diving and to be his buddy when he went into deep water. There wasn't very much when I saw it, and there still isn't. A bit of ship's timber sticking out of the sand, that's all, but it did suggest that the hull would be buried beneath it. I would have said something about it if I hadn't found a couple of antique coins near it. I put them up the sleeve of my wetsuit so I could check them in good light and then decide what I should do. They turned out to be Dutch silver ducatoons and probably worth a lot of money.'

'Probably? You haven't found out yet?' Rogers asked.

'No. I've still got them. I couldn't chance selling them, not after I'd decided to return this year and make a real search. It wasn't possible until now, anyway, because I had to get the equipment and find somebody I could trust to help me. Then, with the winter coming on, it would have been impossible. I knew Seb Quennell at the club and knew he'd be game. He persuaded me that his friend Whitaker would be useful because he was a chap with some scientific know-how.' He scowled, producing more deep creases. 'I wouldn't have had the sod if I'd known the trouble he was going to cause.'

'What about Gough? I've checked on the membership list and he isn't on it. Does he dive?'

'No.' Player hesitated. 'He's my brother-in-law,' he said, not as if that gave him any pleasure. 'He is, or was. I don't know. My sister chucked him out years ago.'

166

'But you obviously didn't. If he doesn't dive, what's his part in all this?'

'He's got contacts. He was going to put the stuff on the market later on, but while he was here he was doing the maintenance – getting the air bottles filled, things like that.'

'What was his attitude towards Whitaker when his girlfriend was taken over?'

'He went off his rocker, of course. I had to push him into letting it be. There was too much to lose for him to quarrel over who had Angela. Seb Quennell did tell me there'd been a bit of a punch-up with Whitaker, but it all cooled down after that.'

Rogers had the distinct impression that there was little affection between Player and Gough. 'Did you know that he was going to leave here last night?' he asked.

'No, I didn't. I think he got cold feet with you lot digging into things. And I don't blame him,' he added bitterly.

'And you also?' Rogers allowed himself a sarcasm. 'Getting rid of your diving gear from the boathouse? Where is it?'

'I buried it in the shingle at the end of the beach.' There was irritation in his voice about that. 'I had to, didn't I, with the police here?'

'Is that what you were about to do last night when you saw Mrs Haggar outside with her dog?'

'She told you, did she?'

'Only that it was a man, and I guessed it was you. Did you also bury the underwater pump engine and the location line?' Rogers had cursed his earlier blockheadedness when the purpose of those had been explained to him.

Player nodded. 'I can get them back now, I suppose. I have to because the engine's only hired.'

'So, mentioning that, what have you taken from the wreck?' Rogers suspected that Player could be approaching the time when he would be regretting his damaging garrulity and begin to hedge and conceal more than he had done so already. 'We shall be searching your home, so tell me straight.'

The sun, shining directly on to Player, made sharp the creases and crevices in his face, gave his hair and beard the appearance of untidy hay and washed the colour from his deeply-sunken eyes. He was gnawing on his lip and, for a moment, Rogers thought that he was going to see him weep. Something was hurting him and it had to be greed. 'Some of those,' he said reluctantly, nodding at the gold coin on the desk. 'Quite a lot of ducatoons and some Spanish reals. There're some gold buttons and bits of ivory – knife handles, I think. Won't I get *anything*?' he burst out. 'I should get a reward for finding it. I mean, I've still got it all, I haven't sold any of it and I could hand everything over voluntarily, couldn't I?'

'It's too late for you to pretend honesty now,' Rogers said shortly, 'so forget that. You've been taking it home as you've found it?'

'Yes, but you don't have to make a search. I've kept it all in a plastic dustbin in the garage.'

'Good.' It had been the reason for sending Lingard for the car keys, having classified Catherine Horn as the most likely of the two to collect it and disappear. Even in that, he had so nearly failed and that must be because he now had more spaces in his skull than he was entitled to. Back to basics, he told himself, before they increased. He asked, 'Were Mrs Horn and Miss Foxton doing any diving?'

'Not diving, no.'

'Only keeping watch and helping you to fish with a broken rod while somebody was diving? Is that it?' When Player kept silent, he said, 'More importantly, what about yourself?'

'I haven't dived recently. I've an infection in my ear-drum.' He pushed a thick finger and thumb into his ear and pulled out a small wad of brownish cotton wool, holding it up for the detective to see.

'And that stops you?' It didn't seem much to Rogers.

'Yes. It could worsen to something more serious if you don't.' He pushed the wad back as if it were giving him excruciating pain.

Rogers was not wholly satisfied. 'You say not recently. When was the last time in the cove?'

He looked unhappy about that, scratching the side of his face as if thinking it out, then said, 'The first two or three days. It began to hurt and I decided then that I'd leave it to Quennell and Whitaker.'

'All right. I'll accept that, but don't go thinking that it lets

168

you off the hook.' Rogers pushed himself from his chair, his elbow joints cracking as he did so. He thought his body must now be running out of synovial fluids. It was also one of those fed-up moments, growing increasingly more frequent, when it felt as though he had spent most of his life looking at talking faces with words booming into his ears like falling rocks. 'I may need to use your boat,' he said, as if the matter had already been decided. 'I don't imagine you can have any objection?'

When Player shook his head, he spoke to Lingard. 'Go with Mr Player to his house, David, and collect what there is to collect. Then return here with him and it. You will not,' he emphasized, 'take Mrs Horn with you. She is to stay here.'

What else Rogers needed to know about the stealing from the wreck he could leave to Lingard. He thought that he had enough information to confirm the identity of the murderer, although proving it would depend on a final verification of his theory. And that was necessary, for he had no wish to be remembered as a detective with rusty handcuffs. Then, thinking of the necessary interview with Catherine Horn, he smiled to himself. Somehow, he was going to sick her off on to the anti-feminist Coltart. It should be a quite interesting encounter.

32

Rogers, wearing his swimming trunks, the wetsuit jacket brought for him by the underwater team and cumbersome rubber flippers on his feet against the harshness of shingle, sat on the pontoon of Player's *Sea Nymphet* at the sea's edge. Unless he chose to sit on the rock floor of a baking boathouse, there was no other shade in the cove and he sweated in the strong smell of seaweed and hot rubber. An oily swell moved on the water and a mountainous formation of grey-bellied cumuli that threatened rain marched towards the coast from the horizon.

With Rogers, and caring for the diving hardwear in the inflatable, was PC Potter. A bony lanky man, he had, apart from restlessly cracking finger joints, scratching at the blond fuzz on his legs and whistling tunelessly through his teeth, whatever attributes it needed to go grubbing with bare hands in the mud and ooze of canals and harbours for often foetid and noisome flesh and to be able to eat afterwards. Rogers couldn't think of anywhere he could justifiably send him, so, thanking God that he wasn't in his department, overrode his irritation by watching the other two members of the team at work.

Below the cliff face of the crescent headland that curved away from the boathouse end of the beach, a navy-blue inflatable dinghy with POLICE in yellow letters on its pontoons and a silent outboard engine in its tail bobbed in the swell. The boat handler, accoutred in wetsuit, life-jacket and air cylinder, held a blue nylon line that moved about in the water. Occasionally, he changed the position of the dinghy, working along the cliff by using its oars. Less occasionally, the glistening goggled head of team-leader Sergeant Lauder appeared, speaking briefly to the handler and submerging again.

With his meerschaum clenched between his teeth and feeling on the pessimistic side of anticipation, Rogers intended to dive, needing to see for himself the vindication or otherwise of a theory that could well prove to be the deadest of ducks. He had done his aqualung diving in the Mediterranean; a short enough time ago to claim that he could do it, a long enough time since to have doubts that he still could without drowning himself. Or that he was in fettle enough, anyway. He waited patiently. He had sent Coltart back to the house to ensure that nobody left, to keep them away from the cove with an authority short of violence. Coltart was also to interview Catherine Horn whom Rogers had, expressionlessly and with tongue in cheek, described as a shy and introverted female to be handled with a generous amount of understanding. A higher rank, he had reminded himself, had surely to have occasional advantages.

Giving room to some sombre thinking about his so-called retrograde amnesia and the fragmentary recalls of memory that bothered him, he had to admit to an apprehension of looming trouble. Nothing of the obvious recognition of himself at the breakwater by the arrogant, positively disdainful woman for whom he could never in a million years have any liking, the

angry face of the unknown man, a woman's voice saying . . .
and I think you should go, and the late hour at which he was
returning from Thurnholme, gave him any comfort. His apparent involvement with these people was so much against the
grain of his normal cautiousness with women, certainly with a
married woman (as the circumstances he had remembered
suggested she must be), that it wasn't a Detective Superintendent Rogers's thing at all. So perhaps it was the product of
his imagination filling in empty spaces, a damaged brain's
concoction of unconnected incidents and meaning nothing.
That was it, and he felt a surge of relief. He need not fret himself
into a lather over fantasies, although that late hour did need an
explanation . . .

His brooding was cut short by the surfacing of Sergeant
Lauder, his pulling away his mouthpiece and saying something
to the handler, then looking towards the beach with an arm held
upwards in a gesture of things having been achieved.

Putting on his life-jacket and strapping a lead-weighted belt
around his waist, Rogers stood while Potter, whistling his
tuneless dirge into an irritated ear, buckled the yellow air
cylinder on to his back and pressed things to ensure its proper
functioning. Rogers neither liked nor wholeheartedly trusted
cylinders with their two-and-a-half thousand pounds per square
inch of compressed air inside. Not after having once been
warned that a total failure of the air demand regulator could
result in either no air at all, or in his quite warmly-loved lungs
being blown up to the vastness of a barrage balloon.

Seated in the inflatable with Potter pulling at the oars away
from the beach, he tried to exude a professional competence as
he checked the proper working of his mouthpiece by sucking in
its thin dry air and testing the watertight fitting of the face mask
and nose pocket, grateful that its securing strap came by design
above the painful lump on the back of his head.

The police dinghy sat about thirty feet out from the base of
the cliff, the jagged tips of exposed rocks cautioning against a
closer approach. Even so, the cliff appeared to be leaning over
them as they pulled athwart the boat, the swell less than gentle
in its shadow. Sergeant Lauder, waiting in the water and
holding on to the side of the dinghy, said, 'It's not too deep, sir,

but be careful with the water surge. And you'd better have my safety line.'

Rogers, busy washing out his face mask with sea water and putting it on, nodded, having no intention of being anything but careful. Tying the line to the back of his belt – suspecting that the sergeant's concern was almost certainly motivated by the fact that losing a detective superintendent would be regarded as being just short of a capital offence – he clamped his teeth and lips around the rubber-tasting mouthpiece, regulated his breathing to what he thought was normal but probably wasn't, and let himself fall backwards from the warm safety of the *Sea Nymphet*, his fingers firmly crossed.

For a few long seconds he was all instability in a boiling of noisy silver bubbles, flailing awkward arms and legs with a brief moment of animal panic at his loss of vision, then finding himself sinking head-first into a dimmer world of bluish-green. Forcing air into his life-jacket to balance his excess weight, he managed to adjust his lack of buoyancy and to untwist the line snagged around his leg. Lauder was already at his side, his face mask and mouthpiece hiding whatever undisciplined laughter Rogers's floundering descent had provided. Holding up a thumb and getting his nodded assurance that he might be under control, the sergeant turned and, with his arms held along his sides, finned away from him.

Rogers followed, astern and slightly above, feeling only the light drag of his safety line in his gliding through what felt like fluid air. Midway between the iridescent blue underskin of his liquid sky and the greenish muddy sand and shingle of the sea bed he was weightless, feeling euphoric at moving so effortlessly, his escaping bubbles of exhaled air the only sounds in a silent world. He was now a cyclops-eyed, pink-fleshed seal carrying secondary lungs on his back, his only possible discontent being that he couldn't smoke his pipe.

Although visibility was limited by a thin mist of suspended sediment, he could already see the rocks ahead of him, appearing as a settlement of squat, church steeples and roofs carbuncled with limpets and furry with a moss-like seaweed. Between and around them were growths of long-stemmed kelp, their fronds moving snakelike in a water surge that was now pronounced. A shoal of small fish showed flashes of silver as they scattered at their coming.

As he followed Lauder between the dark slabs of rock, the light diminishing to a shadowed crème de menthe gloom as the verticality of cliff rose above them, the sergeant held up a cautionary hand to him and unhitched a handlamp from his belt. The cave into which he shone the beam of light was triangular in shape with its upper point dwindling to an above the surface fissure, its floor rising in a gradual slope.

With the water surge nudging him forward and then back, Rogers was never more thankful for the safety line and, suppressing his claustrophobic reluctance, entered the cave's darkness with his nose as close as he dared to Lauder's flippers. It was not, he discovered, too deep, for it ended after three or four yards in a narrow crevice. In the crevice, lit by the handlamp's beam and sharply defined, were a pair of denim-trousered legs appearing to be standing bodiless and ankle-deep in sand. By them, partly buried, was a woman's white shoe. Then the beam moved up to show the gleaming black of a plastic sack covering the head and upper part of the body.

Rogers tapped Lauder's arm, signalling his wish with a raised hand. The sergeant swam forward and grasped the top of the sack, trying unsuccessfully to pull it off. Then, using his diver's knife, he slit the plastic and opened it out, pushing it aside to reveal the rest of the dead Whitaker.

Wedged tightly in a standing position with his arms imprisoned between the jaws of rock, his head was bowed as if he were waiting in the darkness in deep thought, the hair stirring in the water's movement. His eyes had gone, the left side of his throat gashed superficially to furrowed pink flesh, and his flesh bloated to a fish-belly white. The gun-fighter's moustache framed a mouth that seemed opened in a cry of anguish. The fabric of his white shirt, blotched with blood that was now the colour of weak coffee, showed squirming movements beneath it not caused by water currents. Rogers couldn't think that he looked a man – as Lingard had said so flippantly – who had died *in situ* on a high note of happiness.

Moving closer to the body, and with Lauder helping him, Rogers grasped a shoulder – even touching dead flesh through the material of a wet shirt was repugnant to him – and dislodged it, allowing it to sink slowly face downwards to create small clouds of sand where it settled. The saucer-sized hole now visible between the shoulder blades revealed splintered white vertebrae. As it had clearly penetrated where the heart would be, Rogers was prepared to accept, in the absence of Twite's pathological techniques, that Whitaker had died instantaneously with his receiving the ball of shot.

There was nothing else he could do, or wanted to do, in the blackness of this watery lovers' grave from which Angela Foxton had somehow been displaced. It would be Sergeant Lauder and his team's dismal lot to finish the exhumation of Whitaker's body and to return it to the bright light in which its owner had died. As he turned to follow his safety line back to the surface, he knew that what he had seen, whatever Twite might subsequently find in his mortuary examination of the body, was unlikely to tell him who had been shot first; Whitaker or Angela Foxton. And, should there arise a problem about motivation, knowing that could be important.

33

When a dried and re-suited Rogers climbed the steps from the beach, front-running clouds had already darkened the sun, the horizon hidden behind grey veils of falling rain. His footfalls on the rock sounded loud in the brooding hush that preceded a storm. Unarduous as his swimming had seemed, it had drained vitality from his body. It was tiring badly and he was pessimistic of getting it into a higher gear, unsure whether because of a thinning out of the benzedrine in his blood, or of Phaedra's earlier demands on it. Neither of which, however, appeared to affect his mental alertness for, lifting himself achingly over the top step, he glimpsed movement in the bushes at the approach to the headland opposite him. Undoubtedly, he guessed without too much interest, the understandably inquisitive Grice.

Nearing the house, he saw a scowling Coltart skirting the

parked cars and hurrying towards him. 'Did you see Quennell?' he bellowed as if Rogers were a mile away. 'He's slipped me. Mrs Tolliver said she saw him heading for the cove about fifteen minutes ago.'

'Leave him to me.' Rogers had halted, already moving to return, his guess about Grice discarded. 'You stay near the house in case he cuts back behind me. If he does, arrest him. Hold him for whatever reason you can first think of.'

He managed to retrace his steps over the grass at a brisk, if laborious stride, entering the shrubbery the seaward side of the summerhouse. Separated from him by bushes, Quennell was standing openly near the cliff's edge, watching Sergeant Lauder and his team unloading Whitaker's body from the dinghy.

With his squatness emphasized in silhouette against the sombre sky and sea, he turned his head towards the detective on his approach, seeing in his expression a something that moved him to the edge itself. There was desperation and indecision in his face and he breathed as if he had been running. He stared down into the gulf below his feet, made tentative movements with his arms and then stepped back. 'That's enough!' he called out. 'Stay there or I will!'

Rogers halted, still yards away from him. He said nothing, but watched.

'You know.' It wasn't a question, but said as a statement from a shaking mouth.

Rogers, standing too close to a crumbling edge of the cliff for his peace of mind, was, even without the bushes intervening, a good four-second fast sprint from Quennell should he be able to goad his tired leg muscles into running it. 'I don't know anything,' he replied, making his voice sound as though he hadn't understood anything Quennell had said. 'I want to have a talk about things. About your diving for sunken treasure . . .'

'Liar,' Quennell said, shutting him off, although without heat. 'I saw him brought out.'

'And you're intending to jump because of it?' He had to raise his voice to be heard and he cursed. Even Lauder at the far end of the beach had looked up at them, although he need not have understood his words.

'Don't try to stop me.' That had been almost inaudible.

'I can't hear what you're saying,' Rogers called back. 'Can I come nearer? I promise – not too near.'

'I don't care what you do . . . you won't stop me.' Quennell scrambled himself to the ground in a sitting position, shuffling forward until his legs hung dangling over the edge. Rogers, holding back an impulse to make his run, thought that he was going. Instead, he slid down waist-high to rest the heels of his sandals on a narrow ledge, holding himself supported with his forearms on the grass behind him. It wasn't a secure lodgement, but a perch precarious enough for any incautious move to topple him down the sheer slab of the cliff.

Skirting the bushes, Rogers halted a good twelve paces short of him, seeing as he did so his mouth open in silent terror, his head jerking to look below him. 'All right!' he said sharply, 'I won't come any closer.'

He thought about similar situations dealt with successfully or unsuccessfully by other men; of would-be-suicides standing on the ledges of high-rise buildings, on the parapets of lofty bridges, and being urged not to do it. What in the hell was the attitude he should use? He was no psychologist and had no wish to ape one. George Rogers, private citizen, could see no over-whelming reason why he should interfere with Quennell's wish for a self-inflicted and retributive death. As a detective superin-tendent, however, he had to think and act differently, to find and hit the right mental button to counter the man's intent. For the moment, he needed to get him talking. 'Get this straight, Quennell,' he said flatly. 'I've no intention of stopping you. I don't know why you'd think I'd want to. Why should I give a damn? All I want . . .'

He stopped, glimpsing movement at the periphery of his vision. Coltart had seen them and was charging across the grass like a runaway lorry. Without taking his eyes from Quennell, Rogers waved him back, shaking his head in negation. The uncomplicated, no-nonsense inspector was the last man he needed to help him deal with this situation. That done, he took out his wallet of tobacco and his meerschaum, making his movements slow and deliberate, filling his pipe and lighting it while keeping his gaze steady on Quennell. Since he had last seen him, he had shaved the stubble from his jowls and changed from his soiled linen suit into khaki trousers and an olive-green shirt, the shape of his liquor flask bulging out its breast pocket. His moist brown eyes, darker now, were still bloodshot, the flesh of his face fungus-coloured. Even at a distance preventing him from smelling it, Rogers could tell that he had topped himself up with his vodka. Which, he considered, wasn't a bad idea were one intending jumping from a high cliff.

'The fact that you seem so set on it,' he said, changing the tone of his voice to that of an understanding observer, 'is something to your credit. It shows that you've a conscience, somewhere inside you. But before you do it, now might be a good time to unload some of your agonizing on to me. I know you killed both of them and, naturally, you'd have had a reason, some sort of justification. And that's what I'm not sure about.' It wasn't anything Rogers believed, but he had to push him into talking. Men about to die were supposed to feel a compulsion to say something.

Quennell stared at him. 'I don't like you, Rogers,' he said without emotion, 'and I don't give a bugger what you're sure about, or what you're not.' He released an arm from its supporting him, gingerly withdrew the flask from his shirt pocket, then unscrewed its cap with his teeth and spat it out to drop to the rocks beneath. He drank gulping with his eyes rolling at the detective, tossing the emptied flask to curve out and fall away from him. The sound of its impact on the rocks was faint and slow seconds in reaching their ears.

'I don't think much of you either,' Rogers said equably, 'but I'd still like you to tell me what caused it all.' He looked down past his own shoulder at the frightening drop, showing deliberately a grimace and a shudder of not wholly put-on squeamishness. The lesser thing first, he decided. The large dose of vodka Quennell had put back so greedily should loosen any restraint on the need of a man to confess. 'A couple of nights ago we had a man banged on the head in the wood behind the house, put into his car and sent off down the hill. He could have been killed, but fortunately wasn't. Why did you do that?'

'You should know,' he said after a few moments thinking about it. 'You were up there long enough to find out.'

'So I was. You were digging and he disturbed you. How did he know you were there?' He made it sound a matter of no importance to him.

'I don't know. I heard his car pull in . . . I suppose he needed a piss. He must have heard me because he started moving towards me. I had to hit the nosy sod . . . get him away from where I'd been digging.'

'That nosy sod could have been killed,' Rogers pointed out; mildly, he thought, considering.

'I didn't think about that . . . he wasn't, anyway. If you see him, tell him I'm sorry . . . there wasn't anything personal about it.'

'I'm sure he'll understand.' He couldn't quite keep the sarcasm out of his words. 'It changed your mind about burying them in the wood?'

Quennell said nothing to that, shaking his head. His jaws were working as if gnawing on food, his vision directed sideways and away from the depths beneath his feet.

The clouds were fully over them now, the light a steely grey. The sea gleamed a burnished pewter, the soft wind coming from it cool and smelling of rain. Rogers wondered whether a resolve to die would be stronger in the present dullness than in the vanished sunshine. He could take Quennell's change of mind, his refusal to commit himself completely and his shrinking from looking down the cliff face as a growing irresolution, a weakening of any determination he might have had to throw himself from it. Cautious of misreading his mood, he was beginning to wish that he had a psychologist with him, having no desire to take to bed with him the guilt that he had precipitated a man's death.

He decided. 'I've already told you that I don't give a damn what you do,' he said coldly. 'Your death will clear my file, which is what I'm most concerned about. I shall tell the coroner at the inquest on your death that you shot two innocent people for no good reason; two people who'd done nothing to deserve it. I shall say that I was of the opinion that it was done by a brutal and callous homicidal maniac, gutless and without the decency to admit it.' He turned to go. 'What's more,' he growled, 'I'm not staying here to see you do it.'

He hadn't taken four unmeaning steps away before Quennell spoke. 'No!' he called out harshly and, as Rogers stopped in mid-stride, said, 'You've got it all wrong.'

There had been appeal in his bloodshot eyes, but Rogers kept his coldness unchanged. 'So tell me where I'm wrong. Tell me why you shot them.' He strode slowly back, nearer to Quennell than he had been before, although still not near enough for the grabbing dash he might reluctantly have to make. Reluctantly, because he was too aware of the danger to himself in doing it.

Quennell had glanced down between his feet again and Rogers imagined that he could read the inner terror of seeing the plunging void in the face he quickly turned away from it. 'If I'm telling you,' he said in a halting voice, low and barely heard, as though his mouth was full of tongue, 'it isn't because *you* want me to. It's because my parents . . . they shouldn't suffer that . . . not what you said.' His hatred of the detective showed in his eyes.

'They won't if it's not true, and you can convince me that it isn't. Why *did* you kill them?'

Quennell was not meeting his gaze, but looking down at the grass by his side. 'I loved him,' he said softly. 'I thought he loved me . . . he told me he did. I'm sure he did until she threw herself at him.' His voice became a sibilant whisper, his face angry. '*The bitch! The bloody bitch!*' He swallowed, his anger going as quickly as it had come. 'When we quarrelled about her, he called me an interfering old poofter. Now you know . . . that's all I was to him – an old poofter. It hurt me . . . I couldn't trust anyone ever again. But that was all . . . I swear it. I wasn't wanting to do anything more than leave them alone. Filth . . . that's all it was . . . I'd never thought Michael had that in him . . .' He wagged his head in anguish, lapsing into silence.

Rogers was convinced that Quennell was feeling sorry for himself, and, despite his dislike of him, was using him as a surrogate priest to explain away his sins. He said, 'But you did shoot them.'

Quennell's face twisted as he eased the weight on his elbows. 'I didn't mean to . . . that's God's truth. I'd had a few drinks . . . took the gun to bang at some clays . . . hadn't been there a few minutes when I saw them go into the bushes up near the

179

house. I knew where they were going . . . I couldn't stay there, thinking about what they were doing.' His eyes brimmed with tears that ran unchecked down the sides of his nose. 'I had to see to make sure . . . I don't know why . . . I just had to.' He took a shuddering breath. 'The door was open . . . I could hear them and it was horrible . . . hurtful. He was bumping her and she was whispering vile and dirty things to him. I must have lost my mind . . . she saw me standing there, so I had to then . . .'

He was silent again and Rogers waited. Large drops of rain were falling, plopping cold on his head and darkening the shoulders of his jacket. If Quennell was aware of it, he showed nothing. It would be an unnoticed triviality in the misery he must feel and he needed no prompting to continue. 'I don't really remember that part . . . the blood . . . Michael's poor face . . . I hadn't ever thought it would be like that. And seeing him dead there . . . the enormity of it. I prayed for him on my knees . . .'

Rogers noticed that he hadn't expressed any regrets about killing the woman. 'Who were you intending to shoot?' he asked. 'Miss Foxton, Whitaker, or both?' It wouldn't matter that much now and the private citizen in Rogers was preparing not to get too hysterical if the murderous Quennell did make his jump. If he did, he thought it would meet with Angela Foxton's approval.

Quennell shook his head, his jowls wobbling. 'I can't remember. I don't think either . . . it seemed as if somebody else had done it. I don't remember anything afterwards . . . not until I was back firing off at more clays . . . not even that very well.'

'When did you move the bodies?' Rogers believed him to be approaching the point where it would all be whining self-exculpation. And that was something for a credulous jury to hear. If he ever got him before one.

'I hid them in the bushes before I took the gun back. I had to wait then . . . Luther went down to do some shooting, so it was in the afternoon. I took some of my shirts . . . cleaned up what I could . . .' He groaned at the recollection of it. 'Christ! Don't you imagine I've suffered enough already . . . thinking that somebody would find them . . . that somebody could have seen me . . . ?' He trailed of, closing his lips together as though suddenly believing he had said enough.

The rain was drenching down in fluid rods, silver against the slate grey of the heaving sea and stippling it with tiny splashes. It slapped the leaves of the bushes about the two men into violent motion. Quennell's wet hair showed patches of pink scalp, his soaked shirt plastered to his back. Rogers, beneath his thin suit, was almost as wet as he had been in recovering Whitaker's body. It was impossible to keep his pipe alight and his clammy discomfort added to his contempt, his distaste for the man now seemingly delaying the moment when he would take his plunge.

'Don't shut up on me,' he said, more impatiently than he had intended. 'How did you manage to get them to the cave?'

Quennell shook his head, his shiny wet hands clenching and unclenching. 'Michael meant so much to me . . . I didn't mean to . . . she made him . . .' His voice had choked, struggling against his breathing.

Rogers thought that his mind was being screwed up to a decision. The rest of what he wanted would either have to come later, or go with him into whatever was waiting at the bottom of his fall. He looked down the sheer slab of cliff to the rocks below, gleaming black and green now and promising cold and cruel mutilation to impacting flesh and bone. He judged again the distance from Quennell he would have to propel his stale and wearied body, not believing that he could do it. If he couldn't, and had genuinely tried, he didn't believe he would be all that sorry.

'I'm not waiting about any longer for you to make up your mind,' he said, coldly uncaring. 'But before I go I feel that I should tell you something about what you're stupid enough to consider doing. And I speak from experience, Quennell.' He was about to lie and, where he wasn't, to exaggerate bloodily. 'There's about seventy feet of nothing between you and the rocks at the bottom, but that doesn't guarantee that you're going to die. Dying's not always that easy. I've known an intending suicide finish up a similar jump with his thigh bones driven up into his belly and screaming all the way to a hospital that couldn't do anything about stopping the agony. He died in the end, of course, but not for days – and they were all painful ones. Still, if you're lucky, your thigh bones'll push far enough up to stab you in the heart and probably make it a bit shorter.' He waited, wondering if he hadn't laid it on too thick, been too ghoulish; then, remembering Angela Foxton's smashed-up face, deciding that it was proper he should suffer.

Quennell's mouth was shaking and an artery throbbed visibly at the side of his throat. 'No,' he said hoarsely. 'You're just saying that, you heartless bastard.'

'So I am, but only because it's true. Of course, if you spreadeagle yourself across a rock – and you can hardly miss hitting one – you'll most likely break your spine. That could be fatal, although it isn't always. If it's not, you finish up paralysed for the rest of your miserable life, flat on your back in a bed, or in a wheelchair.' He paused to let it sink in. God Almighty! He was even frightening himself. 'And there's another aspect to falling from a height you should know,' he continued. 'When your head hits the ground it can burst open like a ripe tomato and do things to your brain. I'm told the brain part isn't particularly painful, but if you happen to stay alive – and some manage to – it's almost inevitably as a slobbering idiot in a mental institution. Suicide isn't all . . .'

Quennell, looking up at Rogers with a rictus of sudden fright on his face, had jerked as his forearms momentarily lost purchase and slid on the wet grass, loosening small stones and crumbs of soil to fall on the ledge beneath.

Rogers, caught unprepared, took hasty steps towards him, but pulled up short, his heart thumping, when he saw him recover. 'I was about to say,' he said to an apparently unheeding Quennell, 'that I'm now about to leave you. I just don't want to be here when you do it.'

Quennell was shaking, his face strained in despair, the whites of his eyes wholly visible as he goggled into the void beneath him. He made low moaning sounds, his resistance to falling into it clear. Then his legs began to jerk, his sandals scrabbling frantically on the ledge with his full weight on forearms that were sliding on the grass towards the edge.

Rogers was on him then, feeling as though he were moving sluggishly through clogging oil, one hand clutching at the collar of his shirt, the fingers of his other grabbing at the loose flesh of his neck and holding against the sudden heaviness of the gross body as it lost the support of the elbows. Quennell screeched and for a nightmarishly long moment Rogers, wanting to yell with him, found himself leaning over the drop and fighting against the downward drag of him, his legs straining and his shoes slipping on the turf. Heaving with creaking muscles, he flung himself backwards, taking the struggling Quennell with him, the shirt collar tearing in his hand but the flesh of his neck holding, his screeching changing to choked cries of pain.

Lifting himself up from beneath Quennell, now sobbing with his face in the grass, Rogers put a heavy foot on his back, pinning him to immobility as he tried to subdue the shaking of his overstrained muscles. He didn't suppose that he would ever know whether Quennell had seriously intended jumping, or ever know whether he himself had done the right thing or not. If he had, he felt no particular satisfaction. Nor was he believing that Angela Foxton – wherever she might happen to be – was going to think of him with any great gushing of gratitude. That he could understand, for it was Sod's Law that whatever a policeman did, there was always a contrary bugger who considered that he should have done it in a quite different way, or not at all.

Soaked to the skin, his suit probably ruined, the familiar hammering ache returned to his head and a painful something in his back that convinced him he had displaced a vertebra in hauling the mound of soggy flesh at his feet from a deserved death, irritated with the out-of-sight Coltart for not anticipating that he would now be wanted, his disgruntlement was compounded by seeing his well loved meerschaum lying on the ground in two broken pieces. It was a moment when his eligibility for a retirement pension seemed to be an unwaitable and unattainable millennium away.

34

The aftermath of a successful murder investigation held in it, Rogers considered, all the anticlimactic dissatisfaction and disagreeableness of having made love to a frigid woman. It was one o'clock in the morning and he was standing at the window of his sittingroom looking at, but not taking in, the blue flickering of lightning illuminating the storm clouds that were spilling rain on to a sleeping town. His systems had finally run down and, discounting his aches and pains, he felt himself to be a construct of ectoplasm; formless, bloodless, of no weight and with all the cerebral liveliness of a damp sponge.

But enough was left of it for him to accept that, in retrospect, putting the guilt on Quennell had not been all that difficult. Once he had pushed his thinking into working out where Angela Foxton and Whitaker had been concealed, it had been professionally simple. Finding Whitaker's body in its underwater tomb proved without question that the murderer needed to be a diver. The man disturbed in the process of digging a grave, who had hit Rogers on the lower part of his skull, had done so with an upward swinging blow. While not an unarguable conclusion, it did indicate the possibility of an assailant much shorter than the detective, and Quennell and Gough were the only men at the house who could be described as such. The gravedigger and murderer had, logically, to be the one and the same man. He had also to be at the house at shooting time on the Wednesday morning. Gough was not a diver, was away from the house at the time of the killing, and could safely be eliminated. Player could reasonably be crossed off by virtue of his height and, although less certainly, because of the ear infection that prevented him from diving.

It left an abjectly voluble Quennell – now in a cell – who had been making a written statement to Lingard and talking himself into what would be a bolt-hole defence of diminished responsibility. Rogers, seated at his desk, had listened dourly while his suit and underclothing slowly dried on him. What information he hadn't obtained on the cliff was contained in the statement's staccato phraseology that arose from question and answer.

'. . . so during the afternoon I decided I couldn't leave them there. I mean near the summerhouse. I would have killed myself then but I knew I wouldn't rest unless they were properly buried. When everybody was out I went to their rooms. I packed their stuff in their suitcases and put them in the boot of my car. That night when everybody had gone to bed I went to the tool shed and took out a wheelbarrow and two large gardening bags. I went to where I had hidden them and put the bags over their heads. I pulled them down as far as I could. This was because I could not look at something I had done when not in my right mind. Although I pointed the gun at them I would like to say here that I never had any intention of killing them. I must have pulled the trigger without thinking. I was definitely not myself. My intention was to bury them in the trees behind the house. I went back to the tool shed and took a spade and a fork with me. I remember now, I also took a torch from my car with me. It was dark under the trees and I knew I would need it. The man who stopped his car near me must have heard me. Or seen the torch. I was frightened because it was late at night and he might have been violent finding me there. So I hit him first before he was. I carried him to his car and put him in it. I was going to leave him there, not wishing to harm him. He must have left the handbrake off because the car started to move down the hill. I had to jump clear. That was positively unmeant. I couldn't do anything about it so I went back and filled in what I had dug and left before anyone else came. I put the spade and fork in the tool shed and went back to Michael and Angela. I put Angela in the wheelbarrow and went down the steps to the beach. I came back and did the same with Michael. Then I carried Angela to the end of the beach. I left her there and returned for Michael. I am strong and I had no difficulty in doing this. It took me a long time and I began to be worried about when it would be dawn. I went to the boathouse and took my diving gear back to where I had left them. Yes, it was padlocked. I forgot, I went back to the house beforehand and took the boathouse key to do it. I put my diving gear on and lifted Michael into the water. We had already dived the caves in that cliff and I knew where to go. I towed him to it and dived when we were near it. There is a narrow end to it and I* *wedged him into it. I returned to the beach and did the same with Angela, wedging her in front of Michael. I didn't like doing it, but I had to. After I had dressed and put my diving gear away I took the wheelbarrow back to the tool shed. I went to the kitchen and got a bucket of water. I took it to the summerhouse and used my shirt to wash where they had been. By 'they' I mean Michael and Angela. When I got back to the house it was getting light and I went to bed. The next day I drove to Abbotsburn. I parked my car in Cumbria Street near Michael's place and walked to his garage. I had his keys. I drove his car to my shop and put it in the garage. Then I collected my own car, returned to the shop and put the suitcases in Michael's car. I did this because it would support what was being said about them both going away together . . .'*

It had all been as Quennell wished to say it, although Rogers had few doubts that any defence counsel so minded could convince a jury that it had been improperly induced or cozened from him by corrupt and lying police officers.

Overly fatigued and suspecting that his thinking apparatus was less than efficient, Rogers had saddled Lingard with the questioning of Quennell and the taking of his statement after he had returned to the house with a sullen Player and a small dustbin half-full of encrusted coins and the personal relics of dead seamen. An investigation that would have to be left in abeyance, it too was something in which he could anticipate problems over legal claims and counterclaims.

When he had seen Phaedra to tell her that he and his troops were withdrawing from the premises and to thank her for her co-operation and help, she had avoided any opening he would have used to ask if they were to meet again. He had detected an off-putting reserve in her manner that could indicate a regret for what had occurred between them, a something in it suggesting that he was again a borrowed book being returned to the library. Or, perhaps not; only he didn't believe that he would find it in himself to return and ask her.

To compound his feeling of not being the most deliriously happy man in Abbotsburn, there had been a letter waiting for him on his return to his home. The envelope, postmarked Thurnholme Bay with the previous day's date, was addressed in a woman's handwriting. He didn't recognize it, but had a strong foreboding that it had been written by the narrow-faced married-looking woman he had seen from the breakwater and whose letter to his private address promised nothing that would bring a smile to his face. He had dropped it unopened on to the hall table on the theory that if he knew nothing about what was inside it, whatever it was might go away and never happen.

A time may come in the life of the most balanced of men when, possibly because of a temporary chemical imbalance in his body, possibly because of the staleness of the blood reaching his brain, he can do foolish things. Although he knew that it was going to cost him, Rogers pulled the telephone cable from its socket, held the heavy handset for a few seconds with an almost contemplative air, then hurled it as hard as he could to crash through the glass of the window.

Leaving it wherever it might be lying in the rain-swept garden, he climbed the stairs – managing a small grin of satisfaction at what he had done as he did so – undressed and flopped into his bed. Before sleep overtook him, he made a fanciful decision to seek out a monastery, miles from otherwise occupied territory, whose abbot could be persuaded to accept as a novitiate an already tonsured, pipe-smoking, reasonably sexually ascetic ex-detective superintendent who at that moment was deciding not to give a bloody damn for anything or anybody.